THE DATE

Mari Beck

maribeckauthor@gmail.com
Facebook.com/MariBeckAuthor
https://www.pinterest.com/maribeckauthor/
Cover by: *SelfPubBookCovers.com/kerineal*

"I loved her against reason, against promise, against peace, against hope, against happiness, against all discouragement that could be."

— *Charles Dickens*, *Great Expectations*

CHAPTER ONE

The Beginning

January 2015

Emily knew that the man was eyeing her tentatively, wondering maybe if she'd taken a wrong turn before ending up in his shop. She supposed that the fact she was missing all of her hair, eyelashes and eyebrows might have something to do with that. If only he'd seen her when she'd had long auburn hair that reached the middle of her back, perfectly arched brows that framed her inquisitive grey eyes and long lashes, he might not have stared the way he was doing so now.

Once she took off her warm knit hat and stuck it in the pocket of her oversized winter coat it might have been difficult not to notice that she looked different. On the other hand, he'd probably seen all kinds of people walk through his doors so, to some extent, the fact that he kept staring at her bothered her but she'd decided that she would do this and nothing, not even her alien looks were going to stop her from doing it. The man, who was covered in spikes, studs and tattoos, finally left his seat behind the counter and approached her. Emily hoped she'd have the courage to speak loud enough so she wouldn't have to repeat herself. She'd been thinking about this day for a long time and now it was here.

Chemo was done and even if the cancer never came back again, something her doctors could never promise, she knew what she wanted and she was going to keep her promise to herself no matter what. She was getting a *tattoo.* For that reason, she hadn't told anybody about her plans not her best friend Derrick or even her parents. Emily knew what her parents would have said about her idea. It was strictly forbidden by their Jewish faith. Her father - Rabbi Fischer- would have accused her of mutilating her own body. Her mother, Meredith Bernstein- Fischer would have been horrified because no Bernstein woman had ever lowered herself to such an action. Still, Emily couldn't let the idea go and finally she'd had to do something about it which is how she had ended up here.

"Can I help you?" The man asked still staring. She cleared her throat, reached into her pocket and took out a piece of paper she'd been saving for the last few months. Emily had stared at it during every treatment as part of her own personal count down. She unfolded the paper and handed it to the man.

"I want *this.*" She said noticing that her hands were trembling a little. The man looked down at the piece of paper studying it.

"Did you draw this?"

"Yeah." She admitted and he arched an eyebrow.

"It's really good."

"Thanks. So, can you do it?"

"Sure. How big and where?" He asked and Emily held up her hand, spread it out as far as it would go and then placed the hand over her right shoulder.

"Can do." The man said pointing her toward his chair. "Ever gotten a tattoo before?"

"No."

"Just so you know, it's going to hurt like a son of a bitch. You think you can take it?"

"Ever had chemo or radiation before?" She asked as he prepped his tools and she slipped off her coat and then her sweater.

"No." He answered as she exposed the white skin of her shoulder for him to work on.

"They hurt like a son of a bitch too. So, yeah, I'm sure I can take it." She said and the man shrugged.

"Okay. One big ass, green butterfly coming right up." He said turning on the tattoo machine and Emily who'd become used to being poked and prodded with needles during her treatments leaned forward and smiled, feeling better than she had in months.

CHAPTER TWO

The Fight

June 2015

The tattoo was one thing, trying to make the people in her life understand what she wanted was something else. It was frustrating, painful and stressful for all of them but especially for her parents, who hadn't been able to understand that she had wanted to be free-free from pain, free from treatment and more than anything from their ever watchful eyes. They hadn't allowed her to *be* without fearing that anything she'd do outside of her doctor's recommendation would be tantamount to relapse.

The cancer had never really gone away. It was Emily's constant companion and while she didn't consider herself a morbid person she was realistic. There was nothing like losing your health and the ability to do the small things for yourself like walking, going to the bathroom, eating and sleeping not to mention the excruciating pain that came with the treatments designed to save one's life to make a person humble. After each relapse there had been a plan and she'd followed it to a tee but there was something different about this last round of treatment that had her thinking one thing. *Never again.* The fatigue, the loss of every hair on her body, the pain all contributed to the soul weariness she felt that she just couldn't shake this time.

She was only twenty-three years old but she'd felt like she was a hundred. Was it ever going to end? That was the question she'd asked her oncologist only to be met with a long pause and a sympathetic look that told her Dr. Kimberly Lee didn't have the answers she wanted. Then, her parents had *insisted* that she accompany them to Omaha, Nebraska where her father had become the interim rabbi of Temple B'nai Shalom. She'd wanted to stay home. What was there for her in Nebraska? That's when her parents had plied her with brochures for the university's art program. She loved art and had considered herself pretty good at it when she'd felt well enough to draw and paint. Until then, her education had been a little spotty due to years of illness and hospital stays. She had managed to complete her high school degree via homeschooling and she'd even started and completed about 2 years of college before the second relapse landed her back in the hospital undergoing aggressive treatment that left her so weak she'd had to abandon any thought of going on.

Emily had refused to consider going with her parents until she'd realized two things: 1) her boyfriend of two years had been cheating on her while she was undergoing treatment and 2) she'd decided that if the cancer did come back she wouldn't undergo anymore treatment; in fact, when the time came she'd be the one to take matters into her own hands.

She had confided first in her best friend Derrick whom she had known and loved since she was a child.

"You're crazy!" He'd said the night she'd told him about her plan.

"Hear me out. . ." Emily had pleaded but he'd shaken his head and kept shouting at her.

"You want to *kill yourself?*"

"It's not like that!"

"It sounds like it to me."

"Derrick, please, if you'd watch the documentary with me. . ."

"Emily, this is the stupidest idea you've ever had and there have been some stupid ideas. I know, I've been there with you when you acted on them."

"How is wanting to make my own choice stupid?"

"What about your parents?"

"What about them?"

"You haven't told them, have you?" Derrick had asked in an accusatory tone and she'd had to remain silent because it was true. She hadn't had the courage to tell her parents that she wanted to use the Death with Dignity Act, a law that gave a person with a terminal disease and six months or less to live the option of ending their life with the aid of a lethal dose of medication prescribed by a physician. If another relapse came and she met all of the requirements, which judging by the longer pauses and sympathetic looks her oncologist gave her after each time the cancer came back,was a real possibility, she wanted to *choose* the date of her own death. It was all so clear to her but not so to anyone else-especially Derrick.

"I thought you were my friend, Derrick. My *best* friend." She'd said with tears in her eyes. He had looked down at her with tears in his own eyes and pulled her into a tight embrace.

"I *am.* Sometimes, I thought we could have been more, Em. . . the timing is never right." He whispered, "but what you're asking. . .I can't do it."

"You'd rather see me suffer?" She had asked trying to avoid talking about his feelings for her. Emily had never been able to see him as more than just a brother but she had despised herself for hurting him that way. Nevertheless, she needed his support more than ever before. Derrick sighed squeezing her a little tighter.

"Of course not. I'd rather see you *live.*" He murmured into her hair.

"I need your support, Derrick. *Please.*" She'd begged but he hadn't said anything. Instead, he'd lifted her face up, leaned in and kissed her full on the lips leaving her a little dazed. Then, he'd walked to the front door and paused for moment to look back at her.

"I hope you change your mind. I'll be here if you do." Then he'd left without another word and Emily hadn't been able to do anything else but sit back down on the sofa in her parent's living room, put her face in her hands and cry.

CHAPTER THREE

The Move

September 2015

Ultimately, she hadn't had to tell her parents anything. *They had known*. Derrick had told them. She'd felt betrayed. Then, the arguments had begun.

"How could you possibly want this?" Her mother had cried during yet another angry yelling match between she and her parents.

"Mom. . .please. Listen to me!"

"Emily, what about your faith? Have you given any thought to that at all?" Her father the rabbi had pleaded using the best argument he knew how. Still, it had hurt Emily to see him so distraught.

"Papa, I just want to *talk* about it. Why won't you and mom listen to me?"

"How could we ever entertain such a thought when you're talking like a crazy person, Emily!" Her mother had interjected, crossing both arms and avoiding any eye contact. Emily had felt her own emotions overwhelm her and tears had stung her eyes.

"Can you not see what this is doing to your mother, Emily?"

"Papa. . ."

"All these years we've done everything we could to care for you. The best doctors, the best hospitals. . " Her mother had begun to sob.

"I'm grateful."

"Are you? Then why would you want to kill yourself?" Meredith Bernstein-Fischer had demanded to know.

"Mom. . .I'm. . .it's just that. . ." But the words had not come to Emily.

"Derrick told us your plan because he was concerned for your safety." Rabbi Fischer had said calmly and Emily had looked down at her own hands and how her nails were digging into the flesh of her palms. She'd only felt anger and a deep, deep sorrow.

"It isn't what he made it out to be."

"Will you be taking your own life?" Her father's voice had suddenly boomed and echoed through the room. It had startled both Emily and her mother. Rabbi Fischer had never yelled at her like that before.

"It's medication prescribed by a physician."

"It is *murder*, Emily, and it breaks the Law." The rabbi insisted.

"I wish you could see it from my perspective." She had whispered but he had only shaken his head in disgust and disappointment.

"There is only *one* perspective. You know this. It is how I raised you. There is nothing more to be said." Her father had left the room, followed almost immediately by her mother and Emily had found herself alone again.

In the end, she had agreed to go to Omaha under the condition that she be allowed to live on her own in a modest apartment and hold a part-time job. These were things she'd felt would make her feel as normal as any other 23 year-old might. Her parents, surely thinking they had convinced her to abandon her ideas of Death with Dignity had reluctantly agreed. She had even heard from Derrick once in awhile by phone and by text. He'd been given a sliver of hope again by her parents frequent updates she supposed.

Liev Fischer had promised her they would be in Omaha for a year. Just enough time to give the congregation of Temple B'nai Shalom the opportunity to find a permanent replacement. So, she'd tried to show her enthusiasm for the move by enrolling in some art classes at the university, nothing fancy, just some refresher courses. For awhile, things had appeared to be going well and then came the next relapse. This time it had come back fast and furious.

Her hair had barely had a chance to grow back out past her ears and while her eyebrows had sprouted and her lashes had made a valiant comeback, she had still felt like a stranger looking at herself in the mirror. That's when she'd decided to shave off the rest of her hair with the exception of a long swath of bangs that reached right above her chin. She had then proceeded to dye it a bright red and after she'd asked around at school, she'd found a tattoo parlor that did piercings. The next time Emily Fischer had looked in the mirror, the person she saw had been someone of her own creation.

She'd gone back to the doctor to humor her parents and because Derrick, who had been shocked by her appearance when they Skyped one night, pleaded with her to have one last conversation with the oncologist about her options. She loved her parents and in her own way she loved Derrick,however, Emily had always known what she would do if this day came and nothing and *no one* was going to change her mind.

CHAPTER FOUR

The Party

January 2016

As Nick Simon stepped out naked from the pool, the look on the Chinese Ambassador's face told him the party was over, which is why Nick decided to move it upstairs to the penthouse where it was almost impossible to hear the heavy pounding on the door through the ear-splitting techno pop bouncing off the break resistant glass walls. The primal beat coming from the corner of the penthouse, where a DJ was spinning, pulsated through 6,000 square feet and 15' foot ceilings, bypassing the massive wood-burning fireplace, making its way through all seven bedrooms, the ultra modern kitchen with its infinity shaped marble counter and stopping at the bar that looked over the lower Manhattan skyline. That's where Nick Simon was sitting, fully dressed again, away from the dancing with his back to the party-goers, drink in one hand, phone in the other and a near empty vodka bottle sitting next to him.

He was oblivious to the shouts of Francois Delaney, manager of New York's most sought-after luxury residential tower.

"Mr. Simon! Mr. Simon!"

Nick felt a hand on his back but didn't bother turning around. He was too busy texting. Delaney finally grabbed onto the back of his collar and turned him around causing him to spill his drink all over the diamond encrusted t-shirt that had been a gift from Cianti, a world-renowned singer he'd met at one of the several red carpet events for the film adaptation of his last book. She was a *very* big fan of one of his books, (it had *changed* her life) and an *excellent* lover—if he remembered it right. Anymore it was hard to keep track of all his liaisons. They could hardly be called relationships or even flings. They never seemed to last more than the one time.

"What the hell? This is a four hundred thousand dollar shirt, you idiot!" Nick yelling as he turned to find Francois Delaney, red-faced and impatient.

When he'd won Season One of *First Draft/Final Cut*, a reality competition where aspiring authors and screenwriters competed to finish a novel with adapted screenplay in thirty days for the chance at a publishing and film contract, his life had changed overnight. Now five years, six books and four films later, Nick had everything he'd ever wanted. At least that's what his agent Barbara King kept telling him every chance she got—especially the part that involved getting him into one of *the* most coveted pieces of real estate on the entire planet. For Barbara it was less about whom you knew and more about how you looked standing next to him--or her. The purpose of getting the penthouse was to have a place for young Hollywood and sophisticated New York to mingle with Nick Simon as host and Barbara King as mistress of the manse. No party was ever held at the penthouse without Barbara's knowledge, planning, and approval of the guest list, the theme, or scheme. The events were tasteful but trendy and always found their way to the front page of the hottest magazines and celebrity news shows around. Book launches were held near the pool, film screenings in the tower's thirty-seat indoor theater, along with post-award parties in the private dining room with the two- million-dollar chandelier. Everything had been tantalizing but tame, which is why it didn't surprise him when he found Francois Delaney, mouth agape as the poor man took in the music that made the floor vibrate under his feet. The smoky haze coming from a nearby couch as a group of partygoers, smoking a small joint, created a cloud around his head, while several other *guests* spread around the sprawling designer space engaged in activities Nick was certain neither Barbara nor Francois would approve of—but then that was the point.

"MR. Simon!" Francois Delaney yelled in his thick French accent over the music and noise, "This cannot go on!" Nick couldn't help but smile as he put his glass down on the bar and cupped his hand to his ear.

"What? I'm sorry, Frankie. I can't hear you!" Nick had to lean down a good two feet and he knew that there was no better way to irritate the man than by Americanizing his first name. He'd overheard him tell Barbara how much he hated it when some up and coming nobody had done that to him, so he'd committed Delaney's preference to memory. Francois had worked managing some of the best luxury buildings in all of Manhattan and before that in

Paris. He'd been personal friends with Trump, he was on a first name basis with De Niro, he had even been invited to dine with Bardot. Delaney would not stand for any of it. He would *not.* It made Nick smile to see the little man in the fancy suit squirm.

"Mr. Simon!" Francois yelled in his ear. "This *event* appears nowhere in my calendar. I received no word from Mademoiselle Barbara about this, this, party!" *Mademoiselle?* She had been married four times and divorced three times. She preferred to groom all of her men so they could stand next to her while she flaunted her fame and riches rather than marry them for the same. She was ruthless and uncompromising. It's what made her one of the best agents in the business. It could also make her your worst enemy.

Nick saw that Francois was sweating bullets over what was happening at the penthouse and freaking out over how Barbara would react when she found out that Nick had been able to sneak it all past him. It took some planning to figure out who else was having a big event on the same date. No one could just *have* a party, they had to schedule it weeks, sometimes months, in advance so that Francois could handle security, catering and usually one or two paparazzi that continually staked out the building in disguise from across the street. Nick had managed to pull it off but he hadn't followed protocol and from the look of it Francois was about to have a heart attack.

"It's not an event, Frankie. Think of it as more of a small get-together among friends on New Year's Eve." Francois Delaney pursed his lips together and rapidly motioned for Nick to follow him onto the terrace. Nick rolled his eyes but followed. He could see his breath as they stepped out and he wrapped his arms around his thin but expensive shirt.

"Mais non, Mr. Simon. You and your *friends* were found skinny dipping in the pool not even an hour ago."

"What's so bad about that? We were just having a little fun."

"It happened during Ambassador Yang's reception for his country's *Nobel Prize winner,* Mr. Simon!" Francois looked livid.

"Well, who the hell holds a Nobel Prize reception on New Year's Eve?"

"The Chinese New Year DOES NOT take place on December 31, Mr. Simon!"

"Look, Frankie. I can see that you're stressed. You've been hard at work. I know without Barbara here to tell you exactly what to do and when to do it that this seems a little overwhelming. But no worries! I've got it all under control." Nick laughed and patted the frustrated Frenchman on the back.

"Are you *high*, Mr. Simon?" Francois grabbed Nick's face with two pudgy hands and examined his eyes.

"Hey! Get your hands off me," he said defensively. So what if he had smoked a little or snorted a couple of lines? Hadn't he been good for Barbara all this time? He deserved a night off.

"So Mademoiselle King, knows nothing about this?"

"It's my place. I can do whatever the hell I want," Nick scoffed.

"You are right. It is *your* place. But you are not the only tenant in this building and you signed papers where you promised to abide by certain conditions. If you fail to abide by those conditions then you put me in the precarious position of enforcing the owner's explicit instructions. "

"Of what? What can you do? I paid for the place. I'm the owner." Nick smirked.

"You are mistaken, Mr. Simon. You are *paying* for it but you are not the *owner.*"

"What the hell are you talking about? Of course I'm the owner."

"Mais non, Mr. Simon. You are the *tenant.* The *owner* is Barbara King." *What the hell?* The fact that Barbara King could possibly scrape up the funds to buy a penthouse wasn't in question, her clients were top-notch, A-list celebrity clients, the fact that it was *this* penthouse in the city's most celebrity-inhabited towering residence was. There was no way unless. . .

"She used my name. That b-" Nick clenched his fists. But Francois interrupted him putting up a firm hand to stop him from continuing.

"The *particulars* are not important, Mr. Simon. The fact you signed the papers is."

"But I didn't know. . ." Nick protested.

"If the tenant engages in activities on the premises that either break the law or cause the reputation of the residence or its other tenants to be compromised in any way— said tenant may face eviction." Francois recited from memory.

"You've got to be kidding me. . ."

"For both our sakes, Mr. Simon, please. Ask your guests to leave the premises. The *party* is over."

"But it's not even midnight yet!"

"I'm sure—judging by state in which your *friends* currently find themselves— that this will not be a great problem for them. They will scarcely notice the time. Merely have the DJ do a countdown, then ask them to move the festivities elsewhere—agreed?" Nick didn't answer, he turned away and stared out at the skyline, shoving his hands into the silk-lined pockets of his Versace jeans.

"You are a grown man, Mr. Simon, and an esteemed writer." Francois' voice softened. "Do not ruin your career by playing with your reputation. I have seen it one too many times. It only takes one match to light the fire and in seconds, *seconds*, Mr. Simon a whole career, a whole life can go up in flames." Nick didn't reply. After a moment Francois opened the terrace door and made his way back through the crowd of partygoers shutting it behind him. Nick remained on the terrace, staring out into the cold Manhattan sky.

He couldn't believe it. All this time he'd been paying Barbara *rent!* For a place he could easily have afforded himself—no strings attached. But she needed him just like she needed everyone else on her list. That's how she got around, got in, went up in the world. She rode them all like an intricate, 14-karat gold virtual subway all over the world. He was just one of the lines and she'd taken him for a ride alright. She had managed to have him sign over his own penthouse without even knowing it. It made him wonder what else he'd signed over? Barbara and her staff handled all of his affairs. But for now he had no intention of making it easy on Frankie or *Mademoiselle*. If she could make him pay he'd do the same. If Barbara had the balls to evict him for showing a little spunk then he might as well make it a night to remember and with that he decided to return to the party. He opened the terrace doors and walked inside to the cheers of the partygoers nearby. He grabbed another bottle of vodka from behind the bar, took a joint right from the lips of a striking brunette and placed it between his own as he walked by. He tried to remember where he'd put the pills he'd bought from the DJ's assistant right before he led the beautiful blonde gyrating near the fireplace toward his bedroom. Nick Simon, best-selling author, film producer and Barbara King's all around golden boy was about to be very, very bad.

CHAPTER FIVE

The Morning After

Nick felt something vibrate against the side of his face. His eyes were closed but he could still see a neon light shining through the lids. His hands weren't anywhere near the offensive object. *Make. It. Stop.* The vibrating continued until he opened one eye and realized he'd fallen asleep on top of his phone. Everything was blurry even with his contacts, so he couldn't make out who was calling. Either way the list would be short, he didn't give out his private number so it could only mean that Francois or Barbara was calling. *Shit.* Time to pay the piper. He pulled his hands out from under a tangle of long legs and sheets, looked over and saw he was laying up by the headboard of his bed while there was someone (he didn't know who) sprawled across the other end of the bed. Long legs, blonde hair? He didn't have a clue but it must have turned out well for both of them. He grabbed the phone, flopped back onto his stomach, his face in the pillow, and put it up to his ear. While he had very few memories about what had transpired the night before, he hoped that all of his planning would produce something aside from a splitting headache, a massive hangover, and a hook up that he would later regret.

"Hey Barbara." He answered not bothering to lift his face from the pillow. The legs next to him shifted.

"Nick Simon?" It was a male voice but not the one he was expecting.

"Francois?" he mumbled and slowly turned over onto his back.

"No. This is Detective Pat Baker. Is this Nick Simon?"

"Yeah. How did you get this number?" Nick sat up almost fully awake. Fuck that Francois. He'd called the police, and now that it was clear the penthouse wasn't his, there was bound to be trouble.

"We found it."

"I'm sorry did you say you found this number? Where?"

"On a homeless man, Mr. Simon."

"That's ridiculous! Why would a homeless man have my private number?"

"We were hoping you could tell us."

"Who did you say you were again?"

"I'm Detective Pat Baker of the Omaha Police Department."

"Where?"

"Nebraska, Mr. Simon." Nick froze.

"So, what do you want from me?"

"Well, Mr. Simon, we found your number and name among the belongings of homeless individual we found in the city park a few days ago. The director of the shelter near the park thought you might be the man's next of kin. He said he'd mentioned you several times. He told them he was your father."

"Is he alive?"

Nick held his breath.

"No. I'm sorry he's not."

He exhaled.

"Alright. What do you need from me?"

"The director at the shelter has already identified the body. We just need you to come down and confirm the identification and if it's affirmative take possession."

"You mean for burial?"

"Yes."

"Okay. Give me time to make some arrangements. It'll be difficult if not impossible to get a flight out during the holiday. I'll be there as soon as I can, Detective.

"Certainly, Mr. Simon and once again I'm sorry to disturb you on a holiday." Nick ended the call and looked around the room.It was trashed. There were glasses, bottles and baggies everywhere and he was naked, hung over, and starving. First this mess and now the call that changed *everything*. What was he going to do? How the hell was he going to find a ticket to Nebraska on New Year's Day? Better yet how would he keep it all from Barbara? She handled all of his accounts and took care of the details. Usually he called her assistant, Ambrose, told him what he needed—whether it was a car, a jet or a reservation—and voila it was done. He didn't have to do a thing. He didn't even have to carry cash unless he wanted to and even that was handled by Barbara's staff. They'd deliver whatever he needed to the penthouse in a discreet envelope or prepay for whatever activities or social engagements that required it. The cash he'd requested this last time had already been used up, mostly when he'd bought the *party favors* from the DJ's assistant last night. If he had any cash it couldn't be more than a few hundred dollars and that would theoretically get him a one way economy ticket to somewhere in New York State but Nebraska, who knew? He couldn't call Barbara, he couldn't. Not after the stunt he had pulled last night, and certainly not to tell her that he wanted money for a ticket to some place in Nebraska so he could claim the body of a homeless man, found in a city park with his private number in his pocket. It was a publicist's worst nightmare. Nick sighed. He didn't have many options but his mind was made up. He had to go. As he got up from the bed, the long-legged blonde began to stir at the other end.

"Where you going, baby?" Her voice was soft and sultry.

"I've got to go, but you're welcome to stay for awhile. Just make sure you're gone before the French guy comes back," he said, looking for his jeans among the debris scattered on the floor of the bedroom.

"The French guy?"

"Trust me you'll know him when you see him. You don't want him to see you. He'll probably have you arrested," Nick said as he grabbed the diamond encrusted t-shirt and threw it at her.

"What's this?" The blonde asked examining the dazzling diamond sunburst pattern that covered the front.

"A thank you for last night,." he said going to his closet and pulling out a plain t-shirt and matching hoodie.

"Thanks." She flashed him a smile and got up from the bed letting the sheet drop behind her. He pulled out a duffel bag from another closet at the other end of the room along with a pair of shoes, a pair of heavy boots and multiple pairs of socks and underwear. Coming back to the first closet he pulled out additional shirts, jeans and pants, another hoodie, a leather jacket, two caps and a pair of sunglasses. As he did this the blonde came up behind him and held him from behind.

"What's your hurry? Come back to bed," she whispered in his ear. He looked at the image of himself with the beautiful blonde embracing him in the full length mirror that was located right next to the closet. If someone had told him five years ago, before he won the *First Draft/Final Cut* competition, that he would be standing there in designer clothes, surrounded by wealth, living it up in one of Manhattan's most luxurious penthouses with a beautiful blonde model-type begging him to get back in bed with her, he would have laughed his ass off. Now, it didn't seem to matter. He didn't recognize either face in the mirror.

"Come on, baby," she said kissing his neck and running her hands all over his body. He took her hands away and reached down to pick up his bag. She seemed angry.

"What's so damn important that you can't stay here with me?" she demanded..

“Work.”

“On New Year’s Day? Do you really expect me to believe that?" she insisted.

"No," he said and started walking toward the door.

"Call me!" she yelled after him.

He shut the door and kept on walking.

CHAPTER SIX

The Escape

Nick took the private elevator from his penthouse and pushed the garage level button. Leaving had been no easy feat. Once he'd exited his bedroom he found he had to step over people (nobody he knew) to get to the door leading to the elevator on the opposite side of the penthouse. Standing there as the doors closed he still didn't have a clear plan. He needed to make it out of the building undetected, but unlike previous escapes, it wasn't the paparazzi he was afraid would discover him. Instead he knew he needed to do anything and everything possible to sneak out before Francois Delaney discovered him and called Barbara. He had a car he could take, a $65,000 Jaguar he'd bought with part of his winnings from *First Draft/Final Cut*, that he insisted on keeping even though Barbara thought it wasn't expensive enough, and a Cadillac Escalade. He hardly ever got the chance to drive the Jaguar—one because it was New York and there were taxis or you could walk most everywhere and two because Barbara had almost always sent a driver to take him around in the Escalade. If he took the Jaguar, he would clearly be drawing attention to himself and there was no way that the paparazzi would fail to notice him as he raced out of the private garage, especially on New Year's Day. If he took the Escalade, with its tinted windows he might be able to escape discovery. Everybody in the building had an Escalade or something similar in which they went around town from party to party or place to place. The paparazzi guys stationed across the street from the building, one usually disguised as a hipster perpetually walking a tiny designer Pomeranian named Mr. Tippy Toes and the other an exceedingly well-dressed cab driver who never seemed to pick up or drop anybody off, would be more likely to let him go if he took the SUV. The problem was he had the keys to the Jaguar but not to the Escalade. One more damn thing Barbara handled when she sent over the drivers. His head was throbbing. The elevator would soon reach the garage and he would have to make a decision. *Ding!* The doors opened and he stepped out. Looking around he could see both of his vehicles sitting in their designated spaces. He walked past them and kept on walking toward the door near the small booth usually manned by a security guard. *Shit!* It was too late now. He kept going. As he got closer he saw Gerry Fairchild, a large intimidating man, sitting in the booth. Nick always greeted him going in or out of the garage and had even engaged in some very pleasant conversation with him about his family. No time for that now. He had to make it out with the least amount of fuss possible.

"Hey, Mr. Simon! Howsit going?" Gerry said in his cheery Jersey accent. Nick just gave him a nod and kept on walking hoping that the man would buzz him out without any further questions. Working with as many celebrities and influential people as Gerry probably did over the years and now at this building he didn't seem surprised or even upset that Nick had virtually ignored him and walked on by. Nick heard the buzz and click of the door as he pushed on it stepping out into the brightest light he'd ever felt hit his naked eyes. He rummaged in the pocket of his hoodie for a pair of sunglasses and slapped them on. It didn't seem to do much but at least he didn't feel like he was looking directly at the sun. The private garage entrance and exit were located on the other side of the building and usually only covered by one of the two paparazzi who lay in wait for Nick or some other tenant. This time it was the hipster and Mr. Tippy Toes. He had originally hoped that if he could make it out before either one of them made their way back around, he would high tail it the two minutes to the Franklin Street subway line and somehow buy the time he needed to formulate a more concrete plan. But it was not to be. Mr. Tippy Toes spotted him first from across the street as he was relieving himself on one of the lamp posts. He barked when he saw Nick. *Are they training that dog to spot celebrities?* His pseudo hipster owner suddenly looked up and started to discreetly take out his phone. The moment he uploaded the video or shot the Instagram pic and posted it on whatever celebrity site he worked for, Barbara would know it and what would happen next would be like something out of a spy thriller. A black van (more likely an Escalade) with unmarked plates would drive up to a screeching halt. Men in ski masks (probably Barbara's assistant Ambrose and company) would put a hood over his head, throw him inside and drive him to an undisclosed location where she would torture him and he would never be seen again. He'd never make it to Nebraska. He'd never have a chance to end the nightmare once and for all. He couldn't let that happen, so just as hipster boy was about to take his shot Nick ran across the street.

"Wait!" Nick yelled. "I've got a proposition for you."

CHAPTER SEVEN

Consorting with the Enemy

Pseudo Hipster looked shocked and quickly tried to shove his phone into his messenger bag.

"I'm sorry were you talking to me?" the hipster bent down to pick up Mr. Tippy Toes, who was all decked out in doggie winter chic.

"Yes, I was. But then you knew that." Nick said and reached out to pet the Pomeranian. Mr. Tippy Toes growled and snapped at him. He drew back his hand.

"Whoa. Grumpy little fur ball." Nick raised an eyebrow and stuck both hands into his jacket.

"He doesn't like strangers."

"We both know I'm not a stranger. You've been keeping tabs on me and the rest of the poor suckers in this building for months."

"I don't know what you're talking about." The guy said and began to walk away. Nick followed him.

"I know your buddy is out front in a taxi that never moves and that you keep walking the same block over and over without ever going inside. You don't live around here. That's clear."

"I beg your pardon?" the hipster tried to sound offended.

"Come on, man." He leaned in and whispered, "We both know that bag is a knock off and the dog. . ." Nick rolled his eyes.

"What about the dog?"

"No one walks a Pomeranian around this neighborhood anymore. That's so cliché. Bulldogs, Terriers, rescue dogs-yes, but Poms? That was the *real* give away." The man stared at Nick.

"So here's my deal. You and the freaky fur ball take me to your friend out front. You give me a ride and I'll give you one of THE best photo ops you've had all year. It'll be so epic that your colleagues, you know, the ones that are inside somewhere warm while you guys are out here freezing your asses will wish they had taken you more seriously before giving you the crap assignments—like this one." Nick could tell that Hipster was considering it. There was something about the way he chewed on his bottom lip and the way his eyes moved up and down as if he were mentally writing out all the pros and cons.

"What kind of photo op?" Hipster asked finally breaking character. Nick smiled, took his phone out of his pocket and dialed.

"You'll see." He told Pseudo Hipster putting the phone up to his ear as the two of them walked Mr. Tippy Toes toward the unmoving taxi out front.

CHAPTER EIGHT

Seduction

It took some major convincing,especially when he asked for Hipster's phone, but about an hour after making it out of the building Nick was standing in front of one of the city's trendiest new condos. It wasn't quite as trendy as his, but then that was Barbara's plan from the beginning. Stay three steps ahead of everybody who was claiming to be anybody. The plan he had come up with wasn't what he would have called a good plan but it was the best he could come up with on such short notice. The deal he struck was simple. Nick would take Hipster's phone inside with him and snap an *interesting* selfie or two of himself with one of Hollywood's most up and coming young starlets—Cianti. She had started as a global music sensation—the kind that only requires one name that everyone knows. She'd recently broken into film and was one of *the* hottest commodities in the business and the most sought after by the paparazzi. Cianti's obsession with privacy was legendary. On the stage she was the diva—off the stage she faded into the background. There were hundreds of pictures from her concerts but hardly any from her life away from the glaring lights of the stage. It was her private life they wanted to dumpster dive into so Nick promised them a picture to top all pictures. In exchange they would drive him where he needed to go. They reluctantly agreed but as insurance—in case Nick decided to default on his end of the bargain—he would allow them to snap pictures of him holding Mr. Tippy Toes and give them some juicy tidbit about his own private life to include on their sleazy site. Nick agreed and gave the cabbie an address he hoped was the right one.

Looking up at the nondescript building with the warehouse feel as he got out of the taxi with the faux cabbie, pseudo hipster nervously looking at him and the grumpy Pomeranian growling at him from the rolled down window of the back seat, he took a deep breath. *Here goes nothing.* He walked up to the steel doors and pressed on a button off to the left.

"Yes?" boomed a male voice from a small speaker. Nick had to think a moment. There was a password, something he was supposed to say. God, he'd been pretty drunk the night they'd hooked up after one of her concerts. It was Cianti who had sent him complimentary tickets via Barbara of course. She was a fan and wanted to meet him in person but she was also on tour. So, when she was in New York for a performance she asked to see him and he went. She was breathtaking on stage—a sleek, primal force, pulsating rhythm and sex for the adoring masses. He was captivated especially after meeting her backstage. They had a few drinks in her dressing room then she invited him back to her place for another drink and a chat about one of his books. It was her favorite and she wanted him to sign it because it had *changed* her life. So he went and he stood outside this very same set of doors as her bodyguard pushed on the button and gave the password. *Dammit what was it?*

"Yup, yup something." He said racking his brain until he remembered something about that night. It was something she had told him as they headed for her bedroom. She was talking about his book and how it had changed the way she looked at love, blah, blah. Nothing new for Nick. His books tended to get that kind of reaction from his female fans. But he had laughed—partly because he was drunk and because the fact that his books caused his readers to hope for a kind of love that only existed as fiction, *his* fiction, never ceased to amaze him.

"What?" she had said to him in between kisses and passionate gropes. "Don't you believe in *upendo*?"

"What the hell is that?" He'd asked her and she told him it was the Swahili word for love. He'd almost forgotten that Cianti was into the mystical and spiritual aspects of love in all languages. It reflected in her music and her performances. It had even been the title of one of her songs that night. Still he was pretty sure he'd laughed again until he looked at her face. She was dead serious and he wasn't about to miss out on getting laid just because she'd been taken in just like all the other poor schmucks of the world when it came to romance and *true love.*

"Of course I do. I write about don't I? I write about it a lot. How could I do that if I didn't believe in it?" He'd assured her and that had done the trick. It had been one of the best one night stands he'd ever had. That's when it clicked for him—of course he knew the password.

"Upendo!" he yelled into the speaker and he heard the click as doors unlocked. He looked back and flashed the Hipster and the Cabbie a smug grin. Then he opened one of the steel doors and stepped inside.

CHAPTER NINE

Trojan Horse

The inside of Cianti's palatial retreat was anything but palatial. Nick knew she wanted it to look like nothing special. This was part of her elaborate plan to throw off the paparazzi or anyone else looking to intrude on her private life. So when Nick stepped inside he found himself in what looked like the first floor of a warehouse except that it was completely empty. It was nothing but concrete walls, high industrial windows and cold paved floor. Immediately in front of him was an elevator with only one button to push so he pushed it. When the doors opened there was a large, intimidating bodyguard waiting for him. He came toward Nick and forced him to spread his legs and arms for a body search. Funny. He didn't remember that from his previous visit but then Cianti had been with him.

"Name." The bodyguard demanded.

"Nick Simon."

"Nick Simon." The man repeated as he pressed down on an earpiece. After a moment the guard reached over

Nick's head and pressed the only button in the elevator. Neither one of them spoke as they ascended and Nick had a hard time swallowing while he waited for the elevator doors to open. When they did it was onto another sparse concrete hallway. The guard led him down that hallway to another door that was manned by yet a second bodyguard, who after patting him down *again*, turned and knocked on the door. It took a minute or so but the door opened and there standing in the doorway was Cianti dressed in yoga pants and a skimpy tank that caressed the curves of her breasts. She was barefoot and beautiful. Her hair was pulled back, there were droplets of sweat running down her face and she didn't have a stitch of makeup on. This was not the Cianti anyone would recognize on stage. This was a woman who had just finished her morning workout.

"Nick Simon." She said a little out of breath as she motioned for him to come in. He followed her inside and she shut the door.

"Cianti..." He leaned in for a kiss and was met with the palm of her hand.

"You said you would call."

"I did call a little bit ago to tell you I was in the neighborhood but you didn't answer. I thought dropping by in person would be classier."

"Classier?" She scoffed blocking another attempt at a kiss.

"Cianti, you know how it is. I've been busy with my new book and you've been on tour..."

She rolled her eyes. "Yeah, I'll bet. I saw how busy you've been. You're face has been splashed all over *People* this week. Must be tough working on a new book with all those women hanging all over you at parties and premiers. How do you *ever* get anything done?"

"Come on, Cianti. You know how it is in this business. You have to show up or the gig's up." Nick said inching closer. "You know that new book I've been working on is almost done and I'm dedicating it you."

She looked up. "You are?"

"Of course. You were my inspiration. That night we had together was one of the best nights of my life and it meant something." He could tell she was interested and Nick sort of hated himself for lying to her. But a deal was a deal and he needed to get that picture for the two idiots downstairs so he could get to the airport.

"What's it about?"

"Uh, it's about...a singer, who makes it big...but uh...she's lost all of her faith in love. She thinks she'll never find it because she's such a megastar that she can't really trust anyone. Until she meets this guy..."

"What guy?" she asked and he knew he had her hooked.

"Uh, this guy, this ordinary guy, who sees her...really sees her for who she is and...loves her." Wow. He'd just recited the plot line for every novel he'd ever written. There was no way she was going to fall for this.

"He loves her?" she whispered, "Really?" Nick walked over to her and took her in his arms.

"Really." Had he just told Cianti he *loved* her? That was a new low even for him. He had to backtrack somehow.

"In the *book* he loves her, really he does."

"In the book?" she asked, her hazel eyes tinged with gold meeting his head on.

"The one you inspired." He said coming closer, his lips

grazing the top of her forehead.

"What's the title?" she asked placing her arms around his neck. Dammit, of course she would ask him the title of his fake book. He kissed her to buy some time. Her lips were full, warm and salty. Nick smiled.

"Well, I wanted to call it *Upendo*. But my editor said that not enough of my readers speak Swahili." Cianti laughed.

"Is that what you really want to call it?" she asked biting his lower lip. *Almost there.*

"Of course, don't you think it's a great title?" he smiled and began to kiss her again feeling her body respond with every touch of their lips.

"Nick, wait..." she said as he began to kiss her neck. *No! There's no time to wait!* He tried to pretend he didn't hear her as he gently pressed her up against the nearest wall.

"Nick, wait." She said more forcefully. *Shit!* He stopped and leaned away just a bit. They were both breathing heavy, Cianti's hair had come loose and his hoodie had made it to the floor.

"What is it?" he asked trying to keep the impatience and frustration out of his voice.

"Maybe this is a bad idea. I mean, you just call me out of the blue and you show up at my door after all this time? You didn't call after the last time. You didn't even send a freaking thank you note for that damn expensive t-shirt I sent you."

"I'm sorry, Cianti. You're right. I've been an asshole. I didn't call and I didn't thank you for the shirt, which by the way I love. I wore it last night." He almost wished she wouldn't believe him and throw his ass out on the street but in his experience the chances of that were slim. He might not have *done* the right things but by the look on her face he was sure he'd *said* the right things.

"Why don't we start over?" he asked pushing a strand of hair off of her face and behind her ear. She responded by kissing him even more passionately and pulling his t-shirt off. He lifted her up, hooked her legs around his waist, wrapped his arms around her torso and headed in the direction of the bedroom.

They fell onto the bed and Nick tried to ignore the fact that he was still hungover and generally messed up from the night before. He desperately hoped those two facts wouldn't *interfere* with what had to happen next or with the second phase of his plan which required a clear head and a strong stomach.

"Just a second..."he panted. Cianti was almost completely undressed but he still had his jeans on.

"What...no...come on." She said wrapping herself around him.

"My pants are stuck."

"Stuck?"

"I can't get them unbuttoned. Damn skinny jeans." He said and rolled off of her. Nick jumped up and struggled with the button for a moment until it finally came loose. He slipped off the jeans making sure that he took his phone out of the pocket. It only took a moment to set it up on the nightstand. Then he got back on the large King-sized bed and made his way back to a very eager Cianti, who was now as completely naked and aroused as he was. Once their bodies met Nick tried to focus on the task at hand and did his best to forget how easy it had been for him to lie to Cianti. Well- *that* and how easy it had been for him to press the record button on his phone before coming back to bed.

CHAPTER TEN

Deception

Cianti was lying across his chest when he woke up. She was asleep. Nick still had a pounding headache but he had managed to make love to Cianti and for that he congratulated himself. It hadn't taken much to convince his body to get with the plan but there were moments when he thought he might not be able to do it. Thankfully Cianti's own desire and skill in this area had made up for whatever energy and enthusiasm he might have lacked. He looked over at the nightstand. The phone had stopped recording so he reached over and picked it up put it in camera mode and shot a few selfies of the two of them laying together, zooming in on Cianti for another couple of frames. Nick sighed. Part of him knew he was a scumbag for doing this but there was also a part of him that didn't seem to care. So far the apathetic part seemed to be winning out. Nick checked the time. He'd been there for almost three hours and he could just imagine how pissed pseudo hipster and faux cabbie were at having to take laps around the block to avoid being spotted by the bodyguards. Generally he could have cared less but today he was on a mission. He had to get to LaGuardia and, depending on the traffic, it could take 30 minutes or an hour. Then he had to find a ticket to Nebraska and he had to do all of it without Barbara or any additional paparazzi finding out. The two dummies and their psycho pooch were his best bet on getting where he needed to go incognito.

"Are you awake?" Cianti's sleepy voice startled him.

"Yeah."

"Me too. But I don't want to be."

"Then go back to sleep."

"And what are you going to do?" she asked kissing his chest.

"Well, I was supposed to make a meeting in Denver about a new movie deal."

"On New Year's Day?"

"You know how it is..."

"Yeah, Yeah, I know. But it's New Year's Day. Why don't you stay here with me today. We can stay in bed all day." She said and her kisses began to move down his body. It was tempting. So tempting. But he couldn't—not today.

"You know I want to but this is the only chance I'll have to meet with these guys. They're on break so they have a little time. It's really important. Besides, it's going to be the adaptation of your favorite book."

"What?" she stopped kissing him and sat up.

"You know the one. The one that changed your life?" He gave her a wink.

"No way!"

"They're finally going to make it into a movie. Well,

that is if I can get to the meeting. If not there's a pretty good chance they'll move on to some other project."

"I can't believe it! It should have been made into a movie years ago!"

"Well, it's happening now. But there's just one problem."

"What's that?"

"I got a text that my flight got cancelled. There are no more flights going out today being the holiday and all everything's booked." *More lies. It was too easy.*

"Why don't you take your jet?"

"My jet? Are you kidding?"

"What?"

"I don't have a jet, Cianti."

"Of course you do. How else do you get to your book signings?"

"First Class airline tickets. I'm loaded but I'm not that loaded."

"I find that hard to believe," Cianti said raising an eyebrow.

"I *rent* private jets once in awhile. But it's never been practical to own one. Have you seen the price of gas?" He teased.

"That's the silliest thing I've ever heard, Nick. You're a best-selling author raking in millions from your films but you don't own a plane?"

"Not everyone is a global mega singing sensation turned award-nominated actress that's on the road 360 days out of the year." He tickled her.

"Stop it!" she laughed trying to get away. "I just don't get it. How can you afford to live in *that* penthouse and not have a jet?"

"Bingo! You've just figured it out. I had to choose. Penthouse or jet? I get more mileage out of the penthouse." He said with a grin.

"I bet you do." Cianti said leaning down to kiss him on the lips. "Stay with me."

"I can't." He said pulling her on top of him. "I have to get to Denver. Maybe I'll drive." *Nice work thinking up the Denver angle. Much more believable than Omaha.*

"You'll drive? From here to Denver? When is the meeting?"

"Tomorrow."

"There's no way you can drive from here to Denver by tomorrow, Nick. That's insane!"

"Maybe. But I thought that's what you liked about me." He kissed her again feeling aroused as she pressed against him.

"I have a solution. Why don't you take my plane?" *Yes!*

"I couldn't do that."

"Why not?"

"I wouldn't want to impose."

"It's not an imposition."

"I'll call down to make the arrangements. You'll get there in plenty of time for the meeting. But first..." She started to move down his body kiss by kiss. "I'll need a deposit toward that gas money." Nick laid back on the pillow and took in every sensation. He looked over at the phone again but couldn't quite make out the time. It was only a matter of time before pseudo hipster and faux cabbie would get frustrated enough to take off and leave him there at Cianti's. She would offer him her own Escalade as a ride to the airport, of course, but the last thing he needed was for the paparazzi that was used to tailing Cianti to follow him. If he stepped out of Cianti's Escalade and boarded Cianti's plane there would be questions and those would be directed at his agent Barbara King within minutes. He couldn't afford to take that chance. In the meantime, he felt he owed Cianti something for her kindness and attention. So this time as he reached for her he made sure that his body was completely turned on and that the camera phone was turned off.

CHAPTER ELEVEN

The Deal

Nick exited Cianti's place with Hipster's phone in his back pocket and an extra thousand dollars in cash that she'd lent him since he'd 'forgotten' his wallet at home. He tried not to think about what was on the phone. Cianti had tried very hard to convince him to stay with her and it had almost worked. But thinking back to the call he'd received from the Omaha Police Department always put him back on track. Cianti had, as he knew she would, offered him her Escalade and driver for the ride to the airport but he had politely refused saying that he had already made arrangements to get there. When he left her, she was still lying on the bed wrapped in silk sheets and sporting the afterglow of their time together. He almost regretted their liaison. It was the first time he had ever circled back for a second time and he couldn't deny that he had felt something—something he couldn't explain. It bothered him and that was a first too. The more time he had spent in the world of fame and celebrity the more quickly he had been schooled on the hierarchy of how things worked.

Beautiful and famous people hung out, partied and slept with other beautiful and famous people because it got them somewhere. Everybody knew that and no one took it personally because that's the way things worked. Sex was a business strategy. Relationships were a publicity train wreck waiting to happen—career killers. And what was the point of that? They were all here to advance their careers—if they wanted to have loving, monogamous relationships they had better give up on their dreams and go back to being *normal.* There was that rare occasion, however, when the beautiful and famous wanted more and believed they could have it. Nick wondered if such a thing were possible with someone like Cianti. He had seen glimpses of it when they first hooked up and now after their second, technically their third time together if he were to count how many times they had managed to make love since they met. He had to admit that it had been hard to leave her this time. Not just because of the sex but because he actually enjoyed her company. He'd allowed himself to feel something and that alarmed him. He had to shake it off. What choice did he have—especially once he gave Hipster back his phone?

He waited for about ten minutes before he saw the taxi make its way back to the front of the building. Pseudo Hipster and Faux Cabbie looked annoyed.

"Took you long enough." Faux Cabbie scowled.

"I don't think you'll care once you take a look at the phone," Nick said, getting into the front seat. Mr. Tippy Toes growled at him from the backseat.

"Missed you too, fur ball." Nick turned and threw the phone back at Hipster.

"Well, Gentlemen. I think this seals our deal."

"It depends on what you got." Hipster turned on the phone and started scrolling.

"Well?" Nick said putting on his sunglasses.

"Holy Shit! That's Cianti!" Hipster screamed.

"Let me see that!" Faux Cabbie ripped the phone out of his hands.

"Hey!" Hipster protested causing Mr. Tippy Toes to bark.

"Well, I'll be damned!" Faux Cabbie said under his breath. "That is Cianti—but...how?"

"We made a deal. I kept up my end. Now it's your turn. Get me to LaGuardia."

"Wait, we need details!" Hipster demanded.

"Dude—if I need to explain it to you then you're a bigger idiot than I thought and maybe you do deserve to freeze your ass off walking that mutt."

"Come on! You can't just leave us hanging!" Faux Cabbie clamored for the phone again.

"Look, guys. I think it's obvious your readers aren't visiting your site for the articles. I gave you what you wanted and now it's my turn. LaGuardia ASAP." Faux Cabbie and Pseudo Hipster exchanged glances.

"Fine. Deal's a deal." Faux Cabbie said putting the taxi into drive.

Nick stared out the window during the entire ride to the airport and even though they both tried to get more information out of him—not just about Cianti- but others in his circle, he was done talking. He only wished he could stop thinking. The last twenty-four hours had been a whirlwind of activity to put it mildly. At least he was able to push aside his thoughts about the party at the penthouse and his time with Cianti for a few minutes at a time, but the call from the Omaha Police Department was a different matter. That was burned into his brain along with every other memory connected to the place he was headed, and the man whose body he was on his way to claim. He'd been able to escape his past for almost five years and pretend it had never happened. But now it had caught up to him and shaken him to his core. Before he won the *First Draft* reality competition he had struggled to build a life for himself—an identity so different from whom he had been that his own mother would barely have recognized him. The moment they'd opened the envelope on the season finale and read his name, Nick Simon, best-selling author and future film producer, was born. Now he was forced to return to the place where the nightmare began and face his worst fears. It didn't seem fair. He didn't owe anyone anything. But here he was on the way to the airport after having hustled a beautiful and famous woman and conspired with the vultures who circled them both. He'd been willing to lie and betray her just so he could get back home. *Home.* He shuddered at what that meant. It wasn't the penthouse he thought of but that little white house on South 23rd Street by the zoo. Nick shut his eyes to erase the memory. He didn't want to go but he had to because he had to see it for himself. He had to make sure that the man lying in the morgue was really and truly dead.

CHAPTER TWELVE

Leaving on a Jet Plane

Pseudo Hipster and Faux Cabbie dropped him off near one of the terminals. Nick didn't want the dynamic duo to know exactly where Cianti's private hanger was located so he didn't have them drive him there. Besides it was better that he make it there on foot than be seen getting out of a car—any car. It took a while but he found the hanger on the far end of the airport discreetly shielded from the rest of the commercial air traffic. He found the entrance, gave the pilot the note with a confirmation code Cianti's bodyguard had given him on the way out and boarded the jet. When the male flight attendant came to ask him what he wanted for his in-flight beverage, Nick took the opportunity to ask if he could speak to the pilot himself. After a moment or two the pilot obliged and came to meet with him. It was easier than Nick thought to ask if they could reroute the flight to Omaha. He expected there to be a plethora of questions for which he had tried to work out answers on the taxi ride over but there was no need. The pilot informed him that it would be a moment while they submitted a new flight plan and that Nick would be informed when it was time for take-off. In the meantime he was free to enjoy the hospitality provided by the onboard staff. Nick was relieved. Maybe he could relax for the next three hours and forty-five minutes. *Maybe.* When the flight attendant returned with his shot of vodka Nick asked him to leave the bottle. He was going to need it.

"Mr. Simon?" Nick looked up to see the flight attendant. "The pilot asked me to inform you that we'll be taking off momentarily.

"Thanks."

Nick decided to take off his jacket and make an attempt to relax. But as he placed it behind him on the seat he heard his phone vibrate. He half hoped it was Cianti calling to wish him a safe flight but when he pulled it out of his pocket he knew he was in trouble. It was Barbara King, his agent. *Shit.* She'd found him. He could ignore the call, which is what he desperately wanted to do or he could answer it. Either way he would be in for a world of hurt. In the end he decided to answer it because he knew that she would just keep calling. Barbara King was not the type of woman to be ignored.

"Hello,Barbara."

"You sorry sonofabitch! Did you think I wasn't going to find about the little party you had last night?"

"Barbara, calm down. I don't know what Francois told you..."

"*He* didn't tell me anything, Nick! He didn't have to it's all over the freaking Internet, you idiot! Your *friends* posted pictures and video all over Twitter, Facebook and Instagram! You didn't even confiscate their phones? Are you really that stupid?"

"Come on, aren't you the one that always says that there's no such thing as bad publicity?"

"Don't patronize me, Nick! Have you *seen* what they posted? It's *all* bad! *Jesus*, they've got you on video smoking pot, doing lines and I can't even tell what you're doing with that *girl*. Oh my God! *Please* tell me you checked to make sure they were all over 21!"

"Barb-wait-listen to me..."

"Nick....I can't believe you would do something like this! After everything we've worked for! I don't even know where to begin, it's a nightmare. Why would you do this?"

"Are you going to let me talk?" Nick yelled into the phone.

"No, I'm freaking not going to let you talk, you idiot! You're going to listen and then you're going to haul your ass down to my office so we can make a plan. You at least had the good sense to keep the lights low so most of the video and picture are grainy and hard to make out, but there are a few that are going to be hard to make go away. We have to have a strategy—especially when we're only a month away from your next book release and three months away from the next movie. We have to act fast. Ambrose will get you himself. I'm not taking any chances. The paparazzi are going to be all over your building and it's going to be a freaking circus. So, get dressed and be ready in 30 minutes."

"I can't."

"You can't? What the hell do you mean 'you can't'. Whoever she is throw her out and whatever is lying around your place Francois will dispose of -so- jump in the shower, find some sunglasses, slap on one of those freaking knit hats you're so fond of and get your ass down to my office, Nick."

"I can't, Barbara. I'm traveling."

"NO! No, no, no! Where the hell are you, Nick? And you had better say the only trip you're taking has to do with that joint I saw you smoke in that freaking video clip!"

"I can't tell you where I'm going."

"The hell you can't. Nick, this is a career killer, do you know that? You're *the* most popular romance author in America.!"

"I don't write *romance*, Barbara. I hate it when you call it that."

"Of course you do! It's freaking *romance*, Nick! If you prefer I call it romantic *fiction* or romantic *drama* that's fine with me, but it's *romance* to the millions of women who read your crap! Now I made you the bad boy of romance on paper because your readers wanted that but it doesn't work the same way when they find out you're a boozing junkie who preys on young girls in real life!"

"I think you're blowing this way out of proportion, Barb. I think you're pissed because I had the party without you and you hate it when you're not in control." There was dead silence on the other end.

"Where are you, Nick? And you better say New York."

"There's something I've got to do."

"Where. Are. You?"

"I don't think this is as bad as you think. It's just a few pictures and clips on the internet—people are way more interested in YouTube cat videos anyway."

"Not today, Nick. The videos were uploaded to YouTube too and so far you've got more hits than that angry cat singing jingle bells. People are calling my office,

Nick. And when I say *people*, I mean producers, actors and publishers all wanting to know what the hell is going on. They don't necessarily want to be associated with this kind of publicity. Do you understand me? You could lose everything. *Everything.*"

"You mean *you* could lose everything, Barbara. I have to go."

"Nick, dammit, don't you *dare* hang up on me! Nick-" he ended the call and turned the phone off completely. He had enough on his mind. He didn't need to be dealing with Barbara's paranoia too.

The pilot's voice came over the intercom asking him to put on his seatbelt and prepare for take-off. Fastening the belt he poured himself another shot of vodka and leaned back in his seat as the jet began to taxi down the runway. He pulled down the window shade and put his sunglasses back on. Nick hated to fly, it made him nervous and sometimes nauseous but he had no choice. The vodka usually helped but on this trip it didn't seem to have the same soothing effect. Nick's mind was swirling. *What the hell am I doing?* Here he was headed back to a past he had fought so hard to leave behind—a past, that, if Barbara turned out to be right, would cost him his career and the life he'd built in New York. There was still time. He could call the flight attendant and ask him to let the pilot know that Nick had changed his mind. He could tell Barbara where he was and wait for Ambrose to pick him up. He could go to Barbara, like a dog with a tail between its legs and beg her forgiveness and help her strategize in order to save his reputation. *But what about Alex?* Nick had made a promise and he had to keep it no matter what. That's what he decided as the jet left New York airspace and headed for Omaha. It was the only choice. It was the only way. There was no turning back now.

CHAPTER THIRTEEN

Ghosts

Nick fell into a deep, drunk sleep one hour into the flight. That's when the nightmare began. It was a nightmare he hadn't had in almost five years. In it he was standing in one of the back bedrooms of the little white house.

It was the middle of the day but it was dark inside the room. He could barely make out the silhouette sitting on the edge of the bed. Nick took a tentative step toward the figure, a sense of dread filling every cell in his body. His breathing came in short, shallow bursts and he could feel cold droplets of sweat run down his back. He kept walking toward the bed even though he wanted to turn in the opposite direction. The figure was still. Nick had no idea if his presence in the room had been noticed until his foot hit something on the floor near the bed. It was a hand. He called out in fear and disgust. Someone was sprawled, face down on the floor, the hand reaching out as if desperate to escape, to call out for help that never came. Nick was horrified. Words remained trapped in his throat as he looked up and saw that the figure sitting on the bed was staring at him. He knew that face and while it remained mostly hidden in the darkness of the room, he could never forget it. He could never escape it because it resembled his own. Sitting on the edge of the bed was a man, eyes glassy, smelling strongly of booze and holding a long leather belt in his hands. Nick looked at the belt and back down at the body on the floor. He noticed between the shadows and the light coming through the slats of the bedroom blinds that there was blood everywhere.

"I told him what would happen," the man said—his speech slurred and his voice void of any emotion.

Before Nick could process everything he was seeing, the older man stood up and walked the short distance between them. Belt lifted, eyes bloodshot and crazed, the man reached out and grabbed him by the shoulder as Nick put up his hands to defend himself from the coming attack.

"Why won't you boys ever learn?" he yelled, lunging at Nick.

"No!" Nick screamed and that's when he woke up to find the flight attendant staring at him. He had one hand on Nick's shoulder which he promptly removed. Nick's breathing was coming out in quick, short spasms.

"I'm sorry, Mr. Simon. The pilot asked me to inform you that we'll be landing in Omaha in approximately twenty minutes."

"T-thank you." Nick stammered and tried to compose himself. He noticed that the bottle of vodka was still sitting on the tray in front of him. He didn't bother to pour another shot, instead he grabbed the bottle, twisted the cap off and took a long swig. Nick closed his eyes as he felt the burn of the alcohol rush down his throat and into his belly. He felt the heat of it spread through his body and welcomed the numbness of mind that followed. He coughed and wiped his mouth with the back of his hand before taking another swig. He had to erase the dream and everything he'd seen. He refused to go back to the way things had been, to the way *he* had been before he left Omaha behind and made his way to LA and then to New York. He'd wanted to go to Los Angeles, not because he aspired to be an actor or even a writer, he had no real aspirations back then, but because it didn't resemble the place that had birthed, raised and wrecked him. The people were different, the weather was different and the opportunity to recreate himself was *everything*. Nothing he had done or experienced in LA, even at its worst, had ever been as bad as what he left behind. While other transplants complained about the problems of being an outsider, working shit jobs, getting tough breaks, or having their dreams crushed, Nick hustled, networked and got ahead. He bounced from gig to gig but he liked it. The thought of writing had never even crossed his mind until a guy he'd met while tending bar, who worked as a production assistant, told him about an upcoming reality show called *First Draft/Final Cut*, a reality competition where aspiring authors compete to complete a novel in 30 days for the chance at a publishing and film contract. The production assistant had been drowning his sorrows in tequila for about an hour, complaining about how hard it was to find the right people to cast. Nick listened and frowned. How was that possible in a town like LA?

"Have you *seen* many writers?" the very drunk production assistant had asked Nick as he poured him another shot.

"I guess not." Nick shrugged.

"There's a reason they keep them in a locked room working through the night and don't parade them in front of the camera." The guy gulped down his shot and laughed. *Jackass.* But Nick didn't see the problem. In LA there wasn't anything that couldn't be sculpted or fixed with a little nip here or a little tuck there. He said as much to the guy who slapped his hand down on the bar and shoved the shot glass back toward Nick for a refill. He poured.

"No, this is different." The guy slurred. "They're looking for something. . .special." Nick grinned. Everyone in LA was looking for something *special.*

"I thought it was a show about writing." Nick said wiping down the bar. It was the production assistant's turn to scoff.

"Sort of."

"Well, is it or isn't it?" Nick asked. The production assistant looked up and Nick was sure he was probably seeing multiples after all the tequila he'd been drinking.

"Naw, not really. They just need some pretty faces and some fucked up shit heads to come in and fight it out. The coaches will do most of the work."

"The coaches?"

"Yeah, the writing coaches and script writers that've been tapped to work on the show. They each choose teams and then they coach 'em until there's a winner."

"Sounds like a real snooze fest to me." Nick was organizing the bottles behind the bar.

"Yep, that's why they've got to be hot or really fucked up to keep it interesting."

"So skills don't count?"

"Not so much."

"So what's the problem? It's LA. All you have to do is throw a rock in any direction and your problem's solved."

"Tell that to the idiots I work with," the guy whined into his next drink. Then his bloodshot eyes wandered up and down the length of Nick's profile.

"You an actor?" the guy asked and Nick shook his head.

"Nope."

"Writer? Filmmaker?"

"Nope."

"Are you serious?"

"Yeah."

"You're not an aspiring anything?"

"Not me. I'm a bartender here on Mondays, Thursdays and Fridays. "

"Bullshit. Everyone's here to be something else." The guy frowned and Nick couldn't blame him. However, Nick had what he wanted, he had a new life and it was different from his old one. But the guy was right, everyone in LA was there to be *something* else. The difference was that Nick was happy being *someone* else.

"One more." The guy motioned toward the tequila bottle behind Nick. It would be cut off time soon. The last thing Nick needed was this guy passed out on the bar.

"You should think about it," the production assistant said gulping down the shot.

"Think about what?"

"Acting." The guy slurred and Nick cocked an eyebrow. It was definitely cut off time.

"I don't think so."

"Really, I'm not blowing smoke up your ass. You should really consider it. You've got the look."

"You're right, I look like a bartender, maybe three or four given how much tequila's in you right now."

"You're a smartass. I like it. You should try out for this show. You work out?"

"Doesn't everybody?"

"Do you always dress like that or is it the bar's look?"

Nick was starting to get annoyed.

"Maybe we should call you a cab."

"I'm fine." The production assistant tried to get up and almost stumbled. Nick came around the bar and caught him before he face-planted on the floor. He dragged him from the bar to one of the booths nearby.

"Come on, buddy. The bar doesn't have uniforms but it has rules and you're getting close to reaching the limit.

"So this is your own look," the guy mumbled from the booth. "It could work. With some leather and a little 5 o'clock shadow, it could work. You have any tattoos? Any scars? They *love* scars. "

"Thanks, but no thanks." Nick took the empty shot glass and put it in the plastic bin set aside for washing.

"The question is, you the hot one or the fucked up one?"

Nick glared at the guy.

"Oh, I get it. You're *both.* " The guy laughed and laid his head on the table with a thud.

"I'm calling you a cab," Nick said heading back to the bar. He called the taxi service and after about twenty minutes put the production assistant inside.

"Seriously, I think you could do it," he said as Nick was about to shut the door. "Here, take it." The drunk man shoved a card at him through the narrow opening of the window. Nick took it and smacked the side of the cab to let the driver know it was okay to go. He watched the cab pull away and then glanced down at the card. He took about ten seconds to read the information and consider the guy's offer before shoving the card into his wallet. Then, he went back inside and forgot all about it.

Nick opened his eyes and took another drink. The plane would be landing soon and he needed a plan. Once off the plane he needed to call the Sheriff's office and get directions to their morgue so he could go and look on the face of the man that had haunted his dreams for years. The flight attendant came back to the cabin and reached out for the shot glass and the vodka bottle. Nick's grip tightened on the bottle.

"We're getting ready to land, Mr. Simon."

"Don't worry I'll make sure it's safe. You can take the glass." The flight attendant looked flustered but did as Nick instructed and took the glass—after making sure the seat tray was in its upright position. He lifted the window shade and looked out into the open sky. Looking down he saw the sprawling green and brown landscape of Nebraska come into view. He sighed. He'd sworn he would never come back. *Never*. Yet, here he was about to land. Nick could feel the plane begin to descend and pulled the shade back down. He'd seen enough.

He opened the bottle and took another drink. It was almost empty but he didn't feel drunk. Sadly, it didn't have that effect anymore. Now, he was just hoping for numb. He didn't want to feel *anything*, especially when he stepped foot in that morgue. He wanted to reserve any emotion that still lived inside him somewhere for Alex. *Alex*. How often had that name crossed his mind in the last five years? Very few and he had worked hard to keep it that way. If only things had turned out differently. What kind of life would he be leading now? Would he have gone to that audition? Would he have realized that he had a story inside him to tell after all? A story that would go on to win him the *First Draft/Final Cut* competition? But at what price? He'd give anything, even the life he'd built in LA, and New York—the success, the money, the women and that damn penthouse to go back and change what happened that day in the little white house but it was too late. He'd been too late to stop it and Alex had paid the price.

CHAPTER FOURTEEN

The Morgue

The plane was circling Eppley Airfield in its final descent. Overall, it had been a very smooth flight and Nick reminded himself that he should make sure to pay Cianti another visit to thank her in person for the use of her jet. He smiled. He liked Cianti. She was beautiful, talented and deep down a very trusting human being, which is why it bothered him that he had to use her in order to get to Omaha.

He turned on his phone and found he had a dozen messages, eleven of them from Barbara King, his agent. Nick hit the delete button on all of them but one; it was from the Omaha Police Department. He listened to the message from Detective Pat Baker twice. In it the officer provided directions to his office and offered to go to the morgue with him to make the identification. Nick slid his phone in the pocket of his jeans, unbuckled his seatbelt and stood up. The flight attendant met him in the aisle and Nick reluctantly handed him the vodka bottle.

"We have a car waiting for you, Mr. Simon."

"That's all right." Nick said avoiding eye-contact. "I'd prefer a taxi." The flight attendant frowned.

"Ms. Richards always hires a car and driver. We called ahead and reserved one for you." The man insisted, pointing out one of the open cabin windows. Nick could see a black SUV waiting on the tarmac with a driver standing beside it.

"I appreciate that but I'm not Ms. Richards. I prefer a taxi. Please call me one." Nick stuck his hands in his pockets and stared at his feet. The flight attendant hesitated.

"But, Ms. Richards. . ." He began and Nick exploded.

"Look, I don't care what the hell Ms. Richards does. I don't want the SUV or the damn driver!" Nick yelled and the flight attendant retreated without saying another word. Nick chastised himself for being a dick. But he couldn't worry about that now. He had to get to the morgue and the last thing he needed was to have someone keeping track of him and where he was going. He'd been very careful about building his backstory while he was in the *First Draft/Final Cut* competition. Omaha and what had happened all those years ago wasn't part of it. He didn't care about his reputation like Barbara did, but he wasn't an idiot. Sure, if he thought about it, the party at the penthouse had been a stupid move but it wasn't anything that Barbara couldn't fix. He was certain of it because she was motivated to keep her number one meal ticket intact. She'd figure it out, she always did.

A few minutes passed before the flight attendant returned to let him know that the taxi had arrived. Nick felt he should apologize to the man for speaking to him so harshly but once he saw the taxi waiting outside he couldn't concentrate on anything else. He wanted to get to the Police Department. He descended the stairs of the jet and made a b-line for the taxi. It was cold outside but there wasn't any snow on the ground like there had been back in New York. Nick still pulled his jacket tight and shivered. He could see his breath in the air as he opened the door. Once inside, he instructed the driver to take him to the address provided by the detective. Nick watched as they pulled away from the airport and the cityscape got closer and closer..

"Been here before?" asked the driver and Nick hesitated.

"Once or twice."

"Where you from?"

"Back east." Nick said hoping his vague answers would stop the man from continuing the conversation. No such luck.

"Chicago? Boston? Philly?" The driver threw out the names of some cities but Nick didn't answer and the man moved on.

"You picked a lousy time to visit. It's cold out here. But if you're from the east you're probably used to it."

"Yeah." Nick answered.

"Visiting family?"

"You could say that."Nick said under his breath.

"What was that?" The driver asked but Nick didn't repeat it.

"Nothing."

"Me and my family did our thing last night, you know, with the giant ball on TV in Times Square. We watched the countdown, had a few a drinks and a few laughs. Wish I could've gotten wasted like everybody else but I had to work today. What about you? Did you do anything special?"

"No." Nick was starting to get annoyed with the man and he sincerely missed the indifferent New York City cab drivers, who didn't give a shit who you were or where you were going. He missed their passive/aggressive silence and cursed the chattiness and friendliness that was typical of the Midwest. Although the trip from the airport to the Police Department would still be thirty to forty minutes shorter than it took to get anywhere he usually had to go in Manhattan, due to the traffic, traveling with this curious cabbie made it feel like it was taking an eternity.

"How far is it?" Nick asked impatiently.

"Another five or ten minutes. You like football?"

"Sure."

"You follow college ball?"

"Sometimes." He answered and knew immediately that the cabbie was about to entertain him with a liturgy on the state's number one sport: Husker football. He wanted to tell the man that he knew all about it, that he'd sat with the other 77,000 people before in Memorial Stadium on the University of Nebraska campus among the waves of red-clan rabid fans cheering on the team more than once, but how could he?

"If you ever get the chance you should visit in the fall and go to a game. It'll blow your mind." Then, the man started recounting the past season's stats, players and coaching mistakes. Nick already knew the team had blown their chance at their bowl game because he still had a habit of following the team once in a while when the information ticked across the bottom of the screen on ESPN, but talking about it kept the driver from asking

Nick any more questions. He was grateful for that and every once in a while he threw in an 'uh-huh' or an 'are you kidding?' to keep the man talking. Before he knew it they had arrived and the driver had to tell Nick twice that he could get out, before he finally did.

"“You know this here's the Police Department right?” You meeting your people here?" the driver asked as Nick paid him.

"No, I'm meeting them at a restaurant nearby," he answered slipping the man a little extra money, hoping it would stick in his head if anybody asked him. But the man was still skeptical.

"Don't worry, I have the directions. The place is brand new." Nick lied hoping the man would let it go. The driver shrugged.

"Ok, if you need a taxi to pick you up just call the service and someone will come get you."

"Thanks," Nick called as the taxi pulled away and the driver waved. He waved back, took a deep breath and exhaled before stepping inside the Police Department. The nightmare was about to begin. . .again.

CHAPTER FIFTEEN

The Ugly Truth

He found Detective Pat Baker waiting for him in a cubicle at the back of the station.

"I'm Nick Simon." Nick stuck out a hand and the deputy took it in a firm, vice-like grip. The Detective was a tall man with broad shoulders, a protruding midsection and a weary expression.

"I recognize you from your book jacket,"he said, holding up a copy of Nick's latest hardcover. "Turns out my wife's a fan."

Under normal circumstances, Nick would have offered to autograph the book for him, but his brain was too preoccupied with what he needed to do. He just stood there staring at a grouping of photos on the detective's desk. Among the pictures of him with his large, extended family there were several older photographs with his two sons. Nick winced inwardly and looked away.

"Thank you for coming down on such short notice. Normally, I wouldn't expect someone like you to make it down here as quickly as you have, but I assume you want to take care of it and make sure."

"You're right," Nick agreed and waited for the detective to tell him what to do next.

"Well, let's go downstairs and take a look," Detective Baker said, leading Nick out of the cubicle and toward a metal door farther back. Nick started to shiver involuntarily as they descended the stairs to the basement. Within a few minutes they found themselves in a sterile hospital-like room with a stainless steel table in the middle, sitting underneath large examination lights. There was a body on the table covered by a sheet and a woman standing at the head of the table.

"This is our coroner—Dr. Harris." The detective nodded in the direction of the woman. She gave him a slight nod in return. Slowly, she removed the part of the sheet covering the face and Nick stopped breathing.

"Do you recognize this man?" the detective asked and Nick studied the face. It was pale, almost gray and it was covered in a scruffy beard. The eyes were closed. The receding hairline extended to the middle of the head and then grew out long into a frizzy shoulder length river of salt and pepper. He looked like any other homeless man he'd seen sitting near the subway or on the streets of New York. He didn't know *this* man.

"Mr. Simon?" The detective threw him a questioning glance. Nick swallowed. He stared at the face trying to find the man that haunted his nightmares, attacked him, hurt him and screamed insults. Nick was trembling. He didn't look like the same man. He didn't look like the figure that sat on the bed with the belt. This man didn't reek of Jack Daniels and beer; he reeked of disinfectant and death.

"Mr. Simon, is this your father?" the detective asked again and Nick met his gaze with uncertainty.

"You say he had my number?"

"Yes and your name."

"Who gave it to him?" Nick asked nervously and the detective shrugged.

"Are you saying you didn't?"

"No." Nick shook his head emphatically.

"I don't know." The detective admitted.

"What about the man at the shelter. You mentioned there was someone he talked to about me?"

"Yes, the director of one of the shelters near here made a tentative ID and said the man told him you were his son. He seemed very proud of it too. Of course, nobody really took him seriously. But they liked him and they played along. I imagine they'd be fairly surprised if it were true." Nick frowned. He hadn't seen his father in years. Not after what happened to Alex.

"This man is not your father?" Nick stared at the dead man again. He tried to compare him to the man he knew. The drunk, the man who beat his kids and hit his wife. The respectable community man beloved by all and suspected by no one until it was too late. Nick shook his head.

"No, I'm sorry, it's not him."

"Are you sure?" Detective Baker asked studying him intently.

"Yes."

"Okay. Doc, you can put him back," the deputy said to the coroner and she covered up the body.

"What happens if no one claims him?" Nick mustered the courage to ask.

The deputy cocked an eyebrow giving Nick a sideways glance.

"He'll be a John Doe and probably end up in potter's field with a number for a marker."

"I didn't know those places still existed."

"Yeah. Damn shame to end up that way. Means you don't have any family to claim you. You just disappear. I'm glad he wasn't your father, Mr. Simon. But I can't help feel bad for the old man. We can't keep him here. The guy at the shelter said he was nice and good with the younger kids."

"Too bad," Nick said, trying to keep the edge out of his voice. They made their way back up the stairs to the deputy's office.

"Well, I'm sorry you had to come all the way out here and on New Year's Day of all things. But I'm glad it turned out all right. I don't know what to tell you about how the man ended up with your information. I'll keep looking and let you know if I find anything."

"I appreciate that."

"Not to be too forward, Mr. Simon, but my wife will skin me alive if I don't ask. And being that things did turn out okay, would you mind autographing my wife's book?" Detective Baker held out the hardcover and a pen in Nick's direction. Nick put on his best author-at-a-signing smile and took the book.

"Who should I make it out to?"

"Mary Anne Baker. She'll be thrilled." The deputy grinned and Nick signed the inside of the cover. Giving it back to him, Nick shook his hand.

"Thank you for your help, Detective."

"No problem. You have a safe trip back to New York."

Detective Baker said as Nick exited his office and made his way out onto the cold streets of Omaha in search of nearest bar.

CHAPTER SIXTEEN

Memories

The son of a bitch was dead. He was really and truly dead. Nick sat on a barstool five blocks from the Omaha Police Department, nursing a beer and a haphazard row of shots. He still wasn't sufficiently numb. He needed something else, he needed something more to make the memories stop, to keep the guilt at bay. There was a jukebox playing 80's hard rock and a group of tattooed bikers playing pool in the back of the bar. His phone had been buzzing for the last hour but he had ignored it. It was just Barbara leaving more threatening messages. He didn't care. He'd come to see it for himself and now that he had he didn't quite know what to do next. Going back to New York would have to wait until he was in the right state of mind to talk Barbara down from her broom so she could make the arrangements for him to fly home. Given the tenor of her messages, he figured it wouldn't be anytime soon. In the meantime, he planned on drowning his sorrows in beer and tequila, using up a good wad of his cash to make the memories go away. Before he did that he needed to make one more stop. He needed to see Alex and give him the news. The son of a bitch was dead. Even as he thought the words, he didn't feel any relief. He didn't feel anything at all. He knocked back another shot and followed it with the last of the beer. Nick looked up the name of the taxi service that had picked him up at the airport and called. This time the driver had nothing to say. He asked for Nick's destination and quickly got him there. Stepping out of the cab, Nick paid the driver and walked toward the entrance. Passing the chapel on the right, he walked the long gray path that ran through the entire cemetery. Going from memory, Nick made his way past hundreds of headstones and family mausoleums on his way to see Alex. After ten minutes or so, he took the path that branched to the right and found himself near a large oak tree that served as a marker. Alex was nearby. He walked another hundred feet and zig-zagged in and around the marble headstones, many of which were decorated for the season. There were wreaths and plastic holly, miniature Santas and tinsel nativities at the foot of the stones left there no doubt by grieving family members missing their dearly departed during the holidays. Then there was Alex's headstone, cold and bare with nothing but his name and the dates, indicating how long he'd managed to survive in the little white house. Six years. That was all. It hadn't been long enough. Nick stared at the concrete slab on which the headstone rested. There wasn't a sign of a flower living or dead, no ornaments, no tinsel nativities or plastic holly. Nothing. It looked like he was the only visitor Alex had had in a long time and Nick had nothing to put on his grave. He felt ashamed. He should have picked up something on his way here but he was too busy thinking about the man in the morgue. Some things hadn't changed. The bastard had still managed to take center stage, to take up all of his focus to the point that he hadn't given Alex the consideration he deserved. Even in death his father had managed to make him feel worthless and ashamed. Nick took a deep breath. The air was getting colder and he pulled his jacket around him even tighter. There was so much he wanted to say, especially now that it was over. But the words stuck in his throat and the tears welled up in his eyes.

"Hey, Alex." He finally managed to say. "I'm sorry it took me so long to come see you. No good reason, you know me." Nick shrugged and then looked around. There was nobody within one hundred yards but a couple of squirrels running up and down the nearby spiraling oaks that dotted the landscape.

"I came to give you the news, but you probably already heard. He's dead. I saw him myself. He looks different, but it's him." He wiped a couple of rogue tears from his face with the back of his hand. "He can't hurt anybody anymore." The wind picked up and carried a piece of plastic poinsettia from a neighboring grave and settled at the foot of Alex's grave.

"I know. I'm sorry I didn't bring you anything. You know I suck at giving gifts." Nick managed a weak laugh and wiped away another tear. "I promise I'll bring you something before I go back." He stuck both hands in his jeans pockets to keep warm. The weather was turning and Nick knew his own emotions, raw and unchecked, wouldn't hold out much longer. He couldn't stay. The pain was too much and he was too tired from the trip—from going to the morgue and from seeing Alex after all this time. It was time to call the taxi service again and find another place to numb his feelings and maybe something extra to calm his mind. He could go back to the bar near the Police Department or find some place new. He dialed the number of the taxi service and made his way back out of the cemetery to wait. Then, remembering a place he used to go, he gave the address to the driver. When the driver heard the address, the man took one look at Nick and hesitated.

"Are you sure you want to go to that part of town?" Nick sighed. Only in Nebraska would a cabbie ask a fare if he was sure of where he wanted to go. A New York cabbie would have dropped him at Jeffrey Dahmer's doorstep if he'd paid him. But Nick knew what the driver knew. The only people who went to that address did so for one reason, so it was no surprise that he asked. Nick was dressed like a New Yorker, a high end one at that, and while he didn't look like the obvious tourist, he looked different enough that the driver questioned his choice of destination. After all, it wasn't the Old Market, full of colorful shops, restaurants, corner musicians and horse-drawn carriages. It was a place where one could get lost, with the help of some very unsavory characters and never be found. For now, that's what Nick wanted.

"Okay," the driver said. "If *that's* where you want to go." Nick nodded and sat back in the seat. He took out his cellphone and scrolled through his texts and messages. There was one text from Cianti:

Call me.

Nick frowned. No exclamation point, no expletives, just those two words. He went to the PaPaRazzo website to see if those two idiots had put up the pictures he'd given them. Nothing. But what he did see were pictures and video clips from the party at his penthouse. He didn't even bother to look, he closed out the browser, then deleted the next six additional voicemails that Barbara had left him. She was still pissed, even more so now that the pictures and videoclips were making their way around to every celebrity website and entertainment news channel on the planet. He was still news. Yet he didn't care. He wondered how long it would take Faux Cabbie and Pseudo Hipster to put up what he'd given them. What would Cianti do once she found out what he had done? He hated to imagine it, but if none of it had surfaced yet, then why was Cianti calling him? Maybe to ask why he rerouted her plane to Omaha or why he treated her personal flight attendant like shit on the plane? He looked up her number and placed his thumb over the dial button. Nick knew he owed her an apology, if not an explanation. He liked her, he really did. It was more than just sex. There was some sort of connection that he couldn't put his finger on. He hesitated and then reluctantly he turned off his phone completely and put it back in his pocket. Nick took out his wallet and counted the bills he had left. While he'd managed to go through the bulk of it during the party at his penthouse, he still had more than enough left from what Cianti had given him for what he wanted to buy. When the driver dropped him off on a random corner Nick headed to the bar down the street. Compared to the pool hall he'd been at near the Police Department this place was a true hole in the wall, with actual black gaping voids exposing the beams and wiring beneath the drywall. For a holiday, the place was packed with all sorts of people. Some of them looked like they'd spent the night sprawled out drunk, or high, in the booths with ripped vinyl seats. He headed for the bar and managed to squeeze between an old toothless drunk and a large, imposing guy with a bloody skull tattooed on his bald head. The bartender poured him a shot, but before he went on to serve another customer, Nick got his attention. The man came in close, cocking an eyebrow, as Nick tried to whisper something into the ear covered in metal posts, small spikes and studs. Then Nick took a wadded up bill and shoved it discreetly into the man's hand. Lowering his hand under the bar and taking a look, the bartender nodded and waved Nick over to the other end of the bar. Nick gulped down his shot and followed.

The bartender took Nick to a back room where there was a card game going. Several men and two scantily-clad women were sitting around a folding table playing. The bartender whispered something into the ear of the smallest man at the table. He looked fairly regular, no tattoos, no scars and no weird hair or spikes. He was dressed in a Nebraska polo shirt and jeans. The bartender waved Nick over and introduced him to the guy in Husker red.

"Jake," he said, holding out a hand and shooting him a smile. Nick shook his hand without giving his name. The guy didn't seem bothered by Nick's lack of manners.

"So, you're in need of my services?"

"Yeah."

"I work from an a la carte menu. You tell me what you're looking for and I"ll tell you if I carry it on the menu." Husker red waited for Nick to place his order.

"I already told this guy what I wanted and he told me you had it. I've got the money," Nick said, flashing the wad of bills in his hand. He looked over at the bartender and then back to the guy in the polo shirt.

"Dammit, Eddie, why do you go getting ahead of yourself. *I* take care of the menu, you take care of the reservations," the guy in the polo shirt said, rolling his eyes in mock exasperation. The bartender shrugged and gave him a semi toothless grin.

"So do you have what I want or don't you?" Nick was impatient. He could feel the memories and emotions starting to fill his entire being. He couldn't handle it. He didn't *want* to handle it.

"Yeah. I do. And if you've got the time and the money I've got a sale going. It's a combo and I'll throw in some extras," he said, nodding toward the two women. Nick licked his lips and looked from the women to the guy in the polo shirt.

"I'd to like see what I'm getting before I decide." The guy in the polo shirt motioned for one of the large men at the table. The man stood up and disappeared through a door a few feet away. When he returned, he was holding a wooden box. He handed it to the guy in the polo shirt, who opened it for Nick. Inside were a variety of recreational drugs that Nick recognized along with the implements needed for their use.

"How much for the whole box?" he asked eyeing a particular bag.

"Don't you want a sample first?" the guy in the polo shirt asked, picking up the bag Nick wanted.

"Why, are you planning on screwing me over?"

"That wouldn't be good for business, now would it?"

"How much?"

"What you've got in your hand should cover it. If you want to throw in a little more I'll make sure Eddie keeps you hydrated." The guy in the polo shirt flashed him a smile and Nick reached in his pocket and pulled out a few more bills.

"Vodka." Nick called over his shoulder as he handed the dealer the money. The guy in the polo shirt closed the lid on the box and handed it to Nick. Then he motioned the two women over.

"I have a room you can use to enjoy your purchase and your company. You won't be disturbed. Bruno here will take you." Nick followed the large man sporting a tattoo featuring a severed head pierced by a blood-drenched switchblade, with a woman hanging on each arm. He gripped the wooden box tight and pushed all thoughts of anything but getting to the room and finding his own personal oblivion.

CHAPTER SEVENTEEN

The White Light

The women were all over him before the door was closed. If he didn't stop them soon he'd be undressed and in bed with them and he wouldn't be able to stop himself from doing what he was used to doing—what he'd always done. He was still clutching the wooden box under his arm and one of the women was already tugging at it. There was a knock at the door. It was Nick's *complimentary* bottle of vodka. He took it, closed the door and made his way to the bed. He needed to keep it simple.

"Keys." He said to the women and they barely stopped to acknowledge him.

"Keys!" He yelled putting out his hand and clutching the wooden box tightly to his body. The women stopped and stared for a moment.

"There's no reason to get testy, baby." She purred. "What do you want?"

"I need a car. Do you have one?"

"Yeah. It's a junker though. What do you need a car for? You've got everything you need right here." She smiled and returned to kissing his earlobes.

"You can have the box if you'll give me your keys and tell me where your car is." Nick offered and the women looked at each other.

"What's the catch?" asked the second woman.

"No catch. Not really. You take the box minus the white bag and the bottle and a set of keys." Nick said and the second woman eyed him suspiciously.

"That's crazy. You're gonna give us the box and all you want is the vodka and the bag?" She laughed revealing a large gap between her front teeth.

"You know how much I paid your boss for the box. So crazy as it sounds, yes. Do we have a deal?"

"How do we know you're not going to tell him we took it from you?"

"Give me your keys and take me to the car. I'll be out of your hair as soon as you show me where it is."

The two women sat on the bed eyeing the wooden box that he was holding. They looked at each other and finally the woman with the gap between her front teeth reached into her pocket and took out a set of keys. She got up, came up to Nick, and dangled them.

"Ok, baby. Here you go."

He grabbed the keys and turned over the box. She quickly took it over to the bed where the other woman was eagerly waiting. Nick shoved the keys in his pocket.

"Hey, you forgetting something?" he asked as the women began to divvy up the contents of the box among themselves.

"Here you go, baby." The gap-toothed woman threw him a small white bag. Nick caught it midair and stuffed it in his other pocket.

"Where's the car?" he asked and the woman sighed in exasperation.

"Now?" she asked not bothering to hide how annoyed she was.

"Yes. Now."

She rolled her eyes. "Fine. Follow me."

She showed him to the back of the room where there was a large metal utility shelf full of boxes.

"What's this?" he asked impatiently.

"It goes to the alley. That's where I parked my car."

Nick was completely confused. The woman rolled her eyes.

"Just push that way and you'll see."

Nick set down the vodka bottle behind him. He leaned against the shelf and pushed. At first it didn't budge. It was heavy and whatever was in the boxes was making it heavier.

"Come on, baby. You gotta lean into it, like this."

She took over Nick's spot and leaned against it. This time there was a movement and a squeak. The shelf moved a few inches. The gap-toothed woman grinned.

"There I got it started for you."

"You're pretty strong."

"For a woman?"

"You're just pretty strong."

Nick put all of his strength into it this time. The shelf moved almost half way. After one more push it revealed a door.

"Where did you say this leads to?"

"The alley."

"Then why is it covered up by the shelf. What if your boss needs it to get out."

"There are other ways out. Finding a place for inventory was more important," she said, looking up at the boxes marked as different brands of cleaning and automotive supplies. He decided not to ask any more about the *inventory*. He didn't need to know more about the operation than necessary.

"Ok, just show me where the car is."

He bent down to pick up the bottle. The gap-toothed woman reached out and pulled on the door knob. Unlike the shelf it opened easily and led, just like she'd said, into a back alley. There he saw an old beat-up '84 Ford Escort parked by the dumpsters. Nick walked toward it, got in and inserted the key.

"Good luck, baby," the gap-toothed woman called from the door, which she quickly shut, locked, and from the sound of it, was blocking with the heavy shelf again. Nick opened the bottle of vodka and took a long drink. It burned more than his usual brand did. So much for quality. He took out the small white bag and stared at it. He decided to save it for later and started the car. The engine refused to turn. He had to try two more times before it finally squeaked to life. Taking another swig of vodka, Nick put the car into gear, drove out of the alley, and headed down the street at a high speed. He knew where he needed to go but things were starting to blur. Nick shook his head, forcing himself to focus on what he was doing, but little by little the faces and places from the past he'd been trying to avoid for the last five years were catching up with him. If only he hadn't left Alex behind—in that house—with that man. But what could he have done differently? he'd asked himself a thousand times. Then he'd promised himself he would never ask again.

It had all worked out until he'd received that call from Detective Pat Baker. He drove faster. Why had he come here? Did he really need to see it for himself? *Yes.* He did, he knew he did. But now there was a price to pay for seeing things through. The car sped down a street he vaguely recalled passing in the taxi. *Wasn't it a one way street?* It was pretty much deserted even though there was some honking. *Are they honking at me?* He pressed his foot down on the pedal as he turned the corner and heard the tires squeal. He squeezed his eyes tight and laughed. Then he opened them and focused. He knew where he was now. He was only blocks from the cemetery. It was time to go see Alex again and this time he'd brought a gift. Before getting to the bar Nick had asked the taxi driver to stop at a gas station where he'd bought something he'd been carrying around in his pocket ever since. It now sat next to the small plastic bag filled with white powder he'd purchased from the guy in the polo shirt. It was a tiny green teddy bear hanging from a keychain in the seat next to him. *Faster! Go faster!* The memories kept coming and with each one the speedometer climbed.

"I wanna go with you!"

"I can't, Alex."

"I wanna go with you!"

"I know you do, buddy. But you can't. Besides you have school."

"I'm a big boy! I don't wanna go to Kindergarten. I wanna go with you!" he gave Nick a toothy grin minus one tooth. Nick ruffled the hair on the top of his head. Alex jumped on the bed knocking Nick's clothes on the floor.

"Stop it! Come on I'm trying to pack." He looked nervously toward the door. He needed to get out before Charles returned. Nick picked his clothes off the floor and stuffed them in his old duffel bag.

The door creaked open almost giving him a heart attack.

"Sweetheart."

"Mom," he said with relief. She looked sad and worn out. He returned to packing. She reached out to pick up a pair of socks he'd missed off of the floor and handed it him. As he took it from her, he noticed a new set of bruises on her forearm. He paused a moment. Their eyes met. She looked away and then went over to Alex, caught him as he jumped and took him off the bed.

"Mommy, I wanna go!"

"No sweetie, you can't." She said and the little boy began to whine.

"Why not? I wanna go."

"You can't go where he's going." She sat down on the bed. Nick kept packing.

"Do you even know where you're going?"

"Anywhere that's not here."

"Sweetheart. . ." His mother began and he stopped packing.

"Come with me. You and Alex come with me."

"You know that's impossible."

"Why because Charles won't let you? He doesn't have to know. We can leave right now and he would never find us."

"He's your father. I can't just walk out on him. That's not how marriage works."

He yanked her arm up, exposing the bruises in the daylight.

"And this is?" he said angrily as she pulled back her arm and set Alex on her lap.

"There are things that you're just too young to understand."

"Well, it's not my problem anymore. Maybe you want to live with him hitting the shit out of you but I don't."

"He doesn't hit me. He doesn't hit Alex. Sometimes, he just gets angry and you and I just get in the way. You were like that too sometimes. When you were little you used to get so upset when things

didn't go your way that you'd throw things."

"I was five. What's his excuse?"

"Don't leave. What's Alex going to do without you?"

"I have to go."

He picked up his duffel bag. His mother sat on the bed holding Alex and staring after him helplessly. Nick had every intention of walking out of the little white house forever that day. But each step he took, as he heard Alex crying while his mother stopped him from running after Nick, was excruciating.

Memories were coming at him and he couldn't take it. He knew the life he led was all based on a lie. In the end he'd left Alex behind to suffer in that house and when he came back it was too late. Nick drove faster and faster. There was honking and bright light coming toward Nick. He sped even faster. He had to be close now. He glanced over to the items on the seat next to him. More honking. More lights coming at him. Then. . .

I*t was the middle of the day but it was dark inside the room. He could barely make out the silhouette sitting on the edge of the bed. Nick took a tentative step toward the figure, a sense of dread filling every cell in his body. His breathing came in short, shallow waves and he could feel cold droplets of sweat running down his back. He kept walking toward the bed even though he wanted to turn in the opposite direction. The figure was still. Nick had no idea if his presence in the room had been noticed until his foot hit something on the floor near the bed. It was a hand. He called out in fear and disgust. Someone was sprawled, face down on the floor, the hand reaching out as if desperate to escape, to call out for help that never came. Nick was horrified. Words remained trapped in his throat as he looked up and saw that the figure sitting on the bed was staring at him. He knew that face and while it remained mostly hidden in the darkness of the room, he could never forget it. He could never escape it* *because it resembled his own. Sitting on the edge of the bed was a man, eyes glassy, smelling strongly of booze and holding a long leather belt in his hands. Nick looked at the belt and back down at the little body on the floor. He noticed between the shadows and the light coming through the slats of the bedroom blinds that there was blood everywhere.*

"I told him what would happen." The man's speech slurred and his voice was void of any emotion.

Before Nick could process everything he was seeing, the older man stood up and walked the short distance between them. Belt lifted, eyes bloodshot and crazed, the man reached out and grabbed him by the shoulder as Nick put up his hands to defend himself from the coming attack.

"Why won't you boys ever learn?" he yelled, lunging at Nick.

All he wanted to do was die. He accelerated. Nick opened his eyes in time to see a massive set of headlights coming straight at him accompanied by a blaring series of honks. He swerved thinking he could make the corner but severely underestimated the distance. The car hit the large iron fence surrounding the cemetery and everything went black.

When he opened his eyes, a bright white light engulfed him. Was he dead? A face suddenly appeared, but his eyes refused to remain open—especially his left one. It felt swollen. The EMT flashing the light in both his eyes was calling out information for his partner.

"Checking his vitals now. Caucasian male, approximately 25-26 years of age with several contusions and possible concussion. Having trouble breathing. Possible internal bleeding.

"Hey, buddy. Hey. Can you hear me? Can you tell me your name?"

They were trying to keep him awake but Nick kept blacking out. The next time he opened his eyes he was watching ceiling tiles go by as they rushed him into an operating room. He heard voices urging him to hang on but in the end all he wanted to do was let go. The last thing he heard as they put him on the operating table was the sound of the monitor flat-lining.

CHAPTER EIGHTEEN

Handcuffed

He woke up handcuffed to a bed. Nick was no stranger to the scenario but this time he knew it was different—drastically different. No blonde bombshell graced his bedside. It was Detective Pat Baker that sat in the chair next to his hospital bed reading that morning's edition of the *Omaha World Herald.*

"You're awake," Detective Baker said folding the paper. Nick felt like every part of his body had been bruised, battered, or broken. He could only grunt in response.

"That's alright." The detective stood. "I'll let the nurse know you're awake and, once they're done with you, we'll need to have a little chat, Mr. Simon."

Nick's throat was dry and sore. It was hard to breathe. He could barely focus on where he was, let alone what the detective had said. True to his word, Detective Baker returned with a nurse who checked all of the monitors and talked to Nick in a soft, soothing voice.

"Mr. Simon, my name is Charrise. I'm going to be

taking care of you while you're here." She adjusted his blankets. Nick swallowed and winced.

"That'll be from the ventilation tube they had to use during your surgery. I'll get you some more pain medication and some ice chips. That'll help." She eyed Detective Pat Baker.

"When will he be able to speak?"

"Now don't you go getting any ideas, Detective. Mr. Simon is my patient and I'll let you know when the doctor says it's okay."

"I have to talk to him soon. He's got several charges to face and I've got to get the paperwork done."

The detective rubbed his eyes. It looked like he'd been up all night.

"Well he has to heal first. He's not going anywhere. You've got him *handcuffed* to the bed." She gave him a severe look of disapproval.

"It's procedure."

"You know who he is, don't you?" she asked in a hushed tone.

"Of course—which is why he has the means to become a flight risk."

"He's a writer, not Al Capone,." the nurse protested.

"He's a guy with a lot of money. That makes him a flight risk."

"Not the way he's feeling right now, Detective. Lacerations to the face, two fractured ribs, a punctured lung, a ruptured spleen *and* a broken leg. Yes, Detective, he's a flight risk, alright," she said in a tone of definite sarcasm.

"The cuffs stay on," he said firmly.

The nurse scowled as she readjusted Nick's oxygen

tube. "The cuffs are starting to mess with the positioning of my IVs. I'll be back in a minute with those pain meds and ice chips."

She left Detective Baker alone with Nick. The detective sat back down in the chair by his bedside. Nick could hear him trying to get comfortable but had a difficult time keeping his eyes open.

"Well, Mr. Simon. I'll admit I didn't see this coming when we met at the morgue yesterday morning."

Detective Baker let out another sigh. Nick tried to focus on his face but still found it difficult because of the pain he felt *everywhere.*

"What in the hell were you doing in that car? That was a one way street. Did you know that? It's a miracle you're alive and that no one else is dead. You scared the crap out of that truck driver but you're lucky he swerved in time or I'd be visiting *you* at the morgue. Although, given the shape you came in, you almost made it there." Another long silence with the exception of the monitors that continually beeped.

"Your blood alcohol level was off the charts and where do I even begin to talk to you about the contents of the bag we found on the passenger's side?"

The detective continued but Nick was more concerned with the small green teddy bear hanging from a key chain. He wanted to ask but he couldn't force the words through his sore wind pipe.

"EMT says he thought you called for someone named *Alex*? He your dealer, Mr. Simon? Is Alex the individual who sold you the drugs?"

Detective Baker waited as if Nick would suddenly answer. When he didn't the detective simply went on with his interrogation.

"You're facing drug and DUI charges as well as destruction of property. The DA in this county doesn't take these things lightly especially when it comes to out-of-staters, Mr. Simon. He will prosecute you to the full extent of the law and he'll see to it that you serve time."

The detective stood and started to pace. Nick floated in and out of consciousness.

"We attempted to locate your next of kin but the only emergency contact we found in your cell phone was a New York number belonging to one Barbara King. So we contacted her. She'll be on the next plane out."

Nick panicked and made every effort to speak but all he could do was produce another series of indignant grunts. Another moment of silence passed.

"It sure is a shame, Mr. Simon. A person always hopes that you Hollywood types will turn out different than the rest. But then something like this happens and it's disappointing."

Nick wanted to remind Baker that he was from New York, not LA anymore, but it didn't matter. He wondered what the detective would say if he knew that Nick had been born and raised in Omaha?

"I thought I told you to leave my patient alone, Detective."

Nick heard Charrise's voice as she entered the room.

"I'm not bothering him. I'm just chatting. Besides I thought doctors encouraged that sort of thing."

"What sort of thing?"

"Talking to patients that can't talk back."

"That's only if they're in a coma, detective. This patient isn't in a coma."

"But he *can* hear me."

"That's not the point. I don't want him stressed."

"I've got a job to do," the detective protested and the nurse took him by the arm and walked him to the door.

"So do I. Doctor says no visitors until further notice. That means you too, Detective."

"I'll be back tomorrow."

"See you then," the nurse said cheerily and shut the door in his face.

Nick wanted to kiss Charrise, but every bone in his body, especially the broken ones in his leg, were screaming too much for him to focus on anything else.

"It's okay. I have your meds and your ice chips," she said, raising his bed.

"First I'm going to inject your meds into your IV and then I'm going to feed you the ice chips. Okay?"

He tried to blink in response. She smiled and he was grateful for the kindness. He knew that he didn't deserve it, but he accepted it because he knew that when tomorrow came and Barbara arrived, broken bones would be the least of his worries.

CHAPTER NINETEEN

The Vulture

She was circling him, pacing around each side of the hospital bed as he opened his eyes.

"It's about time you woke up," she said sarcastically.

Nick struggled to keep his eyes open, whatever the nurse had put in his IV had knocked him out and it was still running through his system.

"Barbara?" Nick finally said as he squinted through heavy eyelids.

"Who else?"

Barbara King continued to pace. He could tell she was angry. He'd known her long enough to know the signs. Pacing was one of those signs. Extended silence was another. It was as if she couldn't get all of her angry thoughts out at once, so she had to sort and filter them. She was cruel and calculating when it came to what she considered a personal betrayal. Nick knew she felt betrayed and her body language definitely gave away how she was feeling. But it was making him nauseous.

"Could you. . .could you stop pacing. It's making me

dizzy," Nick said

"Making *you* dizzy? You know what's making *me* dizzy, Nick? All the bad publicity we're getting right before the film opens and your next book launch. That's what's making *me* damn dizzy!" she hissed.

"Nice to see you too, Barbara."

Nick covered his face with his free hand to keep the image of her pacing out his mind and the urge to vomit out of his stomach.

"I wish I could say the same, Nick. *Look at you.* You're handcuffed to a goddamned hospital bed. The press is having a field day. . . but you know who isn't so happy about your little escapade, your little joy ride? The studio! You know who else is pissed off? How about the actors it took us ten months to cast for the next movie? They're about to pull out—two weeks before we start filming! Nick what were you thinking? What the hell were you thinking?"

"I wasn't,"

"You're damn right you weren't because here we are in *Nebraska*! *Nebraska!* What the hell was so important that you had to sneak off without telling anyone where you were going?"

"I told someone," Nick interjected. It seemed to make her angrier.

"You. Didn't. Tell. Me." She gritted her teeth.

"It wasn't important."

"You left a shit storm for me to clean up, Nick. You have no idea how bad things really are do you? I tried to tell you over the phone that your little party at the penthouse crossed into dangerous territory. Do you really think you're handcuffed to this bed because of the car crash, the drugs or the DUI? You're being investigated for much more than that. That girl you hooked up with on New Year's, they think she might have been underage. The last thing you want is to be a registered sex offender, Nick. There's no coming back from *that.*"

Nick uncovered his face and opened his eyes. Barbara's silouhette was blurry but he tried to focus.

"Ah, now I've got your attention? Good. So, it's time for a strategy and *this* time you're going to listen to every word I say and do exactly what I tell you. Understood?"

"What do I have to do?" Nick asked.

"Before you can go home again I'm afraid that you'll have to make amends. That means a twelve-step program."

"No!" Nick screamed. He instantly regretted it. His throat was still raw and painful.

"Oh *yes.*"

"I'm *not* an addict or an alcoholic, Barbara."

"Funny. That sounds like something an addict and an alcoholic *would* say."

"What are you up to, Barbara?"

"I'm afraid that after what's happened—as your manager and your agent—you leave me no choice but to make sure that you get the help that you need."

"I'm not checking into any stupid facility." "No worries, Nick. After speaking with the case coordinator of the hospital I've decided that there's no reason to move you elsewhere. You seem to have a special place in your heart for this. . ." she looked around distainfully before finishing, " this *place*, this *town* so I'm leaving you here to dry out and detox. If you manage not to screw it up *again*, I'll consider bringing you back home."

"You've got to be kidding me!"

"Oh, I'm *very* serious, Nick. I warned you not to mess with me. Now, I'm done cleaning up after you. Since, you decided to make a public spectacle of yourself then it seems fitting that you spend your rehab time in a *public* facility."

"That's not fair, Barbara. You can't leave me here."

"It's done. There's nothing you can do about it, Nick so buckle down and do the work so you can come home and help me salvage what's left of your image. Beside, fans love a reformed celebrity. Look at Robert Downey Jr. If we play our cards right you won't have to wear the orange jumpsuit. At least that's what the lawyer is working on."

Nick struggled to get up but the IV tubing and the handcuff kept him from sitting up.

"You made a deal?"

"With the local DA? You bet your ass we did, Nick. You were looking at DUI, drug and destruction of property charges. I know you like the place but I've invested too much in you to have you spend the next five to ten years rotting in a cell. I *still* have to go back to New York and sweet talk the DA there. All this time and you still think these things take care of themselves?" She shook her head disapprovingly.

"You can't do this!"

"I can, Nick. You signed the papers and it's my job to protect the brand and your assets. In fact, I'm on my way to the conservatorship hearing in about a half hour." She looked at her phone.

"Conservatorship hearing?"

"You've given me temporary power to care for your finances and make some of those difficult health decisions that you're clearly not able to make for yourself right now."

"When did I ever do that?" Nick demanded and Barbara smiled.

"Oh, Nick. I told you to have your lawyer look over your contracts before you signed them. Everything's there. There's nothing to hide."

"I had my lawyer look things over and he never said anything about that."

"Well, maybe it's time to get a new lawyer."

Nick pulled at the bedding and attempted to sit up but the handcuff again made it impossible. Barbara chuckled as she took one last look at him before heading for the door.

"Barbara wait! Please!"

"Nick, I waited for you the day you left on that plane. Remember? You had your chance to clean this up, now it's my turn."

"Barbara!"

"Get well soon, Nick. I'm expecting you to be clean and sober by the movie premier."

"I don't *need* to get sober or clean! I don't have a problem, Barbara!"

He yelled at her but she kept walking.

"Acceptance is the first step to recovery, Nick," she called behind her as she waved and the door closed, leaving Nick helpless and at the mercy of Barbara's plan.

CHAPTER TWENTY

Abandoned

Barbara left him in the hospital for the next three months. Recovery was slow and painful. Once he was able to sit up and eat on his own, his days were filled with rounds of brutal physical therapy followed by days of rehab which included individual and group therapy. Nick might as well have been in the seventh circle of Hell. Between the pain medication he needed to get through physical rehab and the detox from his usual self-medicating choices, he was exhausted. Sometimes he lost track of time. Then one day he thought he was hallucinating. It had happened to him several times before during rehab. He saw people and things that simply weren't there. It had cost him a few bruises and bumps along the way. Reaching out to grab what he thought was a bottle of vodka he lost his balance and hit his head on the edge of a conference table. Another time he thought Cianti was sitting next to him and through his stupor he reached out to touch her only to get punched in the face by a large man named Victor, sporting several graphic tattoos featuring death as a theme. But this time as he sat waiting for one of the group therapy sessions to begin he couldn't help but stare at the back of a girl- who looked like a pixie minus the wings, . He closed his eyes to make the image disappear but when he opened them she was still there—a girl with a butterfly tattoo on her shoulder that looked so real it seemed it could fly off at any moment. She was perched on a stool with an artist's sketch pad on her lap and a thin charcoal pencil held tightly between her small fingers. Though all he could see was her back, he could still make out a swath of long bangs dyed a brilliant red sweeping to one side of her face and tucked behind her ear. The back of her head was shaved and also dyed to match her bangs. She was wearing lotus print leggings and a tie-dye tank top that covered most of her back but left the tattoo visible. Her feet were bare and her toenails were painted a bright blue. She was striking even from the back.

Nick tried to maneuver his head to see her face but she kept it turned away, facing the object of her sketches, a large leafy grouping of tropical plants sitting in the far corner of the indoor garden visible to patients on his side of the ward but accessible only to staff and patients or visitors on the opposite side. He wondered if she was a staff member on break from her duties but then doubted it given how she was dressed. Maybe a visitor? It was winter outside and he doubted she'd be walking around dressed in nothing but leggings, a tank top and bare feet if that were the case. Then, she must be a patient but definitely not one on his side of the hallway.

Nick watched as the sketch on her pad came to life with each stroke of her charcoal pencil. It was fascinating to watch. Sometimes, she would stop mid-stroke, tip her head to one side and stare for what seemed a long time at the plants in the corner and Nick wondered exactly what it was that had stopped her from finishing the stroke. Then, she'd begin the stroke again, joining it to the others until another section of the drawing was complete. Nick wasn't an expert or an artist, but he could tell she was talented. What started as a blank page suddenly mirrored what his own eyes were seeing in the little garden through the thick window glass separating him from the girl with the butterfly tattoo. Nick wished she would turn around so he could see her face but, as soon as he had the thought, the other patients began filtering into the room for the therapy session, and he couldn't see her anymore. After a few more moments almost all the participants were in their seats and ready to begin. Nick looked frantically for the beautiful girl. He wanted to stand up but his leg and the last of the stragglers coming in prevented it and he had to be satisfied with waiting for each of them to walk past him and take their seats. Once they had, Nick looked toward the window. His heart sank the moment he saw that the girl with the butterfly tattoo was gone.

CHAPTER TWENTY-ONE

The First Encounter

During one of his physical therapy sessions he and the therapist headed to the meditation garden for a walk. Nick tried to put more weight on his leg but still depended on the crutches for balance. As they came off the elevator on the first floor, where the garden was located, Nick noticed a flurry of activity that began when a man named Chester, whom he recognized from the group therapy sessions, started to run from one end of the lobby to the other with staff not far behind. Then, without warning, Chester stopped and peeled out of his clothes so quickly the staff were hardly aware of what he'd done, until he'd done it. The shock of seeing him had the staff distracted long enough for Chester to take off sprinting down the hallway . So much for a leisurely stroll to the small mediation garden on the first floor. Chester whizzed by Nick in his birthday suit.

Nick had no aversion to nudity, having had the pleasure and displeasure of being naked on several occasions for several reasons including the Chinese

Ambassador's Nobel Peace Prize reception—which came immediately to mind. It was, however, *not* what the hospital staff expected and as soon as they saw the naked man they were after him, leaving Nick on his own. That's when he saw her, the girl with the butterfly tattoo, walking toward him across the lobby. All he could do was stare. She was small in stature, her hair was dyed a brilliant red, short on the sides with a long swath of it, that she kept tucking behind her ear as she walked, sweeping across her face.. She was dressed similarly to the way Nick had last seen her, perched on a stool with a sketch pad on her lap — in bright colors and not at all for the weather. She had multiple earrings in both ears and nothing but a little mascara framing a set of deep gray eyes, and lip gloss on her lips. She was unique. She was beautiful and Nick wondered for a moment if he was hallucinating again.

He hobbled forward. She kept walking but wasn't close enough to acknowledge his presence in her path yet. Then suddenly, when she was but a few feet away, Chester came running up behind her. He was so keen on escaping the hospital staff that he kept glancing behind him and failed to see her in front of him. He knocked right into her, causing her to drop everything and propelling her straight into Nick's arms. She was real.

"What the hell!" She cursed as Nick caught her with one arm while letting one of his crutches fall. He teetered on his one good leg, leaning on the crutch that was still standing, while holding onto her. She smelled like strawberries. Their eyes met and for a moment Nick felt a surge of familiarity, comfort and attraction.

"Hey," he said and she smiled.

"Hey," she said, but before he could say anything else

Chester whizzed by again with the hospital staff in hot pursuit.

"Who is that guy?"

"I think that's Chester."

Nick smiled, tightening his hold on her, as he watched the naked man take the stairs two at a time.

"Chester." The girl repeated. "He's fast."

"Yeah. I guess you could say that." Nick nodded as he followed the chaos with his eyes and found himself standing alone. The girl had extricated herself from his embrace, picked up her bag, and started walking away again without another word. She was fast, too, it seemed.

"Wait a minute!" Nick yelled after her, but he lost his balance trying to turn and ended up on the floor.

"Dammit," he said and the guy from the nearby coffee stand came over to help him. Standing up and retrieving both crutches, Nick tried to follow her, but before long she took a set of stairs, going to what he supposed was the basement, and disappeared. He couldn't maneuver the stairs or find an elevator in time to follow her.

Nick was frustrated. He'd finally found the girl and he'd lost her in a matter of seconds just like that. He'd been so thrilled that his hallucination was real that he hadn't bothered to ask her name. Chester had distracted him from what should have been his number one priority—finding out who she was. He waited for a few minutes hoping she would make it back up the stairs but she didn't. Soon, the staff member who'd accompanied him down from the second floor was back at his side, walking him toward the meditation garden and away from the general chaos Chester had caused. If only he'd asked her name. If only he could stop thinking about her and start concentrating on why he was there—so he could go home to New York.

Suddenly, there was another burst of noise and commotion as Chester made his way back down the stairs and past him once more, still wearing nothing but a smile. Nick watched anxiously for the girl but she never came, giving him the impression for the second time that maybe she had been a hallucination after all.

CHAPTER TWENTY-TWO

Arnie

The next day, he snuck down from the second floor as the staff again pursued Chester from hallway to hallway. Agitated after he found out there would be no chocolate pudding that night because of a mix-up in the hospital kitchen Chester became so anxious that he stripped in three seconds flat. In the scuffle between Chester and the nurses one of their badges came unclipped from its lanyard and fell to the ground. Seeing his opportunity, Nick grabbed balanced himself on his crutches and bent down to pick it up. Hiding it between his fingers he waited until the coast was clear. He held it up to the magnetic strip by the door then he made his way to the elevators and downstairs to the lobby where there was a courtesy phone on one of the walls. He dialed out and placed a collect call. He waited as the phone rang on the other end. *Pick up. Pick up. Come on! Pick up!* Sheila, his lawyer's secretary answered and quickly patched him through.

"Nicky! How the hell are you?" Arnie Schaefer's voice boomed so loudly that Nick had to hold it a good two feet away from his ear. "When Sheila told me who was on the phone I almost choked on my bagel!"

"How do you think I am, Arnie? Barbara's got me locked up me up. Tell me you had *nothing* to with it."

"How could you think that? How far do we go back, Nicky? Since the first day you signed your contract at the end of the show right? Have I *ever* let you down? Well, not counting this, 'cause really you kind of put yourself in the middle of this pickle. . ."

"Arnie, I've got to get out of here."

"Nicky, Nicky, you know you're like the brother I actually like. But this thing has gotten completely out of hand from a legal a standpoint."

"What are you talking about?"

"You never were one for the fine print, Nicky. I told you to read the fine print when it came to Barbara King. Remember? I read it. I told *you* to read it."

"Why the hell did I need to read it if I paid you to read it?"

"Nicky, what's with the tone? It's hurtful. All I'm saying is that it's one thing to read it's quite another thing to live up to."

"What did I miss, Arnie?"

"The morality clause. You missed the morality clause of your contract."

"You've got to be kidding me."

"Wish I were, Nicky, but you took a dump on your contract with that party at the penthouse and then you stepped right in it up to your neck with the crash at the cemetery."

"God, this is a nightmare."

"That's one way to look at it."

"What other way could I look at it, Arnie?"

"Well, what about as a chance to redeem yourself and get back in Barbara King's good graces?"

"Who did you say you work for again, Arnie?"

"Look, Nicky. Here's the deal. You screwed up, and worse, you screwed over the biggest, bad-ass agent in the biz. She's making an example of you and there's nothing to be done—at least not legally—until she's done with you."

"So what you're saying is that I'm stuck here with no money and no place to go."

"Basically."

"You've got to be kidding me."

"Nicky. You know me. I don't kid. I'm not that funny."

"Okay, I'll play along. What do I need to do to get out of this place and back home."

"That's up to Ms. King. She hasn't contacted me personally but the impression her assistant, that skinny kid with the buggy eyes—Ambrose is it?—gave me when I first called is that you'll have to finish your stint in rehab, complete a full psychiatric evaluation, and then do whatever she says. That's the part I'm not so clear on, Nicky. Knowing her, though, it's going to be very public and very painful."

"Shit."

"Nicky, I'm not going to lie to you, I heard she made Al Pacino cry once. In public. At his own movie premiere. It took him years to buy out his contract. Whatever he had to do to get out from under her thumb or any of her other parts, well let me tell you no one talks about it. She's a mean one, Nicky. No heart that one. But I told you that when you signed on with her. You made a deal with the devil."

"Arnie, you're not helping."

"I'm sorry, Nicky. What do you want me to say, that you didn't mess up? You did. You want me to tell you that everything's going to be fine? I can't. You mess with the bull and you get the horns. Barbara King is the biggest bull of all and you're gonna feel every bit of those horns, my friend," Arnie said. Nick could hear him sucking the cream cheese from his fingers.

"Jesus, Arnie. You gotta give me something I can use. You have no idea what it's like here."

"You mean Nebraska or the mental hospital, Nicky? I'm from Jersey and they both sound about the same to me," Arnie Schaefer chuckled.

"Ha, ha, Arnie."

"I'm glad you're keeping your sense of humor, Nicky. That's gonna be important. Who knows what she's planning for you next, huh? I heard she dumped husband number four last week. You could be number five. That would most definitely keep you. . . busy." he chuckled again.

"Dammit, Arnie!"

"Okay, okay, Nicky. I'm sorry. I'm not trying to make light of your serious situation. I am merely trying to impress upon you that I do not have the power to interfere from a legal standpoint in your current status."

"Fine just look over all the contracts again. This time with a fine tooth comb. If there's a loophole I want you to find it!"

"Nicky, I'm hurt that you would think I didn't do that the first time. I'm just your lawyer. I can only advise you and that's what I did the first time when I *advised* you *not* to sign."

"Great. You get to say I told you so. Go over the damn contracts again! What am I paying you for, Arnie?"

"Nicky, you're not paying me a dime. You have to understand, Barbara King has the financial conservatorship in place. One more thing you signed off on that I tried to tell you was a very *bad* idea. That means *she* decides who gets paid while you're in the nut house. But who am I but your *lawyer*? Your nationally award-winning, highly sought-after, Harvard trained, contract litigation *expert. Yep.* Why listen to me?"

"Arnie. . .I'm sorry. . .I'm not myself. . ."

"Actually, I'm glad you're not, Nicky. Usually, you're a bigger pain in the ass. Maybe it's a good thing that I can't swoop in and save you like I usually do. Even like Barbara King does. Understand that *anything* I'm doing for you—I'm doing it from my heart not from my wallet so how about turning it down a notch and not acting like such a schmuck?"

"Sure. I can do that."

"Can you?"

"Yeah. I can do that, Arnie."

"Sounds good. I'll see what I can do. In the meantime, keep out of trouble. You're almost done with rehab. The movie premier is coming up. The last thing you need is any more bad publicity and Nick—whatever you do—-don't piss Barbara King off any more than you already have. Are you listening? This time it's the nut house and your money—next time it's your balls, my friend. Remember Al Pacino. I hear he has no balls. Literally. She cut them off. Do not let that be you, my friend."

"Thanks for the image, Arnie. It's stuck in my head

now."

"It should be a good motivator. I gotta go now. Meeting a new client."

"Who?"

"Someone nicer and a helluva better looking."

"Ah. You're still spending time with Sheila. What about Margie?"

"There's enough of me to go around, Nicky," Arnie said and he could hear Sheila laughing in the background.

"I don't think Margie's going to see it that way, Arnie."

"Look, Nicky. You just keep your nose clean, I mean that both literally and figuratively, by the way. I'll look after things here. You've got enough worries of your own."

"What if Margie kills you while you're working on my case?"

"Don't you worry about my wife. Worry about your agent. Gotta go now, Nicky. Client's getting very agitated that I'm not paying attention to what she's saying."

"Wait, Arnie. . .I have some more questions!" But Arnie Schaefer hung up and left Nick listening to the dial tone. Nick slammed the hospital courtesy phone down.

"Friend or foe?" he heard someone ask in a voice clearly filled with amusement.

"None of your business," he growled and turned around just in time to see the girl with the butterfly tattoo walking away. She was headed for the elevators. He tried to limp after her but the crutches made it difficult and she stepped inside, turning around just as the door started to close.

"Wait! What's your name?" he called out and she gave him a grin.

"None of your business," she mimicked sweetly as the doors closed in Nick's face.

CHAPTER TWENTY-THREE

Support Group

Nick took the next elevator up to the second floor, using the staff badge to get back to his room undetected. He decided to keep it. It came in handy again one day. In the meantime, his mind was completely preoccupied with two things: how to get out and how to find the girl with the butterfly tattoo. But days went by and he didn't run into her again. She wasn't in the patio drawing during group and she wasn't in the meditation garden painting when he passed by during physical therapy either. He continually hoped that Chester would take off, strip and run from the staff so he could make his way out of the ward and into the regular hallways to look for her. Then one day as he was out with the physical therapist for another walk, down in the lobby, he saw her. She was headed across the lobby and down a set of stairs to the basement. Nick was desperate to follow but, stuck with the therapist, he knew he couldn't go after her. Instead he returned to the ward, where he waited a few minutes for the nurses to vacate their station, and quickly hobbled to the door with the badge he'd lifted days earlier. Making his way to the elevator he pushed the button going down to the basement. Once there, he tried to limp quickly down the sparse, gray hallways, lined with carts and shelving. He was relieved to see posters on the walls with arrows pointing in the direction of something called a *Well Life support group.* What were the chances that the girl with the butterfly tattoo had gone there? Slim to none but he had to try. So, he followed the signs until he reached a door. He could hear the sound of muffled talking through it. Nick took a deep breath and opened the door. Immediately he wished he hadn't. The talking stopped and a group of about twenty-five people suddenly turned and stared at him. The girl was one of them. He stood dumbfounded for a moment before the leader of the group, a woman wearing a colorful, tight-fitting turban smiled and motioned for him to take an empty seat next to her.

"Welcome!" she said cheerily and Nick attempted to return the smile as he hobbled over to the empty seat.

It took him a few minutes to get squared away with his crutches before the group finally stopped staring and resumed their topic of conversation. But Nick wasn't paying attention; he was glancing at the girl with the butterfly tattoo every so often, hoping she wouldn't realize it. She didn't. She was too busy doodling away with some colored pencils on a pad of paper and occasionally whispering to the woman next to her The other woman wore a knit cap and looked rather pale. As he studied her features, the dark circles under her eyes, the lack of eyebrows and eyelashes, it began to occur to him that she probably had some type of illness. Maybe cancer? He looked over again at the girl with the butterfly tattoo and realized that her *doodling* was actually a sketch of the woman next to her. It was good, very good, and she had managed to capture something in the sketch that was not there in real life—a look of health and respite. Suddenly, she looked up and for the second time since he'd been *imprisoned* in the hospital their eyes met. This time there was a flash of recognition and a smile. Nick smiled back but she looked away and kept her eyes on the sketch pad until the leader of the group turned to him.

"Well, why don't you introduce yourself?"

"I'm sorry?"

"I said, why don't you introduce yourself?"

"Oh." He paused, mildly embarrassed that he was being put on the spot. "My name is. . .Simon."

"Welcome, Simon," the woman with the turban said.

Nick suddenly noticed that she and the woman sitting next to the girl with the butterfly tattoo seemed to have a lot in common. Both were lacking eyebrows, eyelashes, hair and there were dark shadows under eyes. He tried not to stare and instead turned to look in the opposite direction. Was it him or were there more people wearing knit hats, turbans and bandanas around their heads? Not all but most of them. He frowned. What kind of support group was the girl involved in?

"So, when did you receive your diagnosis?" the leader asked

As she did Nick found that the girl was actually looking at him.

"Excuse me?"

"Your diagnosis. When did you receive your diagnosis?"

"For what?" he asked, truly confused.

"Terminal cancer," she said matter-of-factly. His jaw dropped.

His eyes immediately went back to the girl with the butterfly tattoo, who was still looking at him, her gray eyes full of pain and curiosity.

"Terminal cancer?"

"Yes. This is a support group for terminal cancer patients, Simon. Are you sure you're in the right group?"

Nick looked back across the table at the girl. She was still looking at him. He swallowed hard. There was a lump in his throat and tightness in his chest that he'd only experienced once before.

"Simon?"

Everyone was staring and waiting for his reply.

"Yes?"

"Are you in the right group? Are you terminally ill?"

Nick looked at the girl with the butterfly tattoo before he answered. She had turned the page and started a new drawing.

"Yes," he lied as he watched her look away and return to her sketchbook where he could have sworn she'd begun drawing someone who looked a lot like him.

CHAPTER TWENTY-FOUR

Movie Night

Nick attended as many of the Well Life Support Group meetings as he could but never volunteered to speak. There were plenty of people willing to share and many more willing to listen. The girl with the butterfly tattoo was one of the latter. But, more often than not, the listening was accompanied by sketching, which she did almost every time someone spoke. When she sketched someone, it was as if she returned something they had lost; hope, health and even happiness. Nick was in awe of her talent and wanted the opportunity to reach out to her and rekindle the connection he thought he'd felt between them. The other members of the group, especially the woman with the knit hat kept always seemed to accompany her, though. It also didn't help that he wasn't as fast with his crutches and just couldn't catch up with her once the meetings were over. He kept hoping that other opportunities would present themselves and finally one did.

Movie night in the psychiatric ward left much to be

desired, so he hoped the movie night sponsored by the terminal cancer support group would be better. He could be wrong, but if he went back to the ward he'd be stuck doing crossword puzzles with Vera or taking bets with Calvin on how long Chester aka "Naked Man" would keep his clothes on before his evening 'run.' He'd rather watch a movie. Any movie. At least that's what he'd thought until he realized they were showing one of *his* movies. As a general rule he *never* watched his movies. He'd adapted the screenplays from his novels, but he had never, not once, ever watched one of his own movies. At first it had been fear. Now it was superstition, but he was also curious as to how popular the movie still was. He stuck his head in momentarily and noticed that the room was packed with people carrying their drinks and snacks from the nearby vending machines.

That's when he saw her, sitting in the front row. She was wearing a different tank top and her hair was just like he remembered it, shaved in the back and on the sides with a long swath of bright red bangs swept to the side, framing her face. The tattoo was bright and bold.

There was an empty seat next to her and, without a second thought, he made his way through the incoming stragglers and up to the front row. Apologizing as he stepped over people, he sat down next to her. She was holding a bag of Skittles in her hand and looking straight ahead. He looked straight ahead too. She glanced over in his direction and sighed.

"It's you again."

"Yeah. So?" "Don't you have better things to do?"

"Like?"

"I don't know. You tell me."

"I thought I'd take in a movie."

"You like romance?"

"It's *not* a romance." Nick insisted.

"Have you noticed that almost everyone in the room is female?"

He took a moment to look around. She was right.

"In fact I'd say right now you're the only guy."

"Maybe I'm the only guy with a sense of culture in this place."

"Doubtful."

"So, what brings *you* to movie night?" he asked, changing the subject.

"The movie."

"You *like* this type of movie? What was it you called them—*romance*?"

" God no. I hate romance. But I haven't watched this movie."

"Hmm."

"What?"

"I don't get it. What is it about *this* movie?"

"Well, for starters it's based on the book."

"Did you like the book?"

"No," she said bluntly.

"Why are you watching the movie, then?"

"I'm hoping he didn't screw up the movie half as much as he did the book."

"Who's *he*?" Nick wondered if he was about to be found out.

"The asshole who wrote the book."

"Whoa. That's a little harsh, don't you think?" "Have you *read* the book?" she countered and he stared at her unsure what to say next.

"If I say yes?"

She laughed. It was an amazing laugh. After a moment, he realized he was staring. He looked away and rubbed his sweaty palms over his jeans. He suddenly felt self-conscious and exposed. He was grateful that, since he'd entered rehab, his highlights had grown out, that he'd torn his contacts and had to wear his glasses, and that he'd ended up growing a full beard. At first these things had been part of a long litany of complaints he'd launched at Barbara and the coordinators of the rehab program. But now, as he sat next to the girl with the butterfly tattoo, whose name he realized he didn't even know yet, he was grateful that he was barely recognizable, even to himself.

"What's your name?" he blurted a little too eagerly.

She laughed again.

"Emily. Emily Fischer. What's yours again?"

She waited while he decided on what name he would settle on. He didn't want to lie to her completely but he didn't know if learning his name was in either of their best interests at the moment.

"Simon. Just Simon."

"Nice to meet you, Just Simon."

She held out a hand for him to shake. He took her cool palm in his and held it until she cocked an eyebrow in his direction. He realized he was still holding her hand and abruptly let go.

"Sorry." he said and felt the heat of embarrassment flush his entire face beneath his beard. This had *never* happened to him before. He'd met lots women, had lots of hook ups. So, what was the problem?

"Well then, this is going to be interesting. You're not really a fan of romance are you?"

"Not really."

"So. . .you're here at this movie because. . ."

She waited for him to fill in the blank and he wanted to tell her the truth. He wanted to tell her that from the moment he saw the tattoo of the butterfly with emerald wings tipped in velvet black perched on her shoulder, he'd felt the need to find her, to know who she was. If nothing else, he just needed to know why she'd decided to get this particular tattoo. It had started as sheer curiosity and now. . .

"I wanted to meet you," he blurted and felt relief with telling the truth. Now, she was staring at him and he wondered what was passing through her mind. Did she think he was a stalker? A weirdo? A pervert?

"Nice and direct. That's refreshing." She smiled nodding her head. "But we *did* meet, remember? Naked guy?"

"Yeah. That wasn't the first impression I wanted to make."

"It wasn't like *you* were naked."

"No. You're right. That would have been all kinds of awkward."

"For *you* maybe." She winked and popped another handful of Skittles in her mouth. He could feel the heat rising beneath his beard but he smiled.

"Now that you've met me. What do you think?" she asked and he felt at a loss for words.

"I think you're fun," he said and wanted to shoot himself. *Fun?? I think your'e amazing and I don't even know you.*

"How would you know how fun I am? We haven't really done anything together."

"I-I. . ." He stumbled over his words. "I'm sorry. I

meant that you're really nice." *Nice? Beautiful. You're so damn beautiful.*

"Wow." She let out a small whistle. Fun and nice? Now, I'm the one who's not making a great first impression."

"No. That's not what I meant at all." Nick was struggling. He had never before struggled this much with someone of the opposite sex or the same sex for that matter.

"Nice? My grandmother Bernstein was *nice*!" She stood up, gathered her colorful satchel and bright pink sweater from the chair. Nick panicked.

"What are you doing?" he asked looking around. People were staring.

"Come on!" She called from the door and he stood up to follow.

"I thought you wanted to watch the movie."

"No. He probably messed it up anyway." She led him down the long corridor and back up the staircase to the main hospital floor. She walked to over to the revolving doors that led to the street. Emily started to go through but stopped when she saw he wasn't following. Nick looked nervously over his shoulder, watching for one of the nurses to find him where he shouldn't be—away from the ward and outside of the movie room.

"Come on!" She motioned, giving him a dazzling smile and holding out her hand. He wanted to go. He *really* wanted to step into the night with her, follow her wherever she went but he couldn't. He knew he couldn't. Nick only had days until he was out of rehab. Days until he got his life back. He couldn't risk it but he wanted to more than he had ever wanted anything. He'd made so many mistakes already he couldn't risk one more, especially if it ended up hurting the girl with the butterfly tattoo.

"I can't go with you."

"Why not?" she asked and he hated himself. He looked over his shoulder again. Suddenly, the smile faded from her face and Nick could tell something was wrong.

"Simon?" He heard the stern voice of one of the nurses behind him. "Just where do you think you're going?"

"I. . .uh. . ." He stumbled over his words.

"Simon, you're not supposed to be off the second floor." The nurse said, as she came down the winding staircase.

"You're not a chemo patient are you," Emily Fischer said in a horrified whisper.

"No."

"But you've been going to the cancer support group. Do you even *have* cancer?"

Nick exhaled deeply and shook his head.

"Are you staff?" she asked hopefully.

Again Nick shook his head.

"And Naked Guy? How do you know him?"

"I don't know Chester. . .not exactly. But he's not naked *all* the time. Just when he gets anxious." *Shut up!*

"Simon! It's time to go. Your evening group is about to start," the nurse said and Nick sighed in defeat.

"Please, can I have a minute?"

"Fine. Say your goodbyes. I'll wait by the elevator for you."

Nick heard her footsteps go in the general direction of the elevators on the opposite end of the lobby.

"Oh my God, are you in the psych ward?"

"What's that supposed to mean?" he said suddenly offended for both himself and Chester.

"Nothing, I. . ."

"Emily. . ."

"Please don't follow me. . .I mean. . .ever. I can't deal with this right now." She went through the revolving doors leaving Nick standing all alone.

CHAPTER TWENTY-FIVE

Halfway House

His sponsor was the one who gave him the good news and after the movie night fiasco with Emily he needed some good news. He was being released from the hospital but. . .

"But what?" Nick asked and Joel Stauffer told him what he knew.

"You'll be going to a halfway house nearby."

"A halfway house?"Nick asked trying to wrap his head around that thought. So Barbara wasn't going to let him go home just yet. He frowned.

"It won't be for long. At least that's what they've told me. It's a good place. I know a lot of the guys. You will too. Many of them attend the meetings.

"I thought I'd be going home."

"Back to New York?"

"Yeah."

"I'm sorry, that's not what. . ."

"What Barbara King told you?" Nick interjected and Joel shook his head.

"Actually, it was some guy named Ambrose." Joel said and Nick rolled his eyes.

"Of course it was."

"Look, Nick, I'm you're sponsor. I don't know anything about your life back in New York before the accident or why your agent is the one calling the shots and keeping you here. That doesn't mean, however, that you *shouldn't* be here. We all find our way to the bottom some way or another—this just happened to be yours."

"How long do I have to stay?"

"To be honest I'd like to say that until you're well on your way to recovery but I can't. It's been made clear to me that it's your agent who will make that decision. It's not right in my opinion but my opinion doesn't matter."

Nick nodded and Joel went on.

"Now, once we get you moved over to the halfway house there'll be some rules you'll need to follow."

"Like?"

"For starters no alcohol and no drugs."

"Sounds like no-brainers."

"You'd think so but it happens." He eyed Nick intently. "And. . .no sex on the premises—or, I would strongly suggest, while you're working on your recovery."

Nick briefly thought about Emily.

"I don't think that'll be a problem."

"I wouldn't tell you if someone hadn't *done* it."

"You don't have to worry about me."

Joel Stauffer shrugged.

"Tell me that another thirty days from now and then another thirty days after that. This is a process, Nick."

"I said I understand."

Nick couldn't keep a defensive tone out of his voice.

Stauffer sighed.

"Fine. I'll drive you over when we get the okay that there's a room available."

"Okay. So what do I do in the meantime?"

"What you've been doing, going to group, going to meetings, meeting with me."

"Am I free to leave the hospital grounds?" Nick asked and Joel cocked an eyebrow.

"Why?"

"I'm just asking. I heard from some of the staff that there's some cool things to do and see. Touristy things."

Nick hoped he sounded convincing.

"Once you're dismissed and go to the halfway house, as long as you follow the rules and meet curfew you're free to do what you want but I wouldn't recommend it. It's dangerous at your point in recovery, Nick, not to mention somebody could recognize you."

"Dressed in this getup with *this* beard? Are you kidding? I hardly recognize myself."

"I don't think your agent is going to be on board with that, Nick, but you're a grown man. Your recovery is in *your* hands. How you choose to proceed is up to you."

"I'll be fine," Nick insisted.

His sponsor grinned. "If I had a dollar for every time I heard somebody say that in our group, I might be almost as rich as you."

"Really. I'm okay, Joel."

Stauffer stuck out a hand. Nick took it. They shook.

"Alright then. I've done what I told that Ambrose guy I'd do. As long as you keep up your part of the bargain then I have nothing more to say about it."

"Thanks, Joel."

"Be well, Nick."

Nick sat on his hospital bed lost in thought after Stauffer left. He couldn't stop thinking about Emily. He couldn't stop thinking about how'd he'd messed everything up, which wasn't like him. Nick knew how to act with the opposite sex. But maybe that was the problem he knew how to *act* he didn't know how to *be*. It gave him something to think about in the long days that followed his conversation with Joel. It also consumed his thoughts every time he thought about Emily and going back to the support group to look for her. By now, though, she would have told everyone that he was a fake and that he didn't have terminal cancer. There was no way they'd let him back in now.

After another two weeks in the hospital, Joel took him over to the halfway house. There he put his meager belongings in a small chest they provided, with a lock Joel had helped him purchase.Ambrose had sent money to cover some minimal expenses, which included groceries,since he would be expected to take care of his own meals while he was there. Nick would also have to attend his AA meetings and additional support groups run by staff in the house. He was disappointed that he wouldn't be at the hospital every day, just in case Emily appeared and he'd be able to find the courage to approach her again.

Being that much closer to going home lifted his spirits a little, though. Of course it all depended on when Barbara decided that would be.

In the meantime, he was determined to do what he was told, stay sober and clean. But life at the halfway house was tedious, and before long Nick needed to get out. He called a taxi to take him to the Old Market. He could people-watch and there would be a restaurant or grill where he could get a bite to eat. It beat another night of canned soup and crackers from his stash in the halfway house kitchen.

Before long he was on a corner less than a block from the old Market. It was a cold but decent evening and he enjoyed breathing in the cool air and walking with a boot and cane instead of crutches. He paid close attention to all of the people passing by on their way to the stores or restaurants and committed them to memory. That was how he often created characters in his books, by merging the details and characteristics of people he knew or had seen, and mixing them up to make whole new people. It had been a long time since he'd thought about writing, but now he was out and about it seemed a natural relief. As he neared the restaurant he saw someone that he recognized out of the corner of his eye. It was the Emily Fischer, the girl with the butterfly tattoo.

CHAPTER TWENTY-SIX

The Vintage Point

Nick watched her disappear into a small store with a colorful display window. On one side there were groupings of antiques and mannequins wearing vintage clothing and on the other were vinyl records propped up on old suitcases, hat boxes and chairs. It was called *The Vintage Point.* Nick waited for her to come out, but when she didn't, he decided to cross the street and go inside. The store was much bigger on the inside than it looked on the outside. Every nook and cranny was filled with items from another era. Hats from the 20's, dresses from the 40's and records from every decade imaginable. The Cure's *Boys Don't Cry* was playing on a turntable near the front counter and four or five customers were milling about in different areas; some were searching through the record bins, while others were checking the bottoms of a Carnival glass set located in a hutch, and trying on vintage t-shirts in the far corner of the store. There was a man behind the counter pricing records but Nick couldn't see Emily anywhere. He was certain she'd walked in but, as he scanned the store, he realized she was gone.

"Can I help you find something?" The man behind the counter asked, even as he continued to label records. The question caught him off guard so he stammered a quick, "no," and walked through the store hoping to spot her among the small aisles. Nick couldn't believe how much there was to see and buy. Plates, cups, silverware, bobble heads, candles, picture frames all from another time, all belonging to some previous owner. The customers were also a surprise. The majority of them were in their teens and early twenties. None of them had been alive when the majority of the items in the store had been in use. Nick himself was only three years shy of 30 and didn't have a clue as to what time period the majority of the items for sale belonged to or what they were for. Maybe the mystery was the novelty? He wondered why Emily had come into the store and how she'd disappeared so quickly. Just as he made it to the giant vintage refrigerator magnet collection that seemed to take up an entire strip of wall, a door opened nearly knocking him down.

"Hey!" he called out and there, standing in front of him, was Emily. She was dressed in the same store t-shirt as the man up front and she was wearing an identical name tag. Emily worked at *The Vintage Point.* When he thought about it, it was perfect. Her eclectic style, devoid of any distinctive generational look, and her love of bold color made her the perfect type of person to work in a store like this.

"You've got to be kidding me," she said cocking an eyebrow and walking away from him toward the front of the store.

"Wait, wait. Before you make up your mind just hear

me out."

"No need. My mind's made up."

"Don't you believe in second chances?"

"For what?"

"To make a first impression?"

"You had your chance and you blew it," she said reaching the counter.

"Hey, Emily." The man behind the counter greeted her.

"Hi, Leon," she said and started to go through the pile of records Leon had already priced.

"Oooh, this one's a good one. I might have to buy this one after my shift,/" she said turning over a David Bowie record.

"Are you going to pretend I'm not here?" Nick said and Emily kept sorting through the records.

"Is everything okay?" Leon asked.

Emily shrugged her shoulders.

"Emily, come on, let me explain."

"What's going on, Emily?" Leon asked, giving Nick a stern look.

"Nothing I can't handle, Leon." She continued to ignore Nick.

"I'm sorry for what I did."

"What'd you do?" Leon asked, looking from Emily back to Nick.

"So you're finally going to admit it?" she said, acknowledging his presence again.

"Yes."

"Admit what?" Leon asked, looking disturbed and perplexed.

"You don't have cancer," she hissed at him under her

breathe.

"No. But you do. You have cancer, Emily."

The shock on Leon's face was undeniable. Emily looked angry and Nick realized he must have given away her secret.

"Emily?"

Leon was staring at her now,but Emily glossed over it as if it were nothing.

"Don't worry, Leon. It won't affect my ability to work weekends."

"Please. I just want the chance to explain myself maybe over. . ." Nick continued.

"A drink? No, thanks. I'm not into the bar scene."

"Actually no. I can't drink . ." He said looking away, unable to meet her gaze. "I mean I don't drink."

Nick vainly attempted to correct himself before he saw the awareness suddenly spread across her face.

"You're an *alcoholic*? This just keeps getting better and better. What *else* haven't you told me?" she said a little too loudly, smacking both hands down on the display case separating them and leaning forward.

"Is there somewhere more private we can talk?" Nick asked, realizing that every pair of eyes in the store was staring at them.

"There's the bathroom," Leon offered but Emily waved him away.

"I don't feel like talking to you, Simon."

She shook her head and he winced at the way she said *Simon*. If she was this pissed when she used what she thought was his name how much angrier was she going to be when she found out it was only *part* of his name? Nick shuddered at the thought but knew he had to try to make things right with her.

"Just one more chance, please," he said and she gave him a good hard look.

"Fine. You can meet me here at eight, after my shift."

Nick couldn't hide the smile that crossed his face.

"Are you *sure* you want to do that, Emily?" Leon asked in a paternal voice, even though he was just old enough to be her brother.

When Emily turned to look at him, her face softened, and she put a hand on his shoulder.

"Yeah, Leon. I'll be fine. Let me just say goodbye and we can get back to work, okay?"

Leon gave Nick a dirty look before stepping from behind the counter and heading for a different part of the store. He continued to look over his shoulder at Nick as he went to help other customers.

"Is he your boyfriend?" Nick asked nervously.

"Leon? No. He's a friend—just a good friend," she said turning back, her arms crossed and her pixie face set in a scowl.

"I promise that I'll explain everything tonight," he said and she rolled her eyes.

"You're going to be convinced that this was all just a big misunderstanding."

"Am I?"

"Yes," he said backing away from the counter and toward the door.

"Simon. . ." Emily called out to him as he kept walking.

"What?"

"Watch out. . ." But it was too late and before he knew it he'd backed straight into another customer carrying an armload of vinyl. Records went flying and the disgruntled teen gave him a few choice curse words as Nick helped him pick up the records. When he was done, Emily began to check out the teen. As he reached for the door, she called out to him one last time.

"Simon?"

"Yeah?"

"This isn't a date, okay? I don't do dates."

She frowned as if she were talking about changing a loaded diaper. Nick grinned and shrugged his shoulders, finally, a chance to be completely honest.

"Don't worry. Neither do I."

He stepped out into the chilly afternoon to prep his plans for his brief but interesting evening with Emily Fischer.

CHAPTER TWENTY-SEVEN

The Non-Date

Nick met her at The Vintage Point right as she was getting ready to close the store.

"Wait, don't close up just yet," he said as she went to turn off all of the lights.

"Why not?"

"I thought we could talk right here."

"Seriously?"

"Sure, why not. It's as good as any other place. Looks like there's somewhere to sit," he said, nodding his head in the direction of the turntable listening stations near the bathroom in the back of the store. Emily stared at him.

"Okay. . ." she said hesitantly. Nick grinned and started to walk back toward the tables.

"You said this wasn't a date and it's pretty damn cold outside. We both have to walk home so I thought we could start here. I even brought my own snacks," he said holding up a bag from the local bagel shop around the corner from the store.

"They closed like three hours ago. Those bagels are

rocks by now."

"Good thing I'm not picky—especially after all that hospital food I had to eat," he took out a ziplock baggie full of quarters.

"What's that?" she asked.

"Money for the pop machine," he said, pointing at the vintage Coke machine sitting next to the magnet wall.

"Wow, you've thought of everything"

She sat down.

"And. . .I'm not willing share because this is not a date."

"That's alright. Leon brought me a sub from next door. I'm good."

She watched him reach into the bag, pull out a bagel and take a large bite.

"Wait, we still need music."

"Music?"

She eyed him suspiciously.

"Yeah, I thought you could teach me something about the whole vinyl scene."

"The vinyl scene? Nobody calls it that."

She laughed and Nick couldn't help liking what he heard.

"Alright, whatever it is I want to know more about it. It seems interesting and my. . .my sponsor. . ." Nick hesitated for a moment, "says I need to find a new hobby."

"Oh."

"Yeah."

"How many days?"

"Sober?" Nick asked and she nodded. He exhaled deeply and ran a hand through his hair. How long had it been?

" Thirty-seven days."

"Wow. Congrats."

"What about you?" Nick asked and Emily looked annoyed.

"I'm not an alcoholic. . ."

"I meant chemo. How long?" he asked. There was a long silence as Emily fidgeted with her fingers and avoided eye contact.

"A year and a half since I had the last one."

He was confused.

"A year and a half? But. . ."

"I've still got all my hair? My eyebrows? Eyelashes?"

"Well, kind of?"

"They grow back, you know."

"But you were at the hospital. . .in the support group."

"Sure. I've been there many times."

"Can I ask how many?"

"I've lost track really. The support group helps . .sometimes. But now I go mostly to support my friend Caroline. She's got stage IV breast cancer."

They sat in silence for a moment, then she spoke up again.

"I got sick when I was four and I was in and out until I finally went into remission, well sort of."

"You've had cancer for twenty years?"

"It's very treatable if you get the right one."

"Which one did you get?"

Nick was flabbergasted by how calm she was explaining it to him.

"Does it matter?"

"No, I guess not," Nick said feeling awkward.

"They're all bad, you know. I just got one that's hung on longer than most."

"That sounds like a tough way to grow up. I mean having to deal with being sick. Did you go to school?"

"At first, when I'd feel a little better, but then my hair started falling out and I looked as sick as I felt. Everybody was very nice but it got too hard for me especially when I had to be in the hospital longer. So, my mom homeschooled me, with some help from my dad."

"And now do you go to school?"

"I'm enrolled at the university. I'm an art major."

"What about friends?"

"I have Caroline and now you."

She punched Nick playfully in the arm and he blushed under his beard. She gave him another punch in the arm and this time he reached up to catch her hand in his. She didn't pull away.

"Are we friends?" he asked before clearing his throat and finally releasing her hand.

"I don't know, I guess we could be."

She turned away as if nothing had happened. After another moment of silence, Nick asked the question that had been on his mind for the last few minutes.

"Emily, if you're in remission, why were you at the hospital and in that support group?"

Emily took a deep breath and then exhaled. She looked around the store and then back down at her hands.

"The cancer's back."

Nick didn't know what to say except "I'm. . .I'm so sorry."

"What I should say is that maybe it never really left. It just didn't spread."

"So you've been doing chemo again?"

"No."

"But I thought you said the cancer was back."

"That's right."

"And it's spreading?"

"Yeah."

"Where?"

"Pretty much everywhere."

"But. . ."

"But what?"

"Why no chemo?"

Emily sighed.

"Where to begin. . ."

"But if it could save your life?" he said, hearing the urgency in his own voice.

"It can't."

"What? How can you be so sure?"

"Because that's why I was at the hospital. To run some tests and talk to my oncologists. There's nothing they can do,"

Nick just stared at her, feeling dumbfounded.

"Not now," she added in a whisper and a couple of tears fell down her face. She quickly brushed them away with the back of her hands.

"I don't want to talk about it anymore."

She stood and headed for the front of the store. Nick watched her go behind the counter and grab a record to put on the turntable.

"What are you going to play?"

"It's a surprise," she said placing the needle on the record, "but if you're serious about learning about the 'vinyl scene' then this is a must." A slow and mellow melody began to play and Emily closed her eyes and started to sway with the music.

"What record is it?"

"Don't you recognize it?" she asked still swaying, a small smile on her lips.

"No."

"It's Beck. Sea Change," she said and started to sing along.

Nick watched her, fascinated by the way her body swayed in time to the music and her voice, a soft, sweet child-like soprano followed along with the lyrics. When the song was over Emily opened her eyes and glanced back at Nick.

"That was. . ."He wanted to say 'beautiful' but he knew it would only scare her and ruin the moment, so he chose the next best thing to say.

"That was really cool." Cool?

"Thanks, it's one of my favs. Tell me, why don't you remember it? I thought it was from your generation," she said taking off the record and reaching for another.

"My generation? Just how old do you think I am?" He asked a little bit worried.

"Well, that beard isn't doing you any favors—so thirties, maybe older?"

Nick's jaw dropped.

"I'm not even thirty yet."

She laughed.

"Sorry, but your clothes are screaming thirty-something."

She put on the second record. Nick looked down at what he was wearing and realized that it wasn't what he was used to wearing. That had been on purpose so that everyone, especially the paparazzi, wouldn't suspect that a mild-mannered, bearded, glasses-wearing, quiet patient walking with a cane was really Nick Simon—not even Emily.

"How old are you?" he asked and she smiled.

"Not as old as you, I bet."

"Ha, ha. Come on. How old?"

"Twenty-four," she said as the next record began to play.

This time it was an energetic and loud baseline followed by techno beats and lively vocals.

"Daft Punk?" he guessed.

"That was a lucky guess."

"I actually listen to them."

"Their original albums, not just the one song by Pharell Williams, right?"

"Oh. . ." she had him. It was really the one song.

"My favorites are Robot Rock and One More Time. Alive is pretty good too."

"Weren't most of these records out before you were born?"

"Pretty much all of them. Why?"

"I'm just surprised."

"About?"

"So many things."

"Like?"

She looked at him expectantly and he froze. He wasn't ready to tell her what was swirling around in his mind since he'd first seen her or met her.

"The records, the store. . .the books."

"What do you have against Nick Simon books?"

"Nothing. You said you didn't like them."

"I never said I didn't like them, I said I didn't understand why he would write about something he clearly knows nothing about."

"What's that?"

"Love."

Nick frowned.

"What do you mean?"

"Have you ever read one of his books? Don't get me wrong they're a nice quick read but in the end everything always comes out perfect."

"Wait. . ."

"And that's the problem. There's always some big real-life obstacle the characters have to overcome. That's how he hooks you because you can almost relate, and then just when you think they're not going to make it, they do and love conquers all or. . . worse still, he kills one of them off!"

"I'm sure he has his reasons."

"Yeah. And you know what the problem with that is?"

"What?"

He wanted to know, he really and truly wanted to know.

"It's not how real life happens. It's not how love happens. It all happens somewhere in between," she said and took off the Daft Punk record.

They went a while without saying anything before Nick decided to try his luck and ask the next question.

"Have you been in love?"

She laughed louder and longer than he'd ever heard her laugh.

"Of course I have. Haven't you?"she said and saw that he hesitated.

"Sure." he said and she stopped what she was doing.

"You're kidding right? You've never been in love?"

"I'm sure I have."

"No. . .you'd know. Trust me."

"Maybe it's different for guys."

"Maybe—but it's not."

She insisted.

"I have definitely been in love."

He insisted.

"I said love not lust. There's a difference between a weekly hook-up and a relationship."

"Is there?" he teased and she shook her head.

"I take it back. Maybe we can't be friends."

"I tried to tell you," he laughed. "Seriously, I thought you weren't into the dating thing."

"I'm not."

"But you must've been at one time."

"Isn't everyone?"

"You tell me. Was it serious?"

"Yeah," she said, reaching for a third record and holding it up for him to see. "Here's The Flaming Lips and A Spoonful Weighs A Ton."

"How serious?"

"Vinyl serious. He introduced me to it, you know. Collecting and stuff."

"What does that mean 'vinyl serious'?"

"Pressed and permanent. At least it seemed like it to me but, like I said, some things can't be overcome."

"Like?"

"Cancer."

"He broke up with you because you had cancer?" Nick asked incredulously.

“No.” She said closing her eyes and starting to sway to the song. “I broke up with him.”

“Because of the cancer?” he asked and Emily opened her eyes and grimaced.

“That. . .” she said, “and he was cheating on me.”

“Oh,”

He listened to the record for a while.

“This next song is really great.”

“I get why you broke up over the cheating but why over the cancer?” Nick asked and she sighed again.

“We agreed to disagree on a decision I made.”

“About stopping chemo, right?”

“No. He was fine with that.”

“Then I don’t understand,” he said as she changed the record for a fourth and final time.

“I love Joni Mitchell, especially this song,” she said as a sad, acoustic melody played out on a guitar.

“What’s it called?”

“Urge for Going,” she smiled sadly. “This album was the last gift he gave me before we broke up. "I thought about throwing it away or selling it. But I love it too much.”

“What decision did you make that he couldn’t live with, Emily?” Nick asked and waited anxiously for her to answer.

“To kill myself,” she said quietly and then started to sing along to the Joni Mitchell song in a whisper while Nick sat watching her completely at a loss for words.

CHAPTER TWENTY-EIGHT

The Song

The song ended but her words hung heavy in the space between them and the bagel he'd eaten earlier sat like a rock in the pit of his stomach. *Kill herself? She wanted to kill herself?* Nick tried not to stare at Emily as she put away all of the records and turned off the record player.

"You're staring," she said without even making eye contact.

"I'm-I'm sorry." he stammered as he began to clean up the remnants of the bagel, paying close attention to even the smallest crumb left on the table. There was so much he didn't understand about the girl with the butterfly tattoo and now, just as he was starting to get to know her, to *really* know her, he'd learned two devastating things about her. First, she was dying and second, because she was dying, *she wanted to kill herself.* He felt an inexplicable lump in his throat as he thought about it—a world without Emily in it, without her crazy red hair, inquisitive gray eyes and love of old vinyl records. He couldn't wrap his head around it. He didn't want to.

"It's not what you think," she said from across the room and Nick stopped cleaning the invisible crumbs on the table.

"What?" he asked trying not to give away that he was pretty sure it was *exactly* what he thought it was.

"It's not suicide. Not the way people think it is."

Emily left the front counter and walked back to the listening station and sat down. She brought up her knees to her chin and rested her head on them, wrapping her arms around her legs just the way he remembered her doing back in the hospital.

"Then what is it?" Nick asked, not sure he wanted to know.

"It's called *'Death with Dignity'*. Have you heard of it?" she asked him timidly and he shook his head no.

She sighed and smiled as if she'd already had to explain it several times.

"There's a law in Oregon and four other states that allows a terminally-ill person, who has no other options and only six months or less to live, the right to get a lethal dose of meds from a doctor."

Six months or less? Nick's mind was reeling.

"Is Nebraska one of those other states?"

"No." she said and he couldn't help but feel relieved. "But I'm not planning on staying in Nebraska."

"What? Where are you going to go?"

"I want to go to Oregon, fill out the forms, do what's required and. . .die in peace."

Emily suddenly looked much older than her 24 years.

"But what about. . ." Nick started to say *But what about us and what's starting to happen between us?* Then he corrected himself. "Your parents? Caroline?"

"Wow. Well, you're right. That's a big concern." she said sadly.

"Don't you care about how they would feel. . .losing you like that?"

"Of course. I've thought about it a lot. I love them. I do. But I've got to do what's right for me."

There was such a tone of determination in her voice that he didn't know what to say next.

"It's not as bad as you're imagining. I've done all the research, I've made the calls and even watched some documentaries that show exactly what happens. It seems so. . .peaceful. Everyone you love around you before you. . . fall asleep."

"So you're parents will be there. . .when it happens, I mean."

"No, probably not."

"But wouldn't that be harder for you?"

"Yeah."

"Is it something you could work out?"

"I don't know. We're not exactly on speaking terms right now."

"What about Caroline? Isn't she your best friend?"

Emily grinned.

"Don't get me started on Caroline. If you hadn't noticed from the support group meetings, she's a devout Christian. She doesn't believe in abortion, the death penalty or physician assisted suicide. She has the heart of a saint and I love her. She's been with me through a lot. We met in support group."

"So what you're saying is that you're going to do this alone?"

"I have Mel."

He noticed the look of pure joy that came across her face at the mention of his name. Nick cleared his throat.

"New boyfriend?"

"Alaskan Malamute."

She giggled.

"Mel's a *dog*?" he asked, laughing at himself.

"A rescue dog and the only man in my life right now. The very best one."

"You and Mel in Oregon. Anyone else?"

"I have another friend, Derrick. He might come. Maybe. He's still mad at me, but he'll come around. I know he will." There was another short silence that gave the impression that it was more hope than fact.

"You think I'm crazy," she said giving him another one of her sad smiles.

"Yeah," he said, returning the smile, "but I also think you're brave."

"You'd be the first."

"To think you're crazy?" he teased and she smiled.

"No, to say I'm brave. Usually they say that when you're going *through* chemo and even when you decide to *stop* fighting and let the cancer take you. But doing it this other way. . .well let's just say no one's really on board with it."

"Can't you see why?"

"Absolutely! But what about what *I'm* going through? What this disease has done to *my* body and *how* it's going to kill *me*? Why doesn't anyone want to think about *that*? Everybody wants me to fight but it's for them, not me anymore. The cancer's going to kill me no matter what and it's going to be soon. Why can't I decide when? Why do I have to suffer in order for it to count? Why does it make me less courageous to want to die in peace, surrounded by my family and friends on a date I get to choose?"

"A date? You've already chosen a date?" Nick was starting to panic.

"If everything goes like I planned then yes." She said and Nick's mouth went dry.

"What's the date?"

"I'm keeping that to myself for now."

"I totally understand. . .what I mean is—I can see why you would keep it to yourself," Nick said, even though he didn't.

"Good, cause my parents don't and neither does Caroline."

"I'm sure it's just because they don't want to lose you."

"I know that. . .but I. . .I *can't* do it again. I *won't* put myself through the pain or the side effects of some treatment that isn't going to work. I want what's left of my life to be *different*,"she said with tears in her eyes.

"How?" Nick asked and she smiled, tucking a piece of her bright red hair behind her ear.

"I want to call the shots, to decide what I want to do and do it with the time I've got left."

"And what exactly would you do with your time?"

"For starters I want to finish my record collection. There's a lot of records I still need." He could see a spark of life and energy in her eyes as she said it.

"That explains you working here, then."

"Yeah."

"What else?"

"I don't know. . ."

"Climb Mount Everest, go to Paris, sit in front of the

Taj Mahal?"

"No. More simple things like movies, concerts, art galleries, plays, bike rides, hikes, waterfalls and sunrises, sunsets, full moons *without* the pain, Mel by my side and with all my hair, my eyebrows and eyelashes intact."

"That's all?" he said and felt suddenly ashamed.

"If you knew what it was like to live with this you'd know it's really a lot."

"I'm sorry. I'm an idiot."

"Yeah, I knew that,"

He blushed. "So what's next?"

"I leave Nebraska."

"Just like that?"

"Just like that."

"And then?"

"I get a job, fill out the paperwork, see the doctors I need to and wait."

"It's that easy?"

"No, it's actually really, really, *really* hard."

"Then how is this going to work?" he asked—and waited while she fidgeted with her fingers again.

"We'll see."

"Keeping that to yourself too, huh?"

"I can't bare my entire soul to a complete stranger, can I?"

She laughed. He laughed with her and then got quiet before leaning forward and gently tucking a piece of stray hair behind her ear.

"Is that what I am? A *complete* stranger?" he asked and for a moment their eyes met.

Nick could hardly breathe or explain why he felt this way for someone he hardly knew, at least not by his normal standards. They hadn't played any of the usual dating games or hooked up once. So he was way out of his comfort zone but he couldn't help feeling what he felt. He wanted to kiss her, he wanted to. . .

She kissed him first. He pulled away and she looked back at him, confused.

"Wait."

He couldn't believe it was his own voice he was hearing.

"What?" she said, flushed from their passionate exchange.

"I thought you weren't into dating?"

"I'm not."

"But. . .this. . ."

"It's not dating."

"I know but what about. . ." He didn't know how to say it, how to make his mouth form the words. *But you're dying. . .* The look on his face seemed to give him away and she laughed.

"I'm dying. I'm not dead," she said and kissed him again. He couldn't help but respond and pull her closer to him. He wanted her and she made it clear with every touch and kiss that she wanted him. Nick tried to keep out any external voice in his head, especially his sponsor's, so he could concentrate on what he was doing. He'd never had sex before without having been slightly or completely under the influence. At least not since he could remember and this experience felt new and exciting in a way he couldn't articulate. Everything was more *alive, energetic, enthusiastic*! Suddenly,Emily pulled away and looked around.

"Too bad we can't knock these off and use the tables

like they do in that Nick Simon movie." She said kissing him again and Nick was startled by the use of his own name and the reference to his movie *For the Record*. It had been one of his earliest and biggest literary successes not to mention a big box-office draw. But the last thing he needed to do now was douse himself in a cold shower of statistics so he blocked it out as much as he could.

"What movie was that?" he asked in between kisses and she giggled.

"Really, we're going to talk movies right now?"

"You started it,"he said breathing heavily.

She cupped his face with her small hands and looked at him briefly. Her gray eyes were full of desire and playfulness.

"Always." she said leaving her chair. He groaned with pleasure as she straddled him. Now, things were starting to feel familiar. . .until there was a loud pounding on the door at the front of the store. Nick stopped.

"Just ignore it," Emily said and continued to press herself against him.

"Okay." He agreed, but the pounding got even louder. Nick looked up again.

"What if it's Leon?"

"Leon lives on the south part of town and doesn't own a car. The bus doesn't run this late. Now, shut up and kiss me," she whispered.

The pounding continued and finally Emily turned around and looked toward the front of the door. This time she froze.

"What?" Nick asked.

Emily just sat and stared at the front door.

"Emily, who is it?" he asked and it seemed like an

eternity before she finally answered.

“It’s my father. . .the rabbi.”

CHAPTER TWENTY-NINE

Knock at the Door

Emily stood up and walked to the front door, hair disheveled and lips swollen from their time together, while Nick grabbed and held the paper sack his bagel had come in on top of his lap. He tried to adjust his shirt and pants as best he could but even with the paper sack sitting over his groin and his best efforts to slow his breathing, he knew, what with Emily's outward appearance and obvious indifference to what her father *the rabbi* had seen, it was probably a lost cause. Usually, Nick wouldn't care, but this time he felt guilt and shame he couldn't explain. He was nervous as Emily reached the front door and unlocked it. Nick could make out a tall man wearing a dark colored winter coat. He stepped inside.

"Papa," he heard Emily say.

"Emily." The man greeted her with a brief smile in return but there was no outward sign of affection. No hugs. No kisses. Just an acknowledgement. He had a full salt and pepper beard with mustache, bushy brows and hair of the same color that was covered by what Nick knew,from attending Arnie Schaefer's wedding to Margie, was a *yarmulke,*a skull cap worn by Jewish men when attending religious ceremonies—or if they practiced hard core Judaism. Being a rabbi would *definitely* count as hard core. He also had a pair of rimless, round spectacles perched on the bridge of his nose. He and Emily were staring at each other, having what seemed like an awkward, wordless conversation. It was a visual standoff. Minutes passed before her father finally spoke.

"I hope I'm not here at a bad time," he said glancing back toward Nick and raising a bushy brow of severe disapproval.

"What do you want, Papa?" Emily asked and her father seemed suddenly uncomfortable.

"Your mother. . ."He cleared his throat, "your mother wanted me to ask you to come home for Shabat," he said.

Emily sighed.

"*Mom* wants me to come for Shabat?"

"Yes," Her father said, giving her another tense smile.

"She could have called."

"She tried. She says you don't answer."

"I'm busy when she usually calls."

"You could call her back." His voice sounded a little irritated.

"If I come home are we finally going to talk about it?" Emily asked and his face became stony.

"Emily, your mother simply wants you to come home for Shabat. Go to service and have a family meal. That's all. No arguments."

"It's not an argument for me, Papa. It's what I *want.* You're the ones who turn it into an argument," Emily said.

He pulled on his beard and sighed.

"Emily, *please.* Just this once can we come together as a family? It's been so long since you've been home. Is it too much to ask for us to put aside our differences and celebrate our faith?" he asked.

Nick could detect a note of hope in her father's voice. Emily said nothing at first then, squaring her shoulders, she gave her father her answer.

"Yes, Papa. It is," she said, her voice clear and determined.

Nick thought he saw the older man's shoulders slump a bit in response.

"I told your mother you wouldn't reconsider but I told her I'd try."

"I'm sorry, Papa."

"So am I, Emily."

He turned to go. Then he stopped, as if reconsidering, he turned back around.

"Before I go, won't you introduce me to your friend?" he said as if he hadn't seen them in the middle of a grope fest only moments before. Emily turned to look at Nick. He was discreetly trying to shake his head no. The last thing Nick needed was to come between a dying girl and her rabbi father. Emily hadn't answered when her father simply walked around her. When he reached the listening station area he put out his hand toward Nick.

"I'm Liev Fischer," he said with a smile that conveyed genuine interest and curiosity. . .for the split second until he took Nick's hand. The grip was like angry steel.

"Hello, I'm N-Simon."

He corrected himself and tried not to cry out in pain at the vise-like way he was shaking his hand.

"Simon, I'm Emily's father."

"Nice to meet you."

"I'm sorry for coming here like this and ruining your . . .plans. But my wife and I can't always reach Emily by phone. So I'm forced to wait for her at her apartment complex or come to this store to find her. I guess it's fortunate for me I chose the latter." he said, still gripping Nick's hand.

"Papa. .." Emily called as she made her way back to where they were.

"Are you from the area?" he asked and Nick was about to answer when Emily interceded.

"Papa, please. You have my answer."

Rabbi Fischer ignored her.

"It's been a long time since Emily has come home. Her mother misses her. The congregation misses her."

"The congregation?"

"Yes, the congregation of Temple B'nai Shalom. Do you attend temple?"

"Papa!"

"I'm just getting to know your friend, Emily. How else will I know who is in your life?"

"No, I'd say I'm more of a lapsed Catholic."

"Interesting," He said glancing at Emily.

"Papa, please. Just go," Emily demanded.

Rabbi Fischer put his hands up in the air and shrugged his shoulders.

"Fine. I won't delay you any longer. But give me some good news to tell your mother. Tell me that you'll come to Shabat and that you'll bring your friend."

"Papa. . ."

Her father took Emily's hands in his. "*Please.*"

Emily's determination seemed to diminish.

"I'll think about it," she said softly and he smiled, running a finger across her cheek.

"That's my girl."

He turned back to Nick.

"I look forward to seeing you both on Friday."

"I said I'd *consider* it," Emily called after him as he made his way to the front door.

Her father turned back for a moment.

"Will you come?" Liev Fischer asked looking directly at Nick, who looked back at Emily.

"I don't know," he answered honestly.

"If you do, please do me a kindness and bring my daughter with you, okay?" Nick nodded.

After he gave Emily one final smile, he stepped out into the cold blustery night. Emily went up and locked the door behind him and then marched straight back to where Nick was sitting. She slapped him. Hard.

"Ow!" He yelled. "What was that for?

"How dare you agree to go see my parents?" she demanded and he stared at her, confused, while rubbing the place where she slapped him.

"I never agreed to anything."

"I was standing right here and you talked around me."

I *said* I didn't know if I could go."

"You also agreed to take me with you if you went."

"So? That's not a yes."

"It is in my father's world. You just told him we were going."

"I'm so confused, Emily. I don't know what I did wrong,"

She sat down and pulled her knees up to her chin.

"He seemed. . .nice," Nick ventured.

She gave him a scathing look.

"Of course he does. He's the rabbi of one of the biggest congregations in town. It's his job to be *nice*."

"Are you saying he played me?"

"Like a dreidel."

A small grin spread across her lips. He was still rubbing his face where it stung.

"Who knew you were such a PK?" he said.

"A what?"

"A preacher's kid."

"Not the same thing. He's not a preacher."

"I don't know. Seemed like kinda like a preacher to me. Staunch defender of religious faith, stern look of disapproval, vice-like grip coupled with a confusing but disarming niceness, . . ."

"You're such an idiot."

"You keep saying that, it's starting to hurt my feelings."

Emily reached back across to touch the place where she'd slapped him.

"I want to say I'm sorry about slapping you."

"Okay."

"I said I *want* to, but it's not going to happen."

She laughed and he couldn't help but smile. She was beautiful, full of life and spunk and determination. This time he leaned in and kissed her. She responded by getting up out of her chair and straddling him again. Was she hoping to pick up where they left off? It was tempting.

"Emily. . .I . . .can't."

He was amazed the words had come out of his mouth.

"What? Why?" She continued to kiss him.

"It's complicated."

"There's nothing complicated about it. I'll walk you through it if you want."

"That's not what I mean." He pulled away from her.

"Then, what do you mean?" Her voice was small and quivering.

"I want to I really do. More than you can imagine, but the thing with your dad and everything we've talked about tonight. . .I just want to make sure we're doing it for the right reasons."

"You're kidding right?" Her voice hardened and Nick wished he was.

"No."

She stood and backed away. "Then what's wrong?"

"There are things about me that you need to know."

"Why?"

"Because. . ." He cringed as he said it. "Honesty is part of recovery."

"You're not serious. You're using the Twelve Steps as an excuse?"

"Not an excuse. . .a reason to wait until I have the chance to share with you the way you've shared with me."

"I think you've got it all wrong. I don't want to date you."

"I know that."

"Then what's the big deal?"

"I like you, Emily. I really like you and I don't want to hurt you. I tend to do that to people. I don't want to do that here, not this time."

"It's just a hook up."

"Not for me. Not this time."

"Then this isn't going to work. I can't give you what you want. I'm leaving."

"I know. I just meant we could spend some time together before you go."

"Why, so you can change my mind and we can live happily ever after?"

"No. . ."

"Get out!"

"Emily, wait. . ."

"I said get out."

Nick looked helplessly down at his pants. "Could you give me a minute?"

"No, just get out."

Nick picked up the paper sack his bagel came in and once again held it in front of him as he made his way to the front of the store and out into the cold Nebraska night. When he turned around the store lights had been shut off and Emily was gone.

CHAPTER THIRTY

Daryl

When he returned to the halfway house Jesse at the front counter called him over.

"Hey Simon, you got a visitor."

Nick panicked thinking the paparazzi had finally found him. "Who?"

"He says his name is Daryl." Jesse nodded over in the direction of the den. Nick's heart sank. Daryl was Barbara's driver, bodyguard and all around right hand man (in that pound-you-into-the-ground sort of way).

"Thanks, Jesse." Nick slowly made his way into the den where he saw Daryl seated perfectly still, eyes closed. The man was so large and imposing that Nick was very hesitant to make his presence known. He didn't have to, Daryl knew he was there.

"Mr. Simon. Ms. Barbara sent me to check on you."

"Hey, Daryl. I didn't mean to disturb you."

"Nothing can disturb that which is already at peace." Daryl answered and Nick held his breath as the bodyguard opened his eyes and stood up, towering over him.

"It's good to see you, Daryl."

"It's good to see you, Mr. Simon."

"I would invite you to my room so we could talk, but that's against the rules here."

"I am well aware of the rules, Mr. Simon. Ms. Barbara specifically had Mr. Ambrose research places near the medical center for you to go while arrangements were being made—arrangements for your new living quarters."

"Back in New York?"

"No. I'm afraid Ms. Barbara does not feel that the atmosphere is quite ready for your homecoming."

"So what's the plan?"

"I have collected your things and I will be taking you to your new apartment."

"Where?"

"The Old Market," Daryl said and Nick's heart lifted—that's where *The Vintage Point* was located!

"Wait—exactly where in the Old Market?"

"I believe it is called The Garden." Daryl said and Nick recognized the name. He'd walked by the place several times on his way to *The Vintage Point.* They were *luxury* apartments.

"Daryl—no." Nick protested. Daryl's facial expression never changed.

"Mr. Simon?"

"That's a really nice place."

"That was the point, Mr. Simon."

"I can't live in a place like that—not yet." Nick explained and this time Daryl cocked an eyebrow.

"I do not understand, Mr. Simon. "Certainly, it is not what you are accustomed to but it will surely do." The bodyguard said reassuringly.

"No you don't understand. She can't see me living in a place like that."

This time Daryl sighed and gave Nick a look that might pass on the big man's face as a look of slight disapproval. "Mr. Simon, you know that your sponsor has asked you to refrain from initiating any sexual relations during your recovery. You agreed to this."

"That's not what I'm talking about, Daryl. Well, not exactly anyway."

"Then please explain."

"It's true. I've met someone."

Nick saw the corner of Daryl's mouth twitch. He could imagine how many times Daryl had heard Nick say the same thing after every hook up. "Mr. Simon. . ."

"Really, Daryl. This is different. *I'm* different."

"Mr. Simon. You are not different. You are just sober. Barely sober. It is not the time to begin such a relationship. Ms. Barbara would not approve."

"To hell with Ms. Barbara!" Nick said vehemently and then realizing they were still in the den lowered his voice. "I can't walk away from this, Daryl. I've got to see where it goes."

"It can only lead to heartbreak."

Nick was shocked. Did Daryl know about Emily's situation? Had he been spying on Nick?

"Wait, how did you know?"

"Ms. Barbara pays me to drive and to protect her investments when necessary, Mr. Simon. I also observe. Whoever this lady is, it is best during this time of recovery to leave her be. In my experience, observing your liaisons, it can only lead to heartbreak. . .for the lady."

"But. . .it's different. I swear it is."

"Maybe in a year or two. Not after. . .how many days of sobriety, Mr. Simon?"

This time it was Nick's turn to sigh.

"Thirty-seven," he said.

After a moment Daryl pointed in the direction of the door.

"Shall we go, Mr. Simon?"

"Okay."

Nick reluctantly agreed, waving to Jesse at the front counter and following Daryl out of the halfway house. Nick felt defeated by Daryl's reminder of the fact that he was still Barbara King's *investment* and by the number of days he'd actually been sober. That and the way he'd left things with Emily had made the night a total bust. Even though he and Daryl were on their way to his new luxury apartment in the Old Market, Nick had never felt so lonely or poor.

CHAPTER THIRTY-ONE

Rejection

It had taken lots of persuasion on Nick's part to convince Daryl to drop him off at the hospital several times, without making himself known. Nick couldn't afford to have anyone see Daryl hovering around him and tipping off the media. Daryl wasn't exactly forgettable. The bodyguard reluctantly agreed to Nick's requests partly because it was his job to comply but also because he'd caught Nick trying to leave the apartment complex on three separate occasions. So he finally gave in and discreetly drove him where he wanted to go.

Nick couldn't get Emily off his mind and he waited for her at the hospital, but never saw her walking the hallways. He decided to go back to the Well Life support group, wait outside the door to see if he could find her after it was over, and maybe find a moment when he could speak to her alone. He went several times, making sure that no one saw him, in case Emily had told them he was a fake, but she didn't show up. Then one day he saw Emily make it into the crowded room ahead of him. He waited for her. Caroline had saved her a seat naturally so he spent the next hour trying not to stare at her through the small window in the door while she worked on her sketch pad. Finally, when group ended, he found the courage to approach her but she ignored him.

"Emily. Please talk to me."

Nothing. Her friend seemed confused by their lack of interaction.

"Emily? What's going on?"

Emily kept packing her sketchpad and pencils into her colorful bag. "Trust me, Caroline. You don't want to know."

"Come on. Don't you think it's a little unfair to shut me out because of what happened the other night?"

"*What* happened the other night?" Caroline frowned Clearly, every maternal instinct was on alert.

"Nothing bad. I promise," he said, turning to Caroline.

She didn't seem convinced.

"That's up to interpretation, don't you think?" Emily said angrily and started to walk away.

"Emily, wait up," Caroline called picking up her purse and following, , while glancing over her shoulder at Nick.

He watched them walk away and stood in the middle of the room alone. Suddenly he felt a tap on shoulder and turned around. It was Caroline.She was back, flashing him a big smile.

"Hi, Simon is it?"

She reached out her hand. He took it and they briefly shook hands.

"Yeah."

"I'm Caroline Sterling, Emily's friend."

"Yeah."

He gave her a half-hearted smile. She looked at him sympathetically.

"Look, I'm not sure what happened between you and Emily. I didn't even know you knew each other. But I know that whatever happened has really impacted her and by the look on your face, you too."

"No, it's not like that at all," he protested.

She shook her head.

"I've known her for a while now and I know she can be pretty direct sometimes—to the point where it can come off as rude. She doesn't mean to be that's just the way she is. . .right now."

"I think we just got off on the wrong foot, that's all."

"Maybe." Caroline said. "Or maybe there's more to this than either one of you is willing to admit."

"Don't worry about it," Nick said. He started to limp toward the door.

"She likes you," Caroline called after him.

He stopped.

Turning around, he frowned. "What?"

"That's why she's acting like this. I know, it sounds completely juvenile. I should know, I have a thirteen-year-old daughter at home, but it's not. It's just that you came into her life at a point where she thought she was done with. . ." Caroline shrugged.

"What?"

"Relationships. Love."

"Wait a minute, no one said *anything* about a relationship or love. She made her position absolutely clear on both of those things."

"Don't panic."

Caroline laughed and Nick felt awkward.

"I wasn't."

"Did she tell you why she's not interested in relationships?" Caroline asked and he paused for a moment unsure if he should share what Emily told him, but then if they were really as close as she claimed they were it wouldn't be news.

"Yeah."

"Then you know she's really struggling right now."

Nick scoffed, remembering how angry she had been with him and how harshly she'd reacted after her father had left. "That's not the vibe I got at all. Her mind seemed pretty made up to me."

"Well it is. She told me she saw her father the other night. Did you meet him?"

"Kind of."

"Even though I've never really met him, I believe that deep down he's really a good man."

"He's a very protective one," Nick said recalling the man's steely grip.

"He's her father, how could anything be different?" she said in a motherly tone.

He shrugged.

It took him a moment to find the courage to ask the question he already knew the answer to—because Emily had confirmed it. He wanted to hear it from someone else.

"Caroline, is there really no hope for. . .her illness? Does she really *have* to do it?"

She sighed deeply before answering him. "There's no doubt she's in the support group for a reason if that's what you're asking. But about her decision. . .I've prayed about it so many times. I keep thinking that sooner or later God will give her a miracle and it'll be enough to bring her around."

"She told me you don't agree with her decision."

"No, not at all. I'm a Christian I believe God is the only one who can give life or take it away. I believe that everything happens for his divine purpose and in his divine timing."

"You realize that Emily is Jewish, right?"

"The message of the Gospel is for Jew and Gentile alike. I wasn't always a believer myself, Simon. I'm a born-again Christian so I know a little something about miracles and mistakes."

"Her father is a rabbi and she won't even listen to him, what makes you think she'll ever listen to you?"

"That's not my intent. It's not my place to force her into salvation. It's my job to *love her* no matter what."

"But the differences are so big especially given the decision she's made. How can you two stay friends through this?"

"My job's the same. I love her, I don't judge her and I use my own life or even my suffering as an example. If she chooses to listen, I rejoice. If she chooses something else, I still love her and I leave the rest between Emily and God."

"I'm trying to wrap my head around that idea," Nick admitted.

Caroline placed a hand on his shoulder. "Do you have plans tonight?"

"Well. . ." he thought of Daryl waiting somewhere in the hospital parking lot.

"Good. I want you to come home with me and have supper with my family."

"I don't know if that's a good idea."

He wondered exactly how much Emily had told her

about him.

"Don't worry," she said as if she'd read his mind. "I know you're not dying."

Nick was dumbstruck. A few moments passed before he spoke again.

"Caroline. . ." he began, but she shushed him.

"Remember what I said about judging Emily?"

He nodded. "Well that goes for you too."

"Okay." "My husband Aaron is waiting outside with my daughter. Aaron's a fabulous cook. I promise you won't starve."

"Well, it would be nice change from takeout."

"Or the hospital food. Am I right?"

She laughed her easy-going laugh and Nick marveled at how quickly Caroline Sterling had gone from being a stranger to a friend. He was sure it was her comforting maternal air and laid-back manner that made her easy to confide in and trust.

"I don't want to impose, though."

"You're not. To be truthful, I want to get to know you a little more."

"I thought Emily told you everything."

"Not everything."

"There's not much to tell."

"Isn't there?"

She put her arm through his as they walked slowly out of the room.

"No."

"I think there is."

He gave her a quick sideways glance.

"Like what?"

She paused a moment before going on.

"Well, for starters, how is it that a bestselling author and film maker ended up here in *this* hospital?"

CHAPTER THIRTY-TWO

Dinner with Caroline

Nick froze and very slowly turned to look at Caroline. She was holding up his latest book with the dust jacket opened to the back where the author picture was located.

"Hello, Nick *Simon*." She said with a mischievous grin. He swallowed hard.

"I'm not. . ."

"Don't bother. I *never* forget a face despite what the chemo's done to my brain. It took me a little longer but I knew there was something familiar about you."

"I don't understand."

"The beard and the glasses made it tough. The name, well, it was almost too easy. But the fact is that I'm actually a fan of your work."

"Does she know?"

"Are you kidding me? If she did you'd know about it. Not to mention she's a closet fan."

"She seemed quite the opposite to me,." he said almost under his breath.

Caroline punched him in the arm.

"So you admit it! You *are* Nick Simon!" she said with an almost child-like glee.

"Shhh! Not so loud, Caroline."

"Sorry," she said in a whisper, but a big smile was still plastered across her face.

"If I say yes, what does that mean?"

"It means you'll autograph my book, right?"

He nodded. "I mean what would that information mean to Emily?"

"That's tougher to answer."

"I guess it can't get any worse.".

"How so?"

"Well, she ignores me completely already. She made it clear the other night that she was done with me."

"Okay, tell me what happened the *other* night."

"I thought Emily told you."

"What Emily tells me and what might be the whole picture are two different things. She didn't exactly mention you, just that she had a bad night because her father dropped by unexpectedly. I want to hear your side of the story."

"I'm not sure, Caroline."

"I promise that *all* your secrets are safe with me."

"What makes you think that I have any more secrets?"

"Have you watched TV lately? You've been all over the entertainment news channels for the last two months. Mostly because of those videos they posted."

"Videos?" He asked nervously as he thought about the video and photos he'd turned over to the Pseudo Hipster and Faux Cabbie.

"I told you I'm not going to judge but if there's something you want to get off your chest. I'm a good listener. At least that's what Aaron tells me. He might be a little biased though."

""On second thought, no, that's okay." In the middle of recovery and rehab he'd forgotten all about the penthouse party and the paparazzi. All he'd been able to think about since that day he thought he was hallucinating was finding the girl with the butterfly tattoo.Now he had to know for certain that she was dying and that she wanted nothing to do with him. That was hard enough. Add to that the fact she might learn who he really was and what had gotten him to the hospital somehow bothered him.

"Okay but I'll tell you what you already know. Honesty is always the best policy and I'm not just talking about being honest with others. You have be honest with yourself first. Emily will eventually find out. Do you really want her to learn who you are and how you got here by turning on the TV or through some chance encounter with a scheming photographer?"

"I tried to tell her the truth that night but her father showed up and then all hell broke loose."

"I've never met her father but in between all the complaints Emily has against him he still sounds like he loves her and wants the best for her."

"He refuses to discuss the decision she made."

"As a mom I can understand that. I don't know that I could calmly talk to Abbie about something like that."

He had to admit it sounded logical. They started walking again and, once they were outside, Caroline waved to someone in a car nearby.

"That's Aaron and Abbie. He must have picked her up from school early. He does that sometimes." She got quiet for a moment. There was a deep sadness that he could hear in her voice. "He wants us to have as much time as possible together." He opened the door for her and Aaron greeted him.

"Hey, I'm Aaron. It's nice to meet you."

"I'm. . ." Nick hesitated a moment and Caroline laughed. Aaron grinned and gave his wife a wink.

"Yeah, I know who you are and don't worry I won't go yelling it out. Your secret's safe with me."

"That's what everyone keeps saying," Nick said, getting into the back seat next to Aaron and Caroline's thirteen-year-old daughter Abbie, who just stared at him. He'd seen that look before in the eyes of dozens of fans hundreds of times over the last six years.

"Hi," he said, but she just stared and finally Caroline turned around.

"Abbie, don't be rude. Say hi to Nick."

Finally the girl gave him a quick smile and a wave.

"We're big fans at the Sterling house," Aaron said as he drove them away from the hospital.

Nick glanced back and saw a dark SUV tailing them and cursed under his breath. It had to be Daryl. He'd get an earful when got back to the apartment for sure and it would be harder to go anywhere on his own next time.

"I can imagine."

"You say that as if it's a bad thing," Aaron said laughing.

"I'm not sure yet."

"We're not kidnapping you, Nick, we're gonna feed you, that's all." Aaron said and the black SUV drove faster to keep up.

"Ok."

He let them take him home with them.

CHAPTER THIRTY-THREE

Discovered

Their house was a modest tri-level in a middle class neighborhood. When they got out of the car, he saw a snowman sitting in the middle of the front lawn. He glanced over at Abbie but it was Caroline who filled in the blank.

"It's Aaron's creation. Abbie is far too sophisticated and grown up to make snowmen anymore."

She ruffled her daughter's hair and the girl pulled away clearly embarrassed. "Mom!" she protested.

Nick tried not to smile and followed Aaron into the house instead. Inside everything was tidy. Nothing was out of place but it still had a feel of warmth and coziness. There were pictures of Aaron, Caroline and Abbie everywhere. Nick noticed that in most of the older pictures Caroline had been a striking brunette, her green eyes full of life and energy. He noticed, too, that there were angel figurines and pictures everywhere, on the walls, the end tables, and near the door. Over the fireplace he noticed a large sign that read:

As for me and my house we shall serve the Lord

They all took off their coats and Aaron put them into the closet. Motioning for him to follow Aaron, Caroline and Abbie bounded up the stairs onto the main level. A long-haired gray cat with a sparkling collar, tiny bell and grim expression jumped off the couch, coming to meet them. It wrapped itself around Caroline's legs, before Abbie picked it up held it tightly to her chest, and gave it a big kiss on its furry heard. The cat meowed in protest and Caroline took Nick by the hand, pulling him toward the couch.

"That's Gandalf," she said, sitting down.

"That's an interesting name."

He sat next to her.

"It was Aaron's idea. He's a big fan. We used to have a dog named Snuggles. Abbie named her and Aaron hated taking the dog outside. Calling out her name just about killed him. So after Snuggles passed away we promised him that if we ever got another pet he'd get to name it. So Gandalf it is. Did you like the movies? He's going to ask you know."

"They were okay."

"Don't let Aaron hear you say that or he'll bore you to death with critical reviews stating why they were more than 'okay'." She laughed.

"Gandalf's the perfect name," Abbie gushed and then suddenly turned bright red as if she realized she'd actually spoken in front of Nick.

"Do you have pets?" Caroline asked.

Nick shook his head.

"I'm not really a pet person. I was always too busy."

"All those book signings and movie premiers?"

Nick sighed, remembering the whirlwind of activity that always surrounded him. Barbara made sure to shuffle him from event to event so that he hardly had a moment to himself. He was amazed sometimes how he managed to do so much writing and producing work—but now that he thought about it he realized that every moment he wasn't at an event or doing publicity for Barbara, he was on a plane or in a car jotting down notes and bits of dialogue.

"Did you ever meet Cianti?" Abbie asked, sporting that look that he knew so well.

He smiled and nodded. "A few times."

"Wow!" Abbie gave Gandalf another hug and kiss.

"I'll bet you think that's pretty cool."

Abbie grinned.

"Who went with you?" Caroline asked and Nick looked confused.

"Where?"

"To the events, the premiers, the signings, you know."

Nick shrugged. "Nobody special. Sometimes my publicist sometimes my agent other times I was my own."

"Really? No family or friends?"

Nick felt suddenly uncomfortable. How could he possibly begin to explain the truth. "No, but there were other people who sometimes tagged along."

"Like those actresses and models, right?" Abbie asked.

Nick nodded. "Exactly."

"Wow, that sounds. . ."

"Awesome!" Abbie said.

Caroline placed her hand on Nick's shoulder. "Lonely," she said so quietly that only Nick could hear.

He turned away.

Meanwhile, in the kitchen, Aaron was making lots of

noise as he prepared their meal—which Caroline and Abbie assured him was going to be absolutely 'to die for'.

"No matter what Aaron tells you it's not the cancer that's killing me, it's his *cooking*," Caroline joked and Abbie giggled.

It seemed like a private joke between the two of them. Nick managed a half smile but had a hard time laughing at any joke that had to do with anybody dying.

Suddenly the doorbell rang.

"Oh, Nick, don't be so serious," Caroline said as Abbie let go of Gandalf and went to answer the door.

Nick didn't have a direct view but as soon as Abbie opened the door and greeted the person standing there he knew that he'd been set up.

"Emily!" Abbie cried..

Nick turned to look at Caroline who had suddenly become preoccupied with petting Gandalf. The cat purred while Nick fumed. How was Emily ever going to believe that he hadn't planned this? Why would Caroline think this was a good idea? Abbie and Emily climbed the stairs together. Emily stopped as soon as she saw Nick.

"What is *he* doing here, Caroline?"

"Now, Em, don't get all worked up. Aaron invited him."

She dumped the blame on her husband who was still clanking pots and pans in the kitchen.

"Did you tell Aaron that I didn't want to see this guy again."

"I mentioned it, but you know how he is. He needs to see it for himself. Something about giving him a fair shake or second chance. . .I don't know. You know Aaron served in the Peace Corps. He's all about diplomacy."

Nick was amazed by how convincingly she was, telling these lie, and more so by how easily Emily believed them.

She scowled at Nick. "I don't know if I can stand to be here right now, Caroline."

"You know I'm sitting right here. You don't have talk as if I'm somewhere else. I can hear you," Nick protested.

"Good. Then you know that this was a really bad idea," Emily said frowning.

"That's what I told her," he said, eyeing Caroline.

She shrugged. "Leave me out of it. I'm just going with Aaron's plan."

"Which is?" Emily demanded.

"Have a little dinner, a little conversation, and maybe come to an understanding."

"But, Caroline. . .if you only knew. . ."

Caroline put up a hand. "Let's save that for dinner conversation

"I don't think that's it's something we need to talk about at dinner," Nick countered.

"I'm going to check on Aaron. Come on, Abbie. I'm sure the chef needs our help."

"But, mom, I want to talk to Emily!" Abbie complained.

"You will, but right now we're needed in the kitchen." Caroline dragged her daughter away from them.

When they were out of earshot Nick spoke first. "You know she planned this right from the beginning don't you?"

"Of course. Aaron knows I'd kill him."

"Then what are we going to do about it?"

"I don't know. I haven't decided."

"Can we step outside for a moment and talk. . .away

from everybody?"

"I suppose," Emily said reluctantly, but she followed him back down the stairs and into the cold night air.

"Emily, whatever I did the other night to offend you I want to say I'm sorry."

"I wish I could accept your apology," she said, looking down at her feet.

"So that's how it's going to be?"

She looked up. "I don't get you."

He shifted his weight to his good leg. "There's not much to get."

"That's not true. There's something about you that's so confusing."

"Like what?"

"First you want hook up and then you don't?"

"It's not that I didn't want to—let me make that perfectly clear. I *wanted* to it's just. . .I have to be careful."

"You don't to have be careful with me. That's what I was trying to tell you."

"But I do."

She sighed with exasperation. "Why make it a bigger deal than it is?"

"Because I like you."

"We already went over that. I'm leaving."

He knew that what she really meant was that she was *dying*. "I know." He reached out to touch her face.

She didn't pull away. ``"Then what's the problem?"

"There are things about me you don't know."

"I don't care. Why can't we just hang out and have fun and live in the moment?"

"We can. But I want do it honestly for once."

A look he hadn't seen before crossed her face. She

came closer and he could smell the fruity tanginess her shampoo. Strawberry, he thought.

"Then tell me."

Without thinking he leaned in and kissed her fully on the lips. She tasted like menthol cigarettes and candy. Bubblegum to be exact. She responded to the kiss and for a moment Nick let go of everything that had happened the past few months and let himself live in that very moment with Emily. Suddenly, there was a tremendous flash of light followed by a series of flashes which forced them apart.

"What the hell. . ." Nick cried out.

"Look over here, sweetheart." Nick heard a voice call out from the yard.

"Who is that?" he heard Emily say.Then there was another series of flashes.

"Just a few more. Turn this way, come on, over here." Another voice called out and Nick struggled to open his eyes. When he did he was shocked and dismayed to find two familiar faces standing in Caroline's front yard.

"Hey, Nick. Long time no see." Pseudo Hipster said and Faux Cabbie waved from the other side of the lawn. The paparazzi had found him and now Emily would find out the truth whether he wanted her to or not.

CHAPTER THIRTY-FOUR

The Apartment

"Do you know them?" Emily demanded and Nick hesitated.

"It's a long story."

She rolled her eyes. "It's always something with you!"

She grabbed his arm and jerked him forward. Nick limped quickly after her just as he spied Daryl getting out of the black SUV and coming toward Pseudo Hipster and Faux Cabbie. The bodyguard was about to do his thing, he had that look on his face that meant only one thing for them: trouble.

"Hey! Nick, where you going?" Faux Cabbie called after them.

"We're not going away, Nick! You're a bonafide story and we're gonna get it!" Pseudo Hipster threatened.

"What's your girlfriend's name, Nick?" Faux Cabbie yelled out and then let out a long whistle tantamount to a catcall.

"Why do they keep calling you Nick?" Emily asked as she led him to a yellow VW beetle with a Daffy Duck decal on the back that was parked a block down the street.

"I want to explain. . ."

"As in you want to but you can't?"

She unlocked the doors and motioned for him to get in quickly. Already Nick could see that Daryl was mere feet from both of the unsuspecting paparazzi. He almost felt sorry for them but more than that he was genuinely curious about how they found him and what they wanted. According to Barbara she'd tidied up the whole mess and concocted stories that he was already back in New York working on his next book and preparing for the upcoming film premier. Either Barbara was losing her touch or the two bozos were smarter than he'd thought. He'd hate to find out it was the latter but right now what choice did he have?

"Get in!" she hissed.

Nick obliged, throwing his cane in the back seat and putting on his seatbelt. Emily put it into drive and peeled away from Caroline"s house like a bat out of hell. She was driving so fast that Nick felt he had to hold on to the door handle just so he wouldn't fly out of the windshield.

"What about Caroline and supper?" Nick asked and Emily cocked an eyebrow as she gave him a sideways glance.

"Really? That's what you're worried about? Hurting Caroline's feelings and what you're going to eat?"

"No. I mean you don't know what those guys can be like. . ."He began then he bit his lip to keep from saying anything else.

"You mean as in you do? *Who* are you? What did those guys want? Why were they taking all those pictures?"

"Look, I can explain but it's complicated?"

"Complicated? Okay, let's start with something basic then like. . .I don't know. . .maybe your *actual* name?" She said making a tight corner and causing Nick to hold onto the door handle with an even tighter grip.

"Okay. But can we go somewhere private?"

"Fine. We'll go to my place. It's not too far from here and hopefully those clowns won't be following."

"No, I think they'll have enough to worry about," he said, thinking back to Daryl's large imposing shadow as it approached the two men on Caroline's lawn.

"What does that mean?"

"I promise I'll tell you when we get to your place, okay?"

"Promise?"

"Yeah,. Promise."

She sped all the way to a seedy-looking apartment complex a few blocks away from *The Vintage Point.* Parking the beetle she got out and started walking toward a set of stairs that resembled a fire escape. He felt tired just looking at the steps he'd have to climb with his recovering leg.

"It's going to take me a minute," he called after her and she went on ahead. After a long while of maneuvering his way up to the second floor he saw that she'd left the door open. He made his way inside, closing the door behind him. He was surprised by what he found. In contrast to the outside of the building the apartment itself was warm and inviting even though it was very small. One entire wall had built-in shelving filled with books and records. A couch had been pushed up against the shelving and a small record player had been set up on a small end table nearby. In the middle of the room was a stool, an easel set up with a large canvas. The kitchen was located in the back with a table and chairs crammed into a makeshift dining space. Off to his immediate right was the bedroom with a floor lamp and a bed with a large white dog laying across it. Nick thought it was strange that the dog hadn't come out to greet them yet. As if sensing his thought Emily sat down on the couch and pointed toward the bedroom.

"If you're wondering about Mel, he's not exactly your conventional dog. He's more of an old soul in a dog's body so he doesn't really cater to people the way other dogs do. He likes to lay on the bed and wait for me to come to him."

"Okay, that's different."

"I think it's refreshing. He's his own dog. He doesn't care what anybody thinks. He's just Mel."

Like owner like pet, Nick thought, but he kept those thoughts to himself.

"Has he always been that way?"

"Ever since I got him from the pound."

"So he doesn't come see you at the door when you come home?"

"Nope. He knows eventually I'll come to him."

"Nice."

"Mel and I have a great relationship. Better than some I've had by far."

"Wow."

"A dog is a girl's best friend—at least Mel's mine."

"No one else? What about Derrick?" Nick tried not to sound jealous.

"I already told you, he'll come around."

"Oh, so you're not speaking right now?" he asked and

she brought her knees up to her chin and wrapped her arms around her legs as if she was trying to protect herself from the question.

"Let's not talk about me." She changed the subject. "Let's talk about *you.*"

Nick sighed. It had come down to this moment and he dreaded it. "What do you want to know?"

"Who were those guys and why were they calling you Nick?"

He limped over to the other end of the couch. "May I sit down."

"Sure."

"Remember back at the store when I told you there were things about me I wanted you to know before we. . .hooked up?"

"How could I forget." There was a definite tension in her voice.

"Just hear me out."

"I'm listening."

"Those men were paparazzi."

"Paparazzi?" Emily said in an amused tone. "Like from Hollywood? You're kidding, right?"

"They're from New York and I'm not kidding."

"Okay. But what are they doing here and why were they taking pictures of us?"

"Emily, this may be hard to believe but I'm. . .that is. . .my name is. . .Nick Simon."

"Are you bullshitting me?" She sat up, her eyes ablaze.

"No."

"*You're* Nick Simon. *The* Nick Simon. No way- there's no freakin' way."

"Why not?"

"Well for starters there's that beard and then those glasses? Your clothes? And. . .you're *here*. Why would Nick Simon be here? Have you seen his picture? He doesn't look, like. . .like. . ."

"Me?" Nick filled in the blank and Emily laughed.

"No! Have you ever *seen* him wear what you're wearing?"

"That was sort of the point. I don't want people to know that I'm here."

"Why?"

"Isn't it obvious? The hospital, the rehab. . ."

"Oh, shit. That's right. Nick Simon totally crashed a car and almost killed someone. He was supposedly high and very, very drunk. But I thought that was just some stupid rumor. Those entertainment channels put on lies all the time."

"It's not a rumor. Not this time. It's all true." He avoided making eye contact.

"You have got to be shitting me!" she said in a tone that let him know she was completely unconvinced.

"I'll prove it to you, ask me anything you want about the books or the movies, even the ones you hate. I'll tell you everything you ever wanted to know."

Emily frowned and instead stood up and walked to his end of the couch. She leaned forward and touched his beard with the tips of her finger.

"I have a better idea."

"What's that?"

"If you're really Nick Simon then let me shave off your beard."

"What?" he said, confused by the request.

"Let me shave your beard and look at you."

Nick thought about the ramifications of letting her do it, Arnie's warnings and Barbara's threats that he must keep a low profile. Now that the paparazzi was involved he couldn't afford to be seen but the moment he looked at Emily he felt something he couldn't explain and he realized that he didn't care if he was found out. He wanted her to see him, to know who he was, because he was tired of lying.

"Okay."

She gave him a mischievous grin.

"I'll be right back." She disappeared into the bedroom where Mel the Malamute lay on the bed staring at him. Nick sat nervously waiting when she suddenly appeared carrying a small group of supplies. She laid them down on the couch next to him. There was a razor, shaving cream, a hand towel, and a pair of scissors. Then, she went into the kitchen and brought back a small tupperware container filled with water. Next she climbed on the couch and stood up, reaching for one of the albums on the shelf which she then put on the record player and started to play. Finally, she faced Nick, leaned forward and began to unbutton his shirt.

"What are you doing?"

"I'm going to put this hand towel around your neck to catch the hair."

"Oh."

He watched her pick up the scissors.

"What are you going to do with those?"

"I'm going to cut down the hair, silly. Otherwise the razor won't be able to cut through this mess."

"It sounds like you've done this before."

She suddenly straddled him the way she had the night

at the store. "Nope. Never." She positioned herself in such a way that he couldn't stop his body from responding.

"Emily, what are you doing?" He tried to think of other less stimulating things. Baseball. . .book signings. . .barbells. . .Barbara-*Bingo!* That was working until she leaned closer and he could smell the subtle smell of her body lotion, a crisp melon or cucumber scent?

"I'm getting ready to cut with these sharp scissors. So, if I were you. . .I'd sit very, very still," she whispered, gently pulling on tufts of beard with her hands and cutting. *Snip. Snip.* It was getting harder for Nick to focus so he started to talk.

"Can I ask a question?"

"Sure."

"Why do you hate the books so much? The movies I get. I don't watch them either."

She stopped mid snip.

"Wait, you don't watch your own movies?"

"No. Never."

"But aren't you the one who directs them?"

"No. I leave that to the more seasoned cynics in the industry."

"Well, no wonder they're crap."

"Crap?"

"You've left your work in the hands of someone who isn't you."

"I'm not a director."

"Or a writer according to what you've said so far."

"That's hardly fair."

"But you could have some say couldn't you? That is if you are who you say you are."

"What if I'm not interested?"

"Then what's the point of making them at all?" When he didn't answer she frowned. "Don't tell me. It's all about the money?"

She started to cut again.

"It's a very important part of the process. That's for sure. It's a business."

"I thought it was an art."

"You wouldn't last a second in Hollywood."

"That's why I prefer living here. For now." Nick was suddenly reminded of the elephant in the room. He decided to change the subject.

"I think you'd like New York."

She laughed. "What makes you think that?"

"It's. . .alive," he said without thinking. "What I mean is that it's a living, breathing thing all on its own, it's dynamic, flawed and fantastic in the sense that some things you see are really unbelievable but just as amazing. It's. . ." He stopped and looked straight into Emily's eyes.

"Crazy?"

"Beautiful," he whispered.

Emily smiled and shook her head. "Okay, I'm convinced. You must be Nick Simon."

"Why is that?"

"That was the cheesiest thing I've ever heard." She rolled her eyes.

"Ouch."

"You deserve it. You've got to have better material than that."

"Maybe."

"I hope so or this is going to be the most boring shave you've ever gotten."

"Tell me what book or movie of mine *did* you like? Are there *any?*"

She took her time thinking as she kept cutting.

"There might be one or two."

"What are they?"

"*If* I was forced to admit that you are who you say you are and *if* I had to choose I'd say *Broken Road* and *For The Record*."

"Those were the first two novels I wrote."

"I know. I think they were the best."

"Why?"

"They were the most honest."

"They were the worst reviewed."

"The movies maybe but readers loved the books."

"How do you know so much about it? I thought you weren't a fan."

"I'm not. Not anymore." She put down the scissors and picked up the shaving cream. She sprayed a few pumps into her hand and rubbed them together.

"I'm going to rub this over your face—are you ready?"

"No. But go ahead."

He closed his eyes as she slowly slathered his jawline with shaving cream.

"Open your eyes I'm about to use the razor."

"I'd rather keep them closed."

"Suit yourself." A moment later he felt the blade run along the surface of his skin.

"Why do you write books you hate?" Emily asked.

Nick was taken off guard by the question. "You've made it clear that it's all about the money. It's a business. So why do it now that you have more money than you'll ever need?"

"What makes you think I have that much money?"

"Don't you read *People Magazine*?" She teased.

He laughed. "Not if I can help it."

She kept shaving until there was no more beard.

"I don't hate my books, Emily. I just don't get hung up on them."

"And the movies?"

"Call it superstition. Some guys wear the same socks, don't change underwear, cross themselves or sleep with salami under their pillow for good luck. I don't watch my movies."

"Yeah, how's that working out for you? You slammed your car into an iron gate, fractured your leg and you've fallen for a girl who doesn't have long to live."

They were both quiet as Emily dipped her fingers in the water and deftly cleaned his face of any hair or shaving cream. Then she stared at his clean-shaven face. She took off his glasses and stared some more.

"Holy shit," she whispered, "it *is* you."

"That's what I've been trying to tell you. . ." But she interrupted him by taking his face in her hands and kissing him, deeply and passionately. Pressing her whole body into his quickly brought about a response that he was certain he couldn't and wouldn't stop this time. She paused for a moment and pulled her shirt up over her head and then she began to unbutton his shirt.

"Is there anything else you want to tell me?" She kissed him again.

He thought briefly about Alex, the nightmares and the little white house on South 23rd Street. "No."

"Are you sure? Because this time we're not stopping."

Another kiss, another caress and another opportunity to tell her the rest of his story. He didn't say anything.

"Okay."

She slowly maneuvered herself off of his lap so he could unzip his jeans.

"One thing, Emily."

"What?"

"Is this a hook up?"

She laughed really hard.

"No more questions. No more lies."

She nipped at his lip and straddled him again. They kissed and Nick did everything in his power to keep from thinking about the secrets that still haunted him, the pain that still paralyzed him and the fear that this was more than just a hook up to him. It was a promise, a promise that it would all end in heartbreak.

CHAPTER THIRTY-FIVE

The Problem

At some point in the middle of the night they had made it to the bed. But Mel, was still laying across it—exactly as they'd found him when they arrived. Emily had to ask him to get down. As soon as they got in bed, Mel jumped up between them and lay across Emily's legs, preventing Nick from getting any closer. So they slept and when Nick woke up, Emily was gone, but Mel was still there. Nick managed to get up and reach for the cane, making his way out to the living room where he found Emily perched naked on the stool, the butterfly tattoo on her right shoulder almost taking flight as her arm flowed up and down with the each stroke of a paint brush. Without his glasses, which he'd left back in the bedroom, he had to squint to see what she was painting. Whatever it was, it was colorful and vibrant. He came closer and finally stood behind her.

"Hi," she said, still painting.

"How'd you know I was here?" He traced the butterfly tattoo with his fingers.

"I must have a sixth sense," she said with a giggle.

"Can I ask you something?"

"Sure." Her brush created yet another set of colorful strokes on the canvas.

"Why did you get this tattoo?"

She was quiet for a few moments. "I got it when I made the decision to stop chemo for the last time."

"But why a butterfly?" He traced the tattoo with his fingers again and another minute passed before she answered.

"Because it symbolizes freedom."

"From chemo?"

"From doing what everyone else thinks I should do about my cancer. I got it before I went into the hospital here to do those final tests. I think deep down I already knew what they were going to find. I'd already started the research on Death With Dignity and pretty much made up my mind that if they confirmed what I felt in my heart, I'd be ready. Having the butterfly on my shoulder was like having someone there with me when they gave me the news. I didn't feel as alone."

She kept painting. Nick gingerly kissed the butterfly tattoo.

She stopped painting. Smiling, she reached up, put her arms around his neck and gave him a kiss. The heat he felt coming off her body in combination with the kiss was already causing him to respond and he knew it would lead them back to the couch.

"I'm sorry," she whispered between kisses.

"What for?"

"I have to keep painting. I can't stop. Not even for you."

"What if I could persuade you?" he said caressing her body with that purpose in mind.

"I'm sure you could, but when it comes to something I start, I have to finish it, I have to follow through. Do you understand?"

"What about when it's something you want? Don't you *want* to come back to bed with me?"

"And wake up Mel? Never," she teased. "He'd stop talking to me for days."

Another kiss. Another caress. If only he didn't have a bum leg he could sweep her up in his arms and take her to bed or to the couch. Instead, he would have to settle for a cold shower and the pleasure of watching her bring the canvas to life. . .in the nude. There were worse ways to spend a day.

"Okay. You win."

"Not really," she said breathlessly.

He kissed her one last time before limping back to the bedroom, past Mel's sleepy gaze, and into the bathroom.

Twenty minutes later he was sitting back on the couch, showered and fully dressed in yesterday's clothing, while Emily continued to paint, perched on the stool wearing nothing but the butterfly tattoo and a small necklace he'd never really noticed before. It was a tiny Star of David. That brought his mind back to Emily's father. He wondered if she'd made it over for Shabat or if she'd truly blown it off. He guessed the latter. She seemed like a woman of her word. Nick also thought about her decision to end her life—and soon. Would there be any chance to change her mind? If she was truly the kind of person who had to finish what she started and *insisted* on following through on her promises or her plans then. . . Nick tried to shake off the thought. Instead, he watched her paint and marveled at how slowly but surely the strokes began to take form and substance. It was a naked female form sitting on her haunches, arms outstretched toward a sunrise made up of a cacophony of colors, some of which he'd never seen before, let alone described. It was amazing. Emily was amazing.

"Do you always paint this way?"

"You mean naked?"

"Now that you mention it."

"Sometimes."

"I take it this is one of those times."

"Maybe." She turned and winked at him before going back to the canvas and continuing her work.

"When did you know you wanted to be an artist?"

"Always. When did you know you wanted to be a writer?"

"I didn't. I never *wanted* to be one."

She stopped painting. She turned, cocked her head and gave him a look of utter confusion. "You're kidding right?"

"No."

"I don't understand."

"What?"

"How could you be where you are, do what you do, if you never *wanted* to be a writer?"

"I don't know. It just worked out that way."

"Tell me how that happened."

She balanced the paintbrush between her fingers and pulled her legs up to her chin. He was distracted by the fact that she was still undressed, but he tried to focus.

"It's a long story."

"You know I love those." She smiled. He sighed and shook his head.

"It's boring, really."

"I love boring. Look who I'm hanging out with," she teased, leaving her perch on the stool and coming over to him.

She sat on his lap and painted the tip of his nose with the brush. He felt another wave of desire and kissed her. After a few more kisses and caresses she placed a gentle hand on his chest and pulled away.

"No. Not until you tell me how it all started."

She insisted and Nick tried to distract her again but she refused to give in until he told her what she wanted to know.

"Fine. I was tending bar and some guy came in and asked me to audition for the show."

"Oh that's right. What was it called?"

"First Draft/Final Cut."

"I kind of remember that from the commercials."

"You ever watch it?"

She laughed. "It was a little before my time."

"I'm not that much older than you."

"But you didn't have a rabbi for a father."

He got quiet. For a fleeting moment his thoughts went back to the man in the morgue. She touched his face lifting it up so their eyes could meet.

"Are you still thinking about my father? It's okay really. Don't worry."

"Yeah," he lied and she kissed him. Before they knew it they were on their way to making love again when there was a loud knock on the door.

"You've got to be kidding me," Nick whispered.

Emily ignored him and the door. The knocking continued. Emily ignored it and started to unbutton his shirt.

"What if it's your father?"

"He never comes here."

"How can you be sure?"

"If you haven't noticed, it's not exactly the nicest apartment complex."

"Is that why you chose it?" he asked as the knocking continued.

"Just ignore it. I'm not expecting anybody and whoever it is will go away."

She continued undoing the last of the buttons. Nick struggled to focus as she kissed his cheek and then something occurred to him.

"What if it's Aaron or Caroline?" He said or *Daryl* he thought. Emily stopped what she was doing and got up. She frowned.

"Fine, give me your shirt," she demanded and he hesitantly took it off and handed it to her. She put it on and started to button it. When she finished she walked to the door. Nick could only imagine what reaction her father would have if he saw her come to the door like that and, worse still, what he might do to Nick when he realized the shirt was his. He glanced over at the bedroom and wondered if he could make it before she opened the door. Too late. When she opened it there was a man wearing a suit and holding a manilla envelope in his hands.

"Emily Fischer?"

"Yes."

He handed her the envelope.

"You've been served."
He turned away without another word.

CHAPTER THIRTY-SIX

Sent Away

Emily slowly closed the door.

"What is it?"

"I don't know." She brought the envelope with her to the couch. Undoing the clasp she opened it and pulled out two sets of papers. He watched as she read over the first pages. He could first see tears then tension build up in her face. Finally, when she reached the second set of papers and looked them over she looked angry.

"Tell me, what is it?"

"They're legal papers."

"From who?"

"My parents."

"For what?"

"They've petitioned for a conservatorship hearing and they've cut off access to my trust fund."

"You have a trust fund?"

"It's from my mother's side of the family. My grandmother Bernstein left it for me. It's how I'm living on my own now and what I planned to use when I left here."

Nick's heart constricted at the thought. "So, why would they do this?"

"It's the only thing they can think of to stop me from leaving."

"Can they do that?"

"I don't think so. But I'd have to consult a lawyer—which now I'm not sure I can do without the money from my trust fund."

"But why now?"

The look in her eyes told him everything he needed to know.

"They know the *date*, don't they?" he said softly and she nodded.

"How soon?"

"Nick, let's not talk about this now. Let's go back in the bedroom and make love. C'mon." She leaned forward to kiss him again.

"No."

He was shocked at how forceful and adamant his voice sounded but he meant it. How could he pretend that he didn't know she was planning on taking her life soon and how could she pretend that she wasn't? Her parents knew and were going to extraordinary lengths to stop her from leaving the state. He wasn't a legal expert, but Nick agreed with Emily that it was probably more of a stalling tactic on their part.

"Why can't you just drop it?"

"Why can't you be honest with me."

"You mean the way you are with me?"

"What are you talking about?"

"What the hell is *this*, Nick?"

Emily turned his smartphone to face him. His heart froze. Had she finally found the video of Cianti on his phone?

"You bastard!"

She shoved the phone in his face so he could see the screen. Dammit, he knew he should have set a password on his phone to lock the screen. Barbara was always nagging him about things like that. He'd always scoffed at her nagging. This time it would have proved helpful.

"Emily. . ."

"I thought you understood. You told me you did! I *believed* you!"

He glanced at the text messages between himself and Arnie Schaefer, his lawyer back in New York. He had asked Arnie to find the best oncologist in the country and see if there was a way to get an appointment for Emily as soon as possible. Nick couldn't help it. He wanted her to have a second opinion and he'd hoped to talk to her about it when the time was right. Unfortunately, Arnie had texted him while he was in the shower confirming the appointment and he hadn't even thought twice that his phone might have been in plain sight.

"Let me explain. . ."

"No!" She screamed throwing the iPhone at him, narrowly missing his head.

"How could you go behind my back?"

"Emily, please listen to me."

"I'm not listening anymore. Not to you, not to anyone, Nick. I want you to get out."

"Please don't shut me out. Let's talk about this."

"How could you possibly think this was going to change my mind, Nick?"

"Emily, don't do this. We just found each other again. You can't do this on your own, Nick pleaded.

Emily looked at him, her gray eyes blazing with a fierceness he had never seen before. She shoved him. Hard.

"You think I can't do *what* on my own, Nick?" She shoved him again.

"Em. ." He stumbled back.

"Say it, Nick! Say it!"

"Please. . ." He begged her but she ignored him.

"You don't think I can *die* on my own?" She shoved him against the wall and he knew it was taking all the strength she had. The tears were still coming and all he wanted to do was reach out and wipe them away, apologize for every stupid thing he'd done since they'd met, and hold her.

"I've been dying since I was four years old, Nick. I'm going to die on my own no matter what." Her voice softened. "I'm just tired. I'm fucking tired. All I want do is rest. Don't you understand?"

"Emily. . .I'm sorry."

"It's too late for that,"she cried.

He reached out in an attempt to put his arms around her. Emily pulled away.

"I can't do this anymore, Nick. It's always something with you. First you lie to me about who you are and why you're in the hospital, then all these reporters start stalking me because of the shit you did that got you here and then *this*. . ."

"No, no. . .Emily, this is all a misunderstanding."

"How can I trust you, Nick? How can you promise me anything? You can't."

"Because you *know* me, Emily."

"Do I, Nick?"

"I swear, Emily."

"Why are you really with me, Nick? Are you looking for something to write about, your next best-seller, or do you really support what I want to do?"

He stared at her, caught off guard by the way she changed the subject from the video to what he knew she *really* wanted to talk about. Would he support her decision to die, to leave him, no matter how they felt about each other, and would he stay until the very end? She was looking for a reason to push him away.

"Emily, you know how I feel."

"No, Nick. I don't. I want to hear you say it."

"Why are you pushing me away, Emily? Why start an argument?"

"You're the one who started it by taking the video, Nick. It led those guys here. . .to you! To me!"

"I told you it was a mistake."

"I don't believe you. You're a liar."

"That's not true."

"Then tell me the truth. Tell me it's okay for me to die. Tell me you're fine with it."

They stared at each other for a while. Nick said nothing. His insides were churning with uncomfortable emotions and thoughts he wasn't ready to share. Not now. Not this way.

"Emily. . ." He was at a loss for words.

"Tell me." She cupped his face in her small cold hands.

"No. I'm not okay with it." He whispered.

Her face crumpled into a sob. She turned away but this time he gently grasped her hands and turned her to face him. She was sobbing and it broke his heart.

"I can't lie, Emily. I can't. I want to because it's what you want. But if you're asking me for the truth, right now, right here then no. I'm not okay with it. I don't want you to die."

"You told me you understood," she cried.

Nick pulled her closer. "Emily, I do understand," he said, fighting back tears.

"What do you want from me, Nick? I can't do this anymore."

"I want you to fight, Emily. I want you to live. Please, just think about it. You deserve to do all the things you want to do on your list—Emily we could do that together, you and me. I promise, we'll do every single thing on that list. Just reconsider. I'll be with you every step of the way. *Please.*"

Nick begged and Emily finally allowed him to pull her into an embrace that soon turned into a passionate kiss. He caressed the curves of her thin face and fragile body and found that slowly she responded, answering his kisses and touch with her own. He felt relief and arousal. Suddenly, she yanked herself away from him, fear and grief filling her eyes. Breathless, she stared at him and he was confused.

"What's wrong?"

"This."

"Emily. . ."

"I know what I want, Nick. I've known for a long time. Do you?"

"I want you."

"Not the real me."

"Of course I do."

"I *want* to do this, Nick," she said.

Nick swallowed hard.

"Look at me, Nick. I want you to really look at me when I say this. I *want* to die."

"You don't mean that. . .not now."

"Because I met you? Did you think that was going to change my mind? You're not the first guy I've hooked up with, Nick. It's not like this is. . .love. . .or something. Right? But look who I'm talking to, you know all about that."

"This is different. You know it is."

"No. It's not. Ask me how I know." She said defiantly.

"How?"

"If it was, you'd be okay with it."

"That's not true."

"It is, Nick. If you loved me you'd be okay with it."

"The hell I would be. ."

"And that's how I know it's not different. . ."

"How is wanting you to live so we can be together wrong, Em? What's so wrong about that?!" he yelled at her.

"Because you want me to keep living for you, Nick!"

"What's so bad about that?"

"It's a two-way street, Nick. It's not just about what you want or what you need, it's about accepting what's actually real and right in front of you or moving on."

"Then you're right. I don't understand it! I don't get why you think this is the only option. Don't you want to be with me?"

"Yes! Of course!"

"Then why? Why?"

"If you don't know by now, then it doesn't matter what

I say, Nick. But, I don't have to convince you or anyone else. It's my life and. . . my death." She said and he was quiet. Emily moved toward the door. She opened it. Nick glanced at the door and then at Emily.

"I want you to leave, Nick."

"I don't want this. I know you don't either."

"Stop telling me what I want. I know what I want, Nick. Go."

Mel whined from the couch as Nick made his way to the door.

"I. . .I love you, Emily," he said. He had never said it to anyone before—It had to count for *something*. Emily looked straight into his eyes. His soul.

"Then let me go."

That's when he knew she was right. As Nick stepped into the hallway Emily quickly closed the door behind him. When he turned around, she was gone and so was his last chance to say goodbye.

CHAPTER THIRTY-SEVEN

Love

Nick noticed that they were parked across the street from his apartment almost immediately. Over the years he had learned how to spot paparazzi right away. It was Faux Cabbie and Pseudo Hipster and they were determined to wait him out. So far Nick had been able to go without turning on the news and hadn't seen anything regarding the videos or the photos he'd turned over to the idiotic duo. He sincerely regretted it now, not only because he was certain it had hurt Cianti but because it was certain to hurt his chances with Emily. But there was no way that Daryl was going to let him out of his sight not with this latest scandal. Barbara would see to that. Nick had been stuck inside the apartment for the last three days unable to visit Emily without running the risk that she'd be spotted and that her face would end up on one of those national tabloid magazines linked to him. Not to mention he had to find a way to get to his AA meeting without being followed. He could definitely have used a drink but he was still sober thanks in part to the fact that Daryl was watching him closely. All he could think about was Emily, but he knew that the first thing he had to do was make things right with Cianti. One night when he couldn't sleep he called her and was surprised she even answered.

"Fuck you, Nick," she said as soon as she answered the phone.

"I'm sorry."

"What the hell, Nick! Do you have any idea what you've done?"

"To be honest no. I don't, Cianti. I was really messed up, it was the day after the party at the penthouse, I was hungover and high. I did what I did. There aren't any excuses."

"No there aren't. You *lied* to me. You *stole* from me and you *humiliated* me, Nick. I can't *believe* you took those pictures or that video! And I can't believe I have to move because of your sorry ass. I love this place but I can't stay here because it's always crawling with paparazzi. You know what that's like and you know what it's like when you find a place to call home where they leave you the hell alone. Now, I don't have that, Nick and it's all your fault."

"I don't know what to say, Cianti."

"There's nothing to say, Nick, unless you're talking to my lawyer." She hung up on him.

The call went as well as he expected he supposed.

"What did you expect, Mr. Simon?" Daryl said from the couch where he was meditating.

"I don't know," Nick admitted.

Daryl inhaled, exhaled deeply then opened his eyes.

"You need to follow the plan."

"What is that? That I do *exactly* what Barbara says when she says it."

"I am no expert, Mr. Simon, but the success rate for doing things on your own has been less than stellar."

Nick frowned. "Don't remind me."

"Maybe doing what you should, in this case, would be wise."

"But what about Emily?"

"What about the young woman?"

"I'm not sure that I'm ready to let her go."

"Not even if it is for her own benefit?" Daryl asked.

Nick didn't say anything.

"Maybe that is the problem, Mr. Simon."

Nick shook his head.

"No. The problem is that this amazing girl, someone I barely know, someone. . ."

"Would you have noticed her back in New York?"

"A girl like that? Yes. Absolutely."

"You'd feel the same way as you do now?"

Nick had to stop and think. Life since he'd stopped drinking was so different from his life before when it was party after party and girl after girl. He had never felt this way about anyone so he couldn't answer Daryl truthfully, which the massive bodyguard took as the answer itself.

Nick hung his head in defeat.

"It would be better to leave the girl alone, Mr. Simon. Don't you think?

"I. . .I can't, Daryl."

"What's so different about *this* girl out of all the others?"

"I don't know where to begin."

"Start with the most basic truth, Mr. Simon."

"She's dying."

The news seemed to startle Daryl.

"Dying?"

"She has cancer."

"That is most unfortunate." Daryl gave Nick a sympathetic look.

"That's not the most unfortunate part, Daryl."

"Oh?"

"She doesn't want to wait for the cancer to kill her. She wants to do that part herself."

For a moment neither man spoke.

"How?"

"*Death with dignity*. It's physician-aided death. . .in Oregon."

"That *is* different, Mr. Simon."

"Yeah."

"But it doesn't change what is."

"How can you say that, Daryl?"

"Are you an alcoholic?" Daryl asked.

Nick swallowed hard.

"You know the answer to that"

"Are you an addict?"

"Daryl. . ."

"Are you?"

"You know I am."

"But the question is, Mr. Simon, do *you*?"

"Of course."

"Then why involve yourself in such a delicate situation when you should be working on your own recovery?"

"Because. . .I think I'm in love with her."

Nick knew that Daryl was wondering if he even understood the meaning of the word *love* and to be honest until now he wasn't sure.

"Does she know?'

Daryl broke the silence and Nick thought for a

moment.

"I don't know."

"Then there's still time."

"For what?"

"To extricate yourself."

"You mean to say goodbye? But didn't you hear me? I said that I loved her."

Nick was frowning at the large man. Daryl looked at him and smiled sympathetically.

"Ah, Mr. Simon," Daryl said. "Sometimes love means letting go."

CHAPTER THIRTY-EIGHT

Betrayal

It felt like she'd already died. For weeks she refused to take his calls. She wouldn't answer the door even when he knew she was there. She never went anywhere without Mel and Nick could hear him whine from inside the little apartment. Finally, he stopped calling for Emily and started calling for Mel, who would lower himself so the tip of his nose stuck out under the door so Nick could pet him. He had no idea how much he missed them both until he couldn't be with them and it killed him. Sitting in his own luxury apartment in Omaha's Old Market Nick found himself staring at the walls. He never bothered to turn on the TV. He couldn't bear to see the snippets from the sex tape he'd taken or the pictures of Emily being paraded across the network news channels from that night at Caroline's. In addition, now that the paparazzi couldn't find him they'd started following Emily everywhere. They'd even found out about her court case. The headlines started to buzz all over the internet and they ranged from controversial to cruel:

NICK SIMON TRYST TO END IN TRAGEDY

GALPAL CHOOSES DEATH OVER LIFE WITH NICK SIMON

Emily's court case was coming up and he couldn't forgive himself for not being there by her side. He imagined her standing before a judge, all by herself—she'd rejected having Arnie Schaefer represent her—dressed in one of her best vintage pieces from the store looking thin and tired trying to convince a judge that she was competent enough to make her own decisions.

Her parents would be standing on the other side with their own lawyer, one of the best in the state and a family friend as well as a member of their temple. Rabbi Fischer would look distinguished in his suit and wise with his beard and his wife would look every bit the distraught mother. At the time, when he learned of their plan, to sue their own daughter for the purpose of waiting until her health deteriorated to the point that she would be unable to leave the state and return to a state where a death with dignity would be possible, he was disgusted. But now, as he remembered the look on her face when he admitted that he didn't support her choice—not really—he could hardly live with himself. She expected her parents to go against her wishes, they were her parents. They had devoted themselves to keeping her alive since she was four years old. Nick's betrayal was something altogether different. He'd positioned himself in her life by convincing her that he understood what she wanted, that he supported her, that he loved her no matter what, only to have it be a lie. It must be. How could he say he loved her when he didn't want to let her go? Nick knew she was angry about the appointment he'd made for her with a specialist, but it was this betrayal that hurt the most. The one thing she had confided in him, a stranger, that had brought them so close together. She felt deceived. The thought haunted him, so he begged Daryl to drive him back to her apartment and knock on the door late one night when he thought there might be less of a chance for the paparazzi to see him. It opened and his heart soared until he saw a six-foot man with ripped muscles and the looks of a professional model standing in the frame.

"Yeah?"

The man looked Nick over and frowned. Nick felt his heart sink to his stomach. Had Emily already gone out and replaced him? Hadn't she always called what they had temporary? For a moment Nick was speechless and he kept staring at the man who was clearly getting impatient.

"Do you want something?"

"Uh, yeah, I was looking for Emily."

"She's not here," the man said matter-of-factly and started to close the door.

"Wait!" Nick called out as the door closed and the tall man stepped outside.

"Look," he said ,using the full weight and mass of his body to tower over Nick. "She doesn't need you vultures hanging around here. So, I suggest you get out of here before I make you."

"No, you've got it all wrong. I'm not with the paparazzi. I'm a friend."

"I don't know you," the man frowned.

"I'm Nick."

"Nick?" The man repeated as if trying to jog his memory.

"Sorry. I don't know any Nick."

"Maybe she mentioned Nick Simon?"

"The writer?"

"Yeah. Does that ring a bell?"

"Of course. But what does that have to do with you?"

"*I'm* Nick Simon."

The man stared at him intently then, a slight look of recognition swept across his face.

"You look familiar but why would Nick Simon be here?"

"Did she mention someone named Simon?"

"Simon, yeah. Are you that idiot? 'Cause if you are—*you* I want to punch in the face."

"Why?"

"Are you Simon?" the man asked menacingly.

Nick hesitated.

"I'm *Nick* Simon. The writer. I swear. Look I have ID and pictures on my phone from my last book signing."

"Are you shitting me? Nick Simon? Here? At Emily's place?" The man's demeanor completely changed from one of anger to enthusiasm.

"I'm being honest. Look here's a couple pictures from the book signing." Nick held up his phone so the man could see.

"It *is* you!"

Nick felt a giant wave of relief.

"Do you know when Emily will be back?"

The tall guy was still looking at the photos on his phone.

"She's at the record store, but why don't you go ahead and come in. She'll be back any minute."

Nick wondered what Emily would say about finding

him in her apartment with her new boyfriend. They went inside and Nick was relieved to see that everything was still the same. The record player was still at the end of the couch, which was pushed up against the built-in shelves, which were still filled with records of every kind. The stool was still in the middle of the room and the large canvas remained set up where he remembered it. Nick followed the tall man into the living room doing his best to give no indication that he'd been there before. The man sat down on one side of the couch and motioned for Nick to sit down on the other. The moment he did Mel came bounding out of the bedroom and onto his lap. The man looked astounded.

"That *never* happens. Mel's not like other dogs he just doesn't do that. He stays in the bedroom unless. . .you've been here before." Nick avoided making eye contact as Mel laid his head across his lap.

"Are. . .are you her boyfriend?" Nick finally managed to ask.

"No but it's not for a lack of trying." the man said with a sarcastic laugh. Nick thought it was a strange thing to say.

"She never felt that way about me. I guess I'm more like a really close friend." Suddenly it dawned on Nick who the man probably was and he felt relieved.

"You're Derrick."

"Yeah. She told you about me?"

"Yeah. She did."

"Wait a minute," he said, looking at Nick intently, "You and 'Simon' are the same guy aren't you?"

Nick cringed but knew he had to come clean. "Are you going to hit me in the face now?"

"I should," Derrick said frowning and then he sighed. "You really messed with her head you know. I can't believe you hooked up."

"She told you about that?"

"Of course, we're best friends. I thought she was done with relationships. At least that's what she told me when she explained all the stuff about wanting to die," Derrick paused for a moment.

"Is that why you're here?"

"That and the fact her parents are taking her to court. I couldn't believe it when I found out. I've known them almost all my life. They're suing her to stop her from going back home how crazy is that?"

"It's really insane," Nick agreed.

"I'm not sure that it'll even work but I'm not sure how things work here." Derrick said.

"To be honest, neither do I."

"Aren't you from LA?" Derrick asked and Nick decided he wasn't ready to explain how complicated it all really was so he went for simple instead.

"New York."

"Not one of the states where it's legal."

"I don't think so."

"So where in Nebraska are you from?" Nick asked and Derrick gave him a funny look.

"Oh, we're not from Nebraska. None of us are."

"I'm sorry. What?" Nick felt very confused.

"No. Didn't she tell you? We're all from Oregon."

CHAPTER THIRTY-NINE

Judgement

Nick thought he might pass out. Emily was from *Oregon* one of the states where she could *legally* take her life. How could she have failed to tell him something so simple as where she was from? No wonder her parents were taking extreme measures by taking her to court, questioning whether she was competent enough to make her own decision, and cutting of access to her trust fund. They were trying to stop her from going back to the one place they could do absolutely nothing but watch her die.

"Are you okay?" Derrick asked.

Nick knew he wasn't.

"I'm not sure."

"You *didn't* know?"

"She didn't tell me."

"Hmm."

"What?"

"She's dying and she hooks up with you but doesn't even tell you where she's from? That says something."

"What?"

"I don't know, but something. Look, Emily came because her father is the interim rabbi at the temple here in Omaha. He's doing it as a favor for a friend in the congregation. Emily came along because her parents wouldn't leave her alone until she said yes."

They sat in silence for a while as Mel moved between the two of them in an effort to get each one to pet him.

"How soon before Emily gets back?" Nick asked again.

"Soon. But hey you don't have to stick around. I'll tell her you stopped by."

Nick was tempted to leave. The last thing he wanted was to have a private conversation in full view and earshot of a guy who already thought he wasn't good enough for his friend.

"I think I'll go." Nick got up and made his way to the door just as it opened. Emily stood there and she seemed shocked to see him.

"How did you get in here?" she demanded, looking over at Derrick.

"That would be my bad, Em," Derrick admitted.

Nick glanced at Emily and noticed how tired and worn out she looked. Were those shadows under her eyes?

"Emily, is there somewhere more private we could talk?" he whispered.

Emily looked angry. "We don't have anything to talk about, Nick."

"Please. Give me another chance."

"To what? Talk me out of it? Make another video?"

"Uhm, video?" Derrick repeated getting up from the couch, an angry scowl spreading across his face.

Nick waved him away.

"Never mind."

"I'll tell you later." Emily countered.

Nick reached for her hand. She pulled it away.

"Let's just talk. That's all,"

Emily looked him in the eyes.

"Fine. five minutes." She led him to her bedroom as Derrick looked on.

"Em, do you need me to leave, 'cause I'm not really into that kind of thing where I sit out here and you do your thing back there. If that's the case I'd rather take Mel for a walk."

"It's not like that, Derrick. Not *anymore*." She glared at Nick.

"Okay, then I'll be out *here* in case you need me." He said glaring at Nick and then taking out his cellphone. As soon as Mel saw Emily walking to the bedroom he jumped off the couch and followed. Nick stood in the corner while she closed the door behind her and sat on the bed.

"Well?" she said impatiently.

"How are you?"

"That's the best you can do?"

"It's a start. I really want to know how you are, Emily,"

She sighed.

"How do you think I am, Nick? I'm getting followed around by reporters at the store and at the courthouse."

"Why won't you use the attorney I sent?"

"That schmuck from New York who just showed up out of the blue?"

"You would've known he was coming if you'd taken the time to read your texts or take my calls."

"I told you, I don't need your help," she fumed and Mel whined.

"At least let Daryl drive you to work and the

courthouse."

"Your driver? Are you kidding me? You might as well stick a sign on me that says *paparrazzi follow me*!"

"Why are you making this so hard, Emily?" Nick came closer to the bed.

"It *is* hard, Nick. That's just how it is."

"I want to help, that's all."

"Then go home. Go to New York and live your life and let me live what's left of mine."

"Is that what your really want?"

He looked her directly in the eyes. She hesitated, but after a moment the defiant tone in her voice returned.

"Yeah. That's what I want."

He sighed.

"No matter what you thought, this was always something more to me Emily. I want you to know that."

"Whatever you say, Nick."

"It's true."

"Go home, Nick," she whispered.

He turned to go. Closing the door to the bedroom behind him he stepped into the living room where Derrick looked up from his phone.

"Giving up so easily?"

"Don't," Nick warned.

"Guess the answer to that is yes," Derrick muttered under his breath.

"If you're so smart why don't you tell me what I should do."

"If you don't know, then you *should* go home."

"Look. . "

"I thought you were some big hot shot expert on love," Derrick said, shaking his head.

"I'm just a *writer*. I'm not an expert on anything." Nick was exasperated.

"You've written enough books on the subject."

"They're books not real life. Besides, I thought Emily said you didn't agree with her decision. What are you really doing here anyway?"

"I told you before. I'm still her friend and she needs *somebody* to lean on while her parents take her to court."

"I tried to help, Derrick. I brought down my own lawyer to take on her case. She wouldn't let him go in with her. I offered my driver so she wouldn't have to deal with the reporters and she turned me down. What the hell am I supposed to do?"

"What does she *want* you to do?"

"She wants me to leave,." he said.

The two men stared at each other.

"Then you better do what the lady says."

Nick shook his head in defeat. "I can't win."

"This isn't about winning, Nick Simon."

"I know that."

"Do you?" Derrick got up and opened the door. Nick stepped through it and, for the second time, he found himself outside of Emily's apartment alone.

CHAPTER FORTY

New York State of Mind

Nick stared at the shower walls. He'd been back in New York for only a week and in that time Barbara had already had him working hard to make up for his mistakes. He'd hit the press circuit to promote the upcoming movie premier and been subjected to a plethora of embarrassing questions regarding the party at the penthouse, the crash and rehab in Omaha as well as the videos and photographs of Cianti. There were also several questions regarding the new mystery girl with whom he'd been seen in Nebraska and her recent court case, which 'according to sourccs' had to do with the right to die. It was the controversy they loved and his life right now was full of it not that Barbara was disappointed. She used the controversy to fan the fires of publicity for the premier and to enhance Nick's reputation as a 'reformed' bad boy of romance. Nothing he said or did could stop Barbara from using that word to describe his work, and because he didn't want her to drag Emily into any of the publicityhe kept his mouth shut as promised.

He did the press junkets, the late night shows and the magazine interviews. He let Ambrose hire the stylists that dressed him for each appearance and he barely spoke as Daryl drove him from place to place. Then one night at one of the many parties Barbara was dragging him around to he found himself only feet away from Cianti, who looked stunning as always. He couldn't help but wonder if Barbara had something to do with it. Nick could imagine the publicity if the paparazzi found out that they were both there. He hesitated for a moment before downing his glass of mineral water. Should he discreetly go over and try to make amends one more time? Not because she was suing him but because it was the right thing to do? Nick gritted his teeth, he could hardly believe how much his outlook on life had changed in such a short amount of time. There was a time he would have said the business was a machine that could swallow you whole and if you were stupid enough to fall for its games it served you right. Hooking up with Cianti would have been one of those situations. She knew he was a player and yet she let him into her home and into her bed and she'd paid the price. Or had she? It had all led Nick to Omaha and to Emily and to the second biggest heartbreak of his life. He flinched at the thought of Alex. Shaking off that thought, he turned toward Cianti, who seemed to anticipate his approach. She turned and came straight for Nick, arms outstretched and brilliant smile flashing for all to see. She hugged him and gave him an air kiss. He was confused by her sudden friendliness.

"Nick!" She called out loud enough to make heads turn in their direction.

"Cianti."

"I didn't know you were going to be here. When did you get back?"

"About a week ago."

"You look good. How's the leg?"

"Fine. I'll have a limp for a while."

"That won't stop you from going to the movie premier I hope?"

"You know it won't. Barbara will see to that."

"Speaking of Barbara will you please thank her for passing along her invitation to this party? I'm sure I could have gotten one on my own of course but just the same it was kind."

Now it was all starting to make sense. Barbara had passed on the invite and forced Nick to attend the event with subtle purpose of making him sway Cianti from pursuing the lawsuit against them. Still something was off, he could sense it. It seemed too easy. Cianti had wanted his head on a platter less than a month ago when he called to make amends over the phone and now she was making pleasant conversation?

"What's going on, Cianti?" He whispered, trying to stay out of earshot of the other party guests. Cianti raised her eyebrows in mock surprise.

"I don't know what you're talking about."

"Now I know something's up." He took her by the hand and led her over to the bar. He ordered another mineral water and a champagne.

"Nick, I'm hurt. Why would you think that I was up to something? Isn't that more *your* style?"

It hit home. "Exactly. So why are you being so nice?"

"I think you're confusing my good manners for me actually giving a shit."

"Ah, that's more like it," He took a sip from his drink. "Barbara offered you a deal. What is it?"

She drank from her glass before shrugging her shoulders.

"I get to write the song for the title track of your next movie and the three after that. I also get a cut of the profits."

"The profits? Barbara *actually* said those words. Profits? You know what that means. Nothing. She's blowing smoke up your. . ."

"Those weren't her words, Nick they're mine. We got down to business it's just none of your business. I don't feel like sharing that information with you."

"Does that mean you're dropping the lawsuit?"

"Yes, it does," she took another drink and Nick felt relieved.

"I don't suppose the fact that I apologized matters to you?"

"Not one bit," She gave him a hard, cold look. "By the way, I heard from Barbara that the paparazzi actually followed you all the way to Nebraska. Is that right?"

"Yeah."

"Those were the same guys you gave my pictures to, weren't they?" Nick hesitated for a moment before answering. He felt the guilt sweep over him again.

"I saw on the news that they found your new girl, the one who's dying?" Her voice seemed sympathetic.

"Yeah." His heart constricted at the reference to Emily.

"That must be awful for her not getting a moment's rest, them following her around all the time, at home, at work, probably even at her doctor's office?" The thought of it all was starting to work him up and make him angry.

"I wonder how they found her?"

"Probably by following me," Nick said even though he knew Barbara had made sure to divert the media's attention back to New York. "I don't know."

"It must be hard knowing you can't protect her from all of that. I mean you and me we're used to it. It's our job but someone like her, well it can drive someone insane."

"Yeah."

"That's too bad." Her tone changed abruptly. "But I guess you should have thought of that before you came into my house and took those photos and that video of me and gave it to those two assholes," Cianti said with a look in her eyes that reminded him of Barbara King.

"Cianti. . ."

"Shh, Nick, no need to torture yourself." Then, she leaned forward and kissed him full on the lips and whispered in his ear. "Karma's a bitch, isn't it?"

Nick was horrified as he realized what had happened.

"What did you do, Cianti?"

"You're not the only player in town, Nick Simon."

"What did you do?" he demanded and she smiled like the cat who ate the canary.

"You brought them to my house, Nick, so I sent them to *hers*."

CHAPTER FORTY-ONE

Double Agent

Nick stared at Cianti and felt a surge of pure hatred. She smiled again.

"What? No smart quip and a smile from the witty writer?" Nick wanted to strangle her but he had to keep it together long enough to get back in the SUV and demand that Daryl drive him over to Barbara's office, where she was probably still working after hours, to demand an explanation. But first he had to find a way to part ways with Cianti that wouldn't make a scene, and leave the party without being noticed. The urge to turn around and ask the bar tender for a shot of vodka and, of course, leave the bottle was overwhelming. If he could only have a drink his mind would clear up and he could come up with some sort of plan to get out of Barbara's constant shadow and back into Emily's good graces. He had to do *something.*

"I know what you're thinking, Nick. I can see it all over your face. You want to run. You're always running because that's what you are—a runner. You ran from me and you ran from that girl back in Nebraska and look what's happened to both of us because we trusted you. I'll get over it because I don't need you to be who I am but what about her? You left her all alone with those guys and came back here?"

"I didn't have any choice."

"Didn't you?"

"How could you possibly understand?" he fumed.

Cianti laughed. "Do you think I got to where I am by being stupid? I make mistakes." She looked him up and down. "But I'm not stupid, Nick. It looks to me like the only one who qualifies as stupid here is you. Did you honestly think I was going to just let bygones be bygones? It's not about my heart, Nick. You damaged my reputation and my brand. It's my name you messed with and I can't have that. So I had to hit you where it hurt, although if I'd known she was just a hook-up like the rest of us I wouldn't have bothered to do all that research or send it to those idiots so they could go find her. But now it's too late and that's on you because you walked away."

"She's better off without me."

"I can't disagree with that."

Nick saw that his hand was starting to tremble around his glass of mineral water. More and more he was craving the shot of vodka. He had to get out of there before it was too late. As he made his way toward the exit he was shocked to see Barbara herself walking into the party. Usually, they made their entrance together. But ever since Nick's scandals had hit the news Barbara had distanced herself while continuing to cash the paychecks. Now, she walked in wearing an expensive and exquisite gown that one would have seen on one of her clients rather than on an agent. In Nick's world Barbara didn't see the difference. He decided to confront Barbara then and there. He needed to know if she knew anything about Cianti's plan and he would need her help and connections to thwart it. As soon as Barbara saw Nick she smiled.

"Glad you made it, Nick."

She took his arms and turned him back in the direction of the bar.

"I'd rather not go back there," he said under his breath.

"I'm not going for you, I'm going for me."

"You haven't called me in for any meetings since I've been back. Or returned any of my calls."

"Ambrose is quite capable of managing your appearances and activities."

"But Ambrose isn't my agent, you are."

"You have to understand, Nick, that you've put me in a difficult position. You're not the only client I have."

"You mean Cianti?"

"I don't know what you're talking about."

"Cianti mentioned that she was dropping the lawsuit."

"Oh, that." She gave him a charming laugh.

"You didn't think that was something I should know?"

"You pay me to keep your brand alive and kicking."

"I pay you to keep me in the loop."

"I could say the same thing."

"We've been over this a hundred times."

"Have you learned you're lesson?"

"You tell me, Barbara. Did you know that Cianti sent those two paparazzi guys to Nebraska?"

"Did she? How strange."

"Is it?"

"What are you implying?" She sounded almost offended.

"You're the only one who knew where I was and *who* I was with."

"Nick, you're being ridiculous and *anyone* could have sent them. You're news so now *she's* news and that doesn't have anything to do with me." She cocked an eyebrow taking a seat at the bar, she asked for a cocktail. Nick, swallowed nervously, eyeing the cocktail and wondering if he'd be able to stop himself from ordering a shot of vodka. He figured she probably wouldn't stop him. But she was right. It was all his fault.

"So are you back in?"

"Do I have a choice?"

"No." She took a sip of her drink. "Now, why don't you relax, smile, and look like you're having a good time. Then, we'll go and make the rounds like we always do."

His hand was trembling and his mouth was dry. He needed a drink. He was sweating. He swallowed again.

"Drink?" She asked pointing toward the bartender, who came over with a bottle of vodka.

"Mineral water," he said craving the vodka with every cell of his body.

"Now that's the spirit," she said getting up, taking his arm and leading him out into the crowd of VIP guests.

CHAPTER FORTY-TWO

The Call

His cellphone kept ringing until he finally answered.

"Nick? It's Caroline."

Emily's best friend from the cancer support group had caught him on his way to a book signing and fan meet & greet in the Village. It was Barbara's idea as a way to make up for the mess he'd made, but the moment he heard Caroline's voice he stopped walking.

"What's wrong, Caroline?"

"She's in the hospital."

"What happened?"

"They chased her, Nick. Those paparazzi guys chased her down and you know how she drives."

He heard another sob. "How bad, Caroline?" He wanted to kill them for what they'd done to Emily.

"They don't know yet. . ."

"How *bad*?" He knew he'd raised his voice when he heard her sharp intake of breath.

"She's on a ventilator. They're talking about inducing a coma. . ."

Nick knew what Caroline knew, that if they put Emily into a medically induced coma there was a very good chance she would die without ever regaining consciousness. It couldn't end this way. He knew it wasn't what Caroline wanted, it wasn't what he wanted, but more importantly it wasn't what Emily wanted.

"It's my fault. She was at my house. They must have followed her. We were fighting. I was trying to. . .to convince her to change her mind. I didn't mean to say anything. She couldn't take it. It was the stress. . .the court case. . .her parents. . .me. . . "

"And me," Nick acknowledged.

"She's been in a fishbowl for weeks. Those reporters showing up all times of the day and night, her father kept showing up at the record store, trying to talk her into moving back home with them and I. . .well, I didn't help. She left the house, she was so angry and they followed her. She was trying to get away and she ran a red light. The car went into a tailspin and she hit a post."

Nick sighed. "I'm coming back. I'll be on the next plane as soon as I can."

"Thank you, Nick." Caroline sounded relieved.

Daryl, his driver looked upset. As soon as Nick hit the end button and looked up, Daryl was already shaking his head.

"No, Mr. Simon. No."

"Daryl, how do you know what I'm going to say?"

"I have been driving you from place to place for almost five years now. I know that look on your face and it means trouble for all involved."

"Daryl. . ."

"Absolutely not! I have never seen Ms. King so upset in

the entire time I have worked for her as the day that you left without telling her."

"I *have* to go, Daryl."

"And miss the book signing? That is *not* following the plan, Mr. Simon."

"Daryl, *please*."

"Do you know what you are asking, Mr. Simon? You are asking me to *disobey*, Ms. King and for what? One of your party girls? I cannot. Please get in the car. Ms. King will be waiting for you at the location."

"Daryl, I swear. This isn't what you think! She's. . .Emily's not a party girl. There's been an accident. . .she's hurt badly! It's all my fault, Daryl!"

"Emily? Emily Fischer, the girl you were with back in Omaha? You mean *that* Emily?"

Daryl had raised his voice. It took Nick completely off guard, well that and the fact that Daryl who stood a good three feet taller than he did and was built like a Mac truck, leaned over him like an angry bear. He'd been a linebacker for the Jets, fallen on hard times when Barbara found him and gave him the job as her personal bodyguard/driver and most recently as Nick's babysitter/jailer.

"Yes," Nick answered feeling the shame creep back into his face.

Daryl's words put him right back at Emily's door, back at his total heartbreak that final day before he left for New York.

"Get in the car, Mr. Simon. Get in now before I shove you in myself. " He'd completely lost the Zen tone in his voice and he gave Nick a look that caused him to scurry into the back of the SUV. Daryl stopped him. He put a large bear-sized hand up to Nick's face.

"No you get in the *front*. I'm not driving you around like you're somebody special. You abandoned that girl after you messed up her life with your own problems. You're riding up front and you're watching for pedestrians. If I kill anybody getting you to the airport it's on you, got it?"

"Okay. . ." Nick agreed, getting in the passenger's side of the car.

"And if Ms. King asks who drove you—you give her any name but mine—you understand?"

"Absolutely."

"And if you screw this up hurt that girl any more than you already have, don't try to come back here like nothing happened—I will find you and I will break you in half. You hear me, Mr. Simon?"

"Loud and clear, Daryl."

"Good, now buckle up, 'cause I'm about to burn some rubber!" He gave Nick a wide grin.

"What about the book-signing?"

"This is a matter of life and death, Mr. Simon. There will be other book signings. There's only one Emily and time is short, isn't it?" He sped through traffic and Nick swallowed hard.

"Yeah."

"Well, then I better drive faster," Daryl said, almost taking out a yellow cab and two unsuspecting pedestrians—who promptly cursed and flipped him off in passing.

"Daryl?"

"Mr. Simon?"

"I'm going to lose her," Nick said trying to keep the emotion out of his voice.

"There's no stopping that, Mr. Simon. We all lose

people we love. It's what we do with the time we got left with them that counts,"

Daryl said that kindly and Nick nodded as they sped through traffic on their way to La Guardia.

Once he was on the plane his phone rang and he knew there was no escaping the wrath of Barbara King a second time.

"Where are you?" she hissed.

"I'm on my way to Omaha," Nick said.He could hear the crowd at the signing.

"The hell you are, Nick. We've been over this. We're not doing it again. I need you at the signing as fast as you can get here or you're through!"

"I'm going, Barbara."

"Is it because of that girl in the news?"

"Yeah, it is. There's been an accident. I need to see her."

"Is that what she told you to get you to go back?"

"No. She's. . .she's the one who's been hurt. It was a friend who called."

"Nick, she doesn't want you there! Even if you go, even if you show up all you'll do is cause more trouble. Haven't you already proven that?"

"I'm going Barbara."

"Nick, if you go then you give me no choice," she said in a steely voice.

"Are you threatening me?"

"Yes!"

"I need to go. Give me a few days and then I'll be back. Reschedule the events this week."

"Do you have any idea what that will do to the tour schedule? Not to mention what the rumors will do for what's already been the biggest fiasco of your career?

"There's nothing you can do to stop me, Barbara, and if you can't find it in your heart to let me do this one thing, then. . .you can't be my agent anymore."

There was a stony silence before Barbara spoke again. "You can't fire me, you son of a bitch. I already terminated your contract!" she yelled and the phone went dead.

CHAPTER FORTY-THREE

The News

Caroline ran to meet him in the waiting room when he arrived.

"Have you seen her?" he asked. He saw that Caroline had been crying.

"No. They're not letting anyone see her except for. . ." She paused and another tear made its way down her face, "family." His heart sank. That meant that the only people allowed to be at Emily's side when he needed to be with her the most were the very same ones who had vowed to keep them apart, Rabbi Fischer and his wife Meredith.

Aaron came up behind Caroline and put his arms around her to comfort her.

"It's going to be okay. You'll see," he reassured her, but Nick wasn't so sure.

He knew how the family felt about Emily's friends, even those, like Caroline and Aaron who agreed with Emily's father and his wife in principle, but still supported Emily's right to choose for herself. He had made an uneasy peace with the fact they considered him an enemy, even though he couldn't change her mind despite the way they felt about each other. Now, everything Emily had worked for was in jeopardy and in the hands of the people who loved her so much they refused to let her go on her own terms. How could he blame them?

Didn't he and Aaron and Caroline often talk about how things might be different if she could only see how much she was loved? How could she go through with it if she knew? But then that was it, wasn't it? They had all made it about them and forgotten about her. *They* were the ones unwilling to come to terms with Emily's decision, despite how much they claimed to love her. *They* were the selfish ones, unwilling to let her go. Sometimes he wondered how it made them any better than Emily's parents—the way they tried to manipulate Emily into staying, into changing her mind. Caroline tried through her faith to convince her that she didn't need to take such drastic measures, that there was a purpose to their suffering and that if she would simply look at things from her perspective it would all be worth it. There was a heaven and salvation to be gained.

Then there was the way he'd tried to convince her to stay. He allowed himself to fall in love with her and let her know it. He'd made it nearly impossible for her to continue her journey—by giving her a taste of what life could be like if she only reconsidered, went to yet one more specialist and tried yet one more treatment. Maybe the result would the same, but if it bought them time what would it matter. At least she wouldn't be giving up on them.

He felt ashamed as soon as he had the thought. She's not the one who went back to New York and tried to pretend they'd never met.

They sat down in the uncomfortable waiting room chairs, hoping that somehow they'd hear something, that they'd be allowed to see her, or by some miracle, that she'd suddenly wake up and ask for them. They waited for what seemed hours and were rebuffed time after time when they attempted to get information from any of the attending nurses or staff. All they knew was that Emily was not awake and that her parents hadn't left her side since they'd been notified of her admission to the hospital. Finally around 11 p.m. Nick saw Meredith Bernstein-Fischer coming down the hallway and he didn't think twice as he got up and went to her. She scowled the moment she saw him.

"Mrs. Fischer, please. How is she doing?" he asked and she kept walking. Nick followed her.

"Go away," she said and walked faster. Nick kept pace with her stepping in front of her so that they were face to face.

"Please, I'm begging you. How is she doing?"

"How dare you?" she hissed, "How do you think she's doing? She wouldn't be here if it wasn't for you."

"That's not fair and you know it."

"All that time she wasted with you when she could have been getting the treatment and care she needed, just so you could put another notch in your belt. Don't think I don't know what kind of man you are. I do. So does my husband."

"Mrs. Fischer, you have to believe me. I want her to live as much as you do. I love her. But she knows what she wants and I can't stop her from knowing her own mind."

"You could have convinced her."

"I tried. Don't you think I tried? She wouldn't listen to me. She cut me out her life. I left for New York because she me sent away."

"You gave up too soon. Of all of us you had the best chance of talking her out of it."

"It's not what she wanted."

"What about what she *should* have wanted? A life with her family, her friends and even if we didn't approve, a life with you? That would be better than what's happened."

"It was the stress of it all. You didn't have to take her to court."

"We had to do something. What would you have done in our position, Mr. Simon? It's something only a parent can understand. You'd do anything to protect your child. That's what we were doing."

"But she's not a child. She's a grown woman," he said and Meredith Bernstein-Fischer seemed taken aback by the thought as if it had only just occurred to her that this might be true.

"Well, it doesn't matter now does it?" she said and walked around Nick.

"Wait! What do you mean if doesn't matter now?" he called after her feeling a wave of panic overtake him. He ran after her and stopped her again.

"Please. Let us see her. If. . .if this is the end of Emily's life, please let us see her or least let Caroline see her."

"I don't think my husband would agree to it, Mr. Simon. You've all had her long enough. We'd like to spend what's left of her life with her if you don't mind."

Nick helplessly watched her walk away.

CHAPTER FORTY-FOUR

Awake

They waited for hours. Nick refused to leave the hospital waiting room even though there was nothing he could do and no one he could talk to about Emily's condition. Not even Caroline. Aaron had finally taken her home because of the physical and emotional toll the situation was taking on her. He asked Nick to call if anything changed, but other than that, he was on his own. He had glimpses of Emily's parents here and there as they exited her room to go get coffee or a quick bite to eat, but they refused to make eye contact or acknowledge his presence. Nothing he did could make them talk to him and, because he wasn't family, every nurse and doctor he pleaded with reminded him over and over that he wasn't really a part of Emily's life. Soon he wouldn't be part of her death either. He had hours to replay all of their conversations and encounters, all of the mistakes he'd made—especially the one where he left and went back to New York. He should have stayed but, he was scared to feel, to have his heart broken again, and to lose her forever. Now, it didn't matter. All of that would happen and he would be helpless to stop it.

He didn't know how long he'd been asleep when a nurse shook him awake. At first Nick was confused and disoriented. Where was he? Then, he remembered that he was at the hospital and panic set in. Was the nurse there to let him know that Emily was gone?

"Mr. Simon? Nick Simon?"

"Yeah." He tried to rub the sleep out of eyes and ignore the pain in his neck from sleeping at a weird angle.

"She's awake, Mr. Simon and she's asking for you." Nick quickly got out of his chair.

"Where is she?"

"Room 209. They moved her out of ICU early this morning." The nurse led him down a long corridor. When he stepped in the door to room 209, he found her father and Mrs. Fischer standing by Emily's bedside. They looked up and the expressions on their faces were somewhere between anger and utter relief. Emily was lying, bruised and battered, attached to a set of IVs and monitors. His heart stopped when he saw the blue and purple bruises around her eye and the large stitched gash across her forehead. He went to her and reached out for her hand.

"Nick," she cried out hoarsely. "You're here. I'm so glad you're here."

He lifted her hand to his mouth and kissed it. "Of course, I'm here and I'm not going anywhere ever again," He stared across at her parents, determined to let them know that each word was a matter of fact. Her father kept gazing at Emily but her mother scowled at him, determined to let him know that the fight between them wasn't over yet.

"Caroline?" Emily asked.

Nick squeezed her hand.

"I'll call her as soon as I can,"

She managed a weak smile before falling back to sleep, probably due to the pain medication the nurse had administered as soon as he'd entered the room. He let go of her hand and walked back out into the hallway to call Caroline with the good news just as Emily's father caught up with him.

"Nick!"

"Rabbi."

"Can you spare a moment?"

Nick nodded.

"Let's go get some coffee, please."

Nick agreed and they made their way to the cafeteria where they bought two coffees and found a place for them to sit, away from the larger groups of people eating their meals.

"What is it you wanted to talk to me about?"

"First I want to apologize."

"For what?"

"For not allowing you to see my daughter when we thought we were going to. . .lose her. My wife was. . .is having a hard time with what's happening and this accident. It put her over the edge."

"I suppose I can understand that."

"Are. . .are you a father, Nick?" Liev Fischer asked looking him directly in the eye.

"N-no." Nick stumbled over his words. Emily's father had that effect on him.

"I think if you were you would understand just how

difficult this whole ordeal had been for us."

"What about Emily? What about how hard it's been for her?" Nick asked.

The older man sighed.

"Of course. I recognize that. But you must know what it's like to care so much for Emily and feel helpless in the face of this decision she's made."

"Sure. But because I care I don't force her to do something she doesn't want to do and I sure as hell don't take her to court over it," Nick said angrily.

Liev Fischer hung his head. "We regret that desperately. We see how the stress of our actions has caused Emily to decline."

"Are you going to drop the lawsuit?" Nick asked, waiting for the man to launch into a defense of why they would continue the court fight.

"As it turns out, Nick, we no longer have to pursue the case."

"Why? What happened to change your mind?"

"You."

"Me?"

"Yes. As soon as Emily woke up today she began asking for you and when her mother explained that we wouldn't let you see her she was inconsolable. She said she would do anything to see you and, while we know she could just as easily change her mind again, I want you to know what she promised. So you can understand what that means to us and to our faith. It's not something we take lightly and Emily knows that. "

"What did she promise?"

"She promised to try chemo again, Nick. For you."

CHAPTER FORTY-FIVE

Time in a Bottle

She straddled him, reaching up as far as her arm would go and grasped the Jim Croce record off the shelf above the sofa with the tips of her fingers.He gingerly caressed the sides of her pale, almost translucent ribs through the thin material of her t-shirt. He stared up at her and tried to memorize the lines of her gaunt face, the dark hollows of her eyes, the dull sheen of her once vibrant red hair. Nick wanted to love this Emily too; the Emily who was in constant pain, who doubled over when she walked—if she felt like walking at all. He wanted to remember the sound of Emily's voice when she cursed under her breath each time a new unseen jab of pain attacked her, the Emily who pulled herself up into a fetal position to comfort herself when she couldn't bear for him to hold her while she slept—as if an invisible barrier cocooned her and kept him away. This Emily, who cried and wailed and whose shoulders he held as she vomited until there was no more to vomit and who looked up at him with pleading eyes that broke his heart over and over again.

As she brought the old vinyl album down off the shelf, it fell and hit him in the head.

"Ow!"

"Sorry." She managed a small apologetic smile.

"No worries." He rubbed his head, handing her back the album. She opened it, took out the record, and reached over him to put it on the turntable. His heart lurched as *Time in A Bottle* began to play. She laid back down on top of him and he wrapped his arms around her. She'd lost so much weight there was hardly anything left to hold. They lay in silence listening to the song until he realized that she'd fallen asleep. She was rarely able to get any sleep anymore due to the pain and discomfort from the side effects of the chemo.While he couldn't feel his left arm, he didn't care. He let her sleep,counted each and every breath she took, and treasured them.

After a while she woke up briefly and he gently picked her up like he always did and carried her to her bed where Mel waited to take his turn at vigil. Not long after he put her to bed, he heard Mel whine from the bedroom and he went back in to check on her. He had to admit that she was frail, like a tiny bird with wings fluttering on a cold December night. She had a fever, but was shivering beneath the layers of blankets he'd been piling on top of her for the last few hours. It wasn't helping. The fevers kept climbing. Nick kept vigil from the chair he'd set up next to the bed. Time was running out. If it continued this way they would have no choice but to return her to the nearest hospital and she would die the way she feared.

He felt selfish. He felt ashamed. She had chosen to suffer like this for *him* because he dared her to prove her love for him instead of doing what she had planned all along. How was this living? It wasn't—not for Emily and it was killing him to watch her suffer. He could hardly take it anymore but he felt responsible so he did what he could to make her comfortable and to let her know that he loved her. But he always had Daryl's words in the back of his mind. Sometimes love meant letting go. The problem was he didn't want to let go, not now and not ever. So what did that say about the way he loved Emily?

The worst thing was, she never threw it in his face, never used it if they argued, which was rarely, since she had barely enough energy to talk. She had made the decision to give the chemo one last shot and what had he done in return? He'd been there to watch her hurt. It was torture for both of them and when, not if, she lost the battle with the disease the whole thing—the fight with her doctors, the court, her parents, Caroline— might have been in vain. But Nick thought selfishly, he would have her for a few more hours, maybe even a few more days. The girl with the butterfly tattoo wouldn't fly away forever. . .not just yet.

CHAPTER FORTY-SIX

The Secret

Nick woke up, his body and hands intertwined with Emily's. The room was still semi-dark and Mel lay across both their legs, still asleep. He listened to the rhythm of Emily's breathing and counted the space in between.

"You were talking in your sleep," he heard her murmur.

He was surprised that she was awake. She wasn't an early riser and, with the chemo, she was so tired that even if she did wake up she didn't have the energy to move.

"I did?"

"Yeah."

"Who's Alex?"

His heart stopped. He didn't want to meld his two heartbreaks into one giant one.

"Who?" he tried to pretend he hadn't heard the name—as if he could ever forget.

"I know you heard me, Nick."

He sighed.

"What did I say. . .in my sleep?"

"It some pretty awful stuff. So, who's Alex?"

"He was family," he said finally.

Emily turned herself around to face him.

"Did he get hurt, Nick?"

"Yeah."

"That's what it sounded like."

"What did I say?"

"You were asking him to forgive you. Forgive you for what?"

The look on her face was sympathetic and curious all at the same time.

"I'm not sure that I can talk about it now." He felt all of the emotions he'd bottled up for so long battle their way up to the surface.

"Then when? It's not like we have all the time in the world, Nick." he had to look away. She gently forced his head back to face her. "I'm sorry. It's just you're so used to keeping secrets and I'm not. I'm past that point now, Nick. I don't have time to keep any more secrets. So tell me. Tell me about Alex."

They lay in silence for a while until Nick let the secret come out one ugly piece at a time.

"Where should I start?"

"At the beginning is always good," she said and smiled.

He frowned. The beginning was the very place he'd been trying to avoid all this time and now he had to return because she'd asked him. He wanted to stop running. He wanted to stop walking away every time it got too hard, too painful and that time had to be now.

"Okay. For starters I'm not from LA or New York. I'm from Omaha."

"Really?" She was actually surprised.

"I grew up in a house not far from the zoo with my parents. Alex came along later."

"How much later?"

"Fifteen or sixteen years." He swallowed hard to keep the lump from rising in his throat.

"Wow. That's a *lot* later. So, I bet your mom and dad weren't expecting him."

"None of us were."

"So what happened to him?"

Nick got very quiet. "My father, Charles, was a drunk. He'd go into these detox programs and do alright until he came home and then it would all start over again. He used to beat on my mom and me until I got old enough to fight back. Then he went into a program where he was gone for six months and it looked like he might make it, but Alex came along and it was stressful. He stopped for a while and he didn't hurt Alex, not at first. But I got tired of it and I decided to leave home. I wanted my mom and Alex to come with me, but she wouldn't leave my dad. She believed in marriage and always thought he would change."

"But what about Alex?" Emily asked.He could hear the sorrow in her voice—maybe even the disappointment she felt at knowing that he had abandoned Alex—left him behind to live with the monster that his father turned into when life didn't go his way.

"I didn't have much contact with them after I left. I decided to go out west and eventually ended up in LA."

"Acting?" she asked.

Nick laughed. "Bartending."

"While you were waiting for your big break?"

"No. I was happy just bartending."

"Then how. . ."

"An assistant producer on *First Draft/Final Cut* came into the bar one day and thought I was right for the part."

" That's right. But I thought it was a *reality* show."

"There wasn't much that was *real* about it."

"But the writing?"

"That may have been the only thing. The coaches were as shocked as I was."

"That's when you wrote *For the Record*?"

"Yeah."

"And I thought you didn't know anything about the 'vinyl scene'." She said kissing his bare chest.

"Not the way you do." He kissed the top of her head. "Besides I didn't do the research, I had help for that."

"But the story. . .I *loved* that book and the movie wasn't too bad."

"Give me a break, it was my first novel *and* my first script," he laughed and she gave him a squeeze.

"I'm teasing you, you know." Then she paused. "How does Alex figure into all of this, Nick?"

Nick thought a moment before he continued. "After I won the competition and signed my contract with my new agent, I got my lawyer to let them give me a little time off before starting on the new projects they had waiting for me. So, I decided to go home, visit my mother and Alex—maybe convince them to come out LA to live with me but. . ." He stopped and he wasn't sure he was ready for the truth to come out.

"What happened?"

"I made it home okay but I wanted to surprise Alex. I remember I picked up this ugly green teddy bear at the airport with a baseball cap for him and I knocked on the door to the house. No one answered and I noticed that the door was open a bit. I pushed it open and called for my mom because it was early in the day and I knew she'd be home and my dad would have been at work. I thought if I could convince her to come with me we could pack a bag and pick up Alex from school and still make the evening flight back to LA before my dad got back but. . ." He stopped again Emily reached up to touch his face.

"It's okay, Nick. Go on," she whispered.

"I found her first, on the floor in the kitchen. Her head was. . .bashed in." His voice was trembling. "There was nothing I could do and then I thought about Alex. His room was in the back of the house. When I opened his door it was dark, the blinds had been partly closed and there was just enough light for me to see that someone was sitting on the bed." He cleared his throat because he felt the lump rising again. "I knew it was him—my dad—he was drunk. I could smell it on him. But Alex. . .I didn't see him anywhere until. . .until. . .my foot. . .I took a few steps toward the bed and my foot hit. . .a hand. . .on the floor. I looked down and.. . .it was Alex. There was so much blood." The tears were starting to overflow. He brought a hand up to wipe them away but Emily caught it and held it tight.

"It's okay, Nick. Keep talking."

"Before I could check on him. . .my dad came at me with the belt he'd used on Alex and I had to fight him off. It wasn't hard. He was so drunk he could hardly stand any more. I knocked him out cold. I think I could have kept hitting him, hurting him except that I wanted to help Alex, so I called 911.It was too late. Too late for both of them. He killed my mother and he killed Alex."

Nick was sobbing now and Emily was holding him tight as if to keep him from falling apart.

"I'm so sorry, Nick. I'm so sorry." she said as the tears streamed down her own face.

She was trying to sooth him but Nick couldn't be consoled—not now that he was about to tell her his deepest darkest secret—the one that had almost cost him his life the night he crashed the car near the cemetery gates.

"He *wasn't* my little brother, Emily. He was my son."

CHAPTER FORTY-SEVEN

Revelations

They held onto each other for a long time while Nick let the pain of a lifetime pour out of him.

"Alex was your son?" Emily asked.

Nick nodded. "I was fifteen and I hooked up with a girl from the neighborhood. Long story short, we were young and she couldn't care for him, so my mother offered to raise him. It was the only time I ever saw her stand up to my father about something. He'd been in that detox program for six months and had been doing so well that he didn't say anything against it. I was Alex's father, so when his mother relinquished her rights, I agreed to let my mother raise him. The plan was that we'd tell him I was his big brother and we'd all live happily ever after, but it didn't work out like that. I was young and I was stupid. A day doesn't go by that I don't wish I could go back and change it so he hadn't been born."

"How can you say that?"Emily said.

"He suffered, Emily."

"Did you love him?"

“Of course, but I left him there.”

“You were just a kid yourself.”

“I should have made my mother come with me or gone to court to take him out of the house, but all I could think about was myself.”

“You have to find a way to forgive yourself, Nick.”

“Why?”

“Because life is short,.” she whispered.

They were quiet again.

“Let’s not talk about it anymore,” he said.

She kissed him. “You have to get it all out. How did you end up in Nebraska?” He sighed. “I got a call from a detective that a homeless man had been found with my contact information. He was dead and they wanted my help identifying him. I decided to fly out and do it.”

“Why?”

“Because I knew who it had to be.”

“Your father?” she said.

Nick nodded. “Back when Alex died, after I called 911, I had to wait while they questioned me. I called my lawyer and he called my agent who told me to keep my mouth shut until they both got out here. So, I did and before I knew it I was out of the whole thing. My name, the fact that I found them in the house, my relationship to them.”

“How is that possible?”

“I don’t know. What I do know is that Barbara’s owned me ever since. At first I thought she’d done everything out of kindness because that’s what a kid from Nebraska *would* think. She arranged for the funerals and even made it so I could go visit the graves before we left on a private jet for New York. The only condition was that I never speak about what happened or what she did and that I follow her instructions regarding my career. I did that until I couldn't anymore. That's when I threw that party at the penthouse."

"The one that's all over the internet?"

"Yeah."

"How did you end up in that crash?"

"I made it out here, I got wasted, I got in the car and I crashed."

"But *why*?"

"I went to the morgue. I had to see for myself. For my mom. For Alex. It was him but it looked *nothing* like him. He'd ended up serving some time for killing them but not enough and they let him out. He'd wandered around from shelter to shelter telling people he was my father. No one believed him. When I realized it was him, I don't know, something snapped inside. I went to a bar, bought some coke, got ahold of some booze and decided to go to the cemetery."

"Oh no!"

"Not the best idea, I know."

"The news channels all said you tried to kill yourself. Did you?"

"I wanted to die and, the more I thought about it, the faster I drove. So, yeah. I guess I tried to kill myself—until that last moment when I saw those headlights coming straight for me. Then I must've chickened out. I tried to swerve but I ended up crashing into the gates instead."

"Oh, Nick. It's a miracle you *didn't* die."

"Maybe."

She traced the outline of his face with her fingers.

"It's a miracle," she said. "Did you ever figure out how he ended up with your contact information?"

"I don't know. I may never know. Barbara had my name expunged from all the family records so that the only son listed as part of the family was Alex."

"But how could she just *erase* you? People would've remembered you from school or the neighborhood."

"Nick Simon never lived here, Emily. He didn't exist until the producers of *First Draft/Final Cut* created him."

"Nick Simon isn't even your *real* name?" She was clearly shocked by the revelation.

"No, it isn't."

CHAPTER FORTY-EIGHT

What's in a Name?

"So, what should I call you?"

"I'm Nick Simon. At least I am now. I can't ever go back. Not after what happened."

"Okay," she said. "But if I had known you then, what would I have called you?"

"Danny Clearwater."

"Danny?" she said and giggled.

"What's so funny?" He managed to smile despite the pain and embarrassment he felt.

"You don't look like a Danny to me."

"I didn't look like a Nick Simon either until the producers of the show got ahold of me."

"I liked you as Simon." She kissed him again. He lay his head up against hers and closed his eyes, taking in her scent, a faint smell of strawberries.

"I'll be whoever you want," he murmured and he meant it.

"I'm sorry."

"For what?"

"About everything. You've already lost so much and now I'm going to. . ." Her own voice choked up.

"It's okay," he said, even though every part of him knew he was lying.

"No it's not. Not really," she said and he shrugged.

"Okay. Enough with the sad." He wiped what was left of the tears and kissed her. "We've got to get out of this bed and do *something.* So, let's get going. Let's do some of the stuff on your list."

"My list?"

"Remember the night at the store when we were talking about what you wanted to do with your time?"

"Yeah."

"So, let's do it. Movies, concerts, bike rides, walks, hikes. . ."

"Not all at once. . .I don't have the energy for that."

"What do you have the energy for?" he asked, winking at her.

She smiled. "Not even that." She frowned."You know, I'd love to go to the store and see if they've gotten any new records in. Could we do that?"

Nick stroked her cheek.

"Of course." He rolled over to the opposite side of the bed causing Mel to wake up. He growled, unhappy to have been awakened so unceremoniously. As Nick stood up he looked down on Emily, whose small frame had become even more emaciated as the chemo treatments continued. She looked so tiny lying in the middle of all those blankets.

"Do you want me to get your clothes out for you?"

She grimaced as she made an attempt to sit up. "Please," she said.

Nick went to her closet and pulled out something for her to wear. Then, he went into the bathroom to get her comb. After helping her dress, he sat on the bed,running his fingers through the hair that framed her face until he had to stop. Feeling the sudden pause, Emily turned around slightly and brought up a hand to her mouth in surprise. Her eyes filled with tears. There in Nick's hands was a clump of her hair.

"Em. . ."

"No. Don't say anything, Nick. Go get your electric razor. Do it. Now."

Nick got up and did as he was told.

"Shave it off. Do it before I change my mind."

"But, Em. It's just a little piece. . ."

"Today it is. Tomorrow. . .trust me, Nick. Please. Do it." She insisted and he pushed the power button on the razor so it came to life with a noisy roar.

"Are you sure?" he said, his hands trembling.

"Yes."

Mel inched closer to her lap with a whine. She placed her hands on top of his head and squeezed gently.

"Do it, Nick!" She'd raised her voice, startling him, and he started to shave . He didn't stop until all of her short red locks were gone. He stared at Emily's bald head. She put her hand over it.

"You missed a spot." She said reached for the razor. Nick relinquished it and she started it up again going over different spots until finally she turned it off.

"There are hats in the closet, will you bring me one?" Her voice was small and childlike.

"Yeah," he said, going to the closet, picking one and handing it to her.

"I'd really like to go to the record store now."

"Okay." He hesitated for a moment before getting up, kneeling in front of her and seeing the tears stream down her face.

"Em, I'm sorry."

"It's only hair."

He wrapped his arms around her grabbing some Kleenex from the nightstand and handing them to her so she could wipe her eyes and blow her nose.

"Ready?"

She nodded.

He helped her get up and make her way toward the front door. He carried her down the stairs and put her into the passenger's side of the car. Getting into the driver's side and shutting the door he spied the paparazzi that had been following them around ever since he'd returned from New York. He didn't care, not any more. There were more important things to think about, like driving the girl he loved to her favorite record store. As he pulled away from the apartment complex, Emily reached out and took his hand.

"I love you," she whispered.

For once he didn't try to keep his emotions in check. He let the first thing that came to mind fall out of his mouth.

"I love you too."

CHAPTER FORTY-NINE

The Results

Nick and Aaron helped Caroline and Emily into the chemo treatment center on a sunny day. Both women struggled out of the car as the men held onto an arm or a hand and led them through the front doors. Then, holding onto each other, the women walked into the treatment rooms with their bags filled with their iPods, blankets and a small pile of Nick's paperback books. Emily's blanket was new. It was a non-sew blanket covered in colorful butterflies made by Caroline's daughter Abbie. Emily had a sketch pad and charcoal pencils with her, like she always did. Aaron and Nick were welcome to sit with them but Caroline and Emily preferred to go in as they always had—together. It wasn't until the treatment was over and they were on their way out that Emily's oncology nurse told them Dr. Johnson wanted to see them before they left. Dr. Johnson, Emily's oncologist, led them to her office.

"Emily has given me consent to share the results of her exams with you." She looked in Nick's direction. Then she paused for a moment looking over the file in her hands before sighing.

Nick felt his whole body tense. The oncologist looked up and faced Emily. Their eyes met and Emily looked away, staring down at her hands. She knew something and Nick knew it couldn't be anything good. The doctor finally spoke.

"The chemo hasn't made the difference we hoped it might," she said.

Nick's heart sank to his feet. His mouth was dry. "What does that mean?"

Emily reached for his hand.

"It means it's time to consider palliative care or any of the other options we discussed previously."

"Palliative care—what's that and what other options?"

"She means pain management and hospice, Nick," Emily whispered.

Nick glanced at Emily, who was staring at their hands, clasped together tightly.

"That's it? That's the option?" Nick's voice was rising.

"Nick..." Emily tried to interrupt him.

"We want a second opinion. There's an oncologist Dr. Manzitti in Cleveland she's considered the best in the field, no offense Dr. Johnson, but I gave your nurse the name..."

"No offense taken Mr. Simon. I know Gina and you're right, for Emily's type of cancer she's considered one of the best, which is why I consulted with her before meeting with you. She's in agreement. We tried the new drug but the disease is too aggressive at this point. I'm sorry, Emily."

Nick sat stunned at the news and Emily didn't speak.

The doctor looked truly sorry and for a few moments no one spoke. Finally Dr. Johnson stood up.

"I'm going to give you some time. If you decide to go forward with the palliative or hospice care my nurse can set up the first appointment with Cathy Zimmer, the coordinator. Again, I'm sorry." Dr. Johnson reached out to shake their hands before she left the room.

"What now?" Nick whispered.

"It's time to go home,." she answered.

"Back to the apartment?"

"No." she said, "back to Oregon."

Nick kept quiet as they gathered up Emily's things and headed back out to the waiting room where Aaron and Caroline were waiting.

"Well?" Caroline asked hopefully but Emily just kept walking toward the exit and Nick shook his head.

"I'm sorry, man." Aaron gave him a sympathetic pat on the back.

Nick wanted to tell Aaron that it was okay. That neither he nor Caroline had to worry about Emily or for that matter Nick, but it wasn't true. Inside Nick was in panic mode and the craving for a drink was strong. Stress. It did that to him. He would have to call his sponsor, he knew that, and he hated it. He hated that he was so weak when it came to loving someone so strong. But there it was and it was the painful truth.

CHAPTER FIFTY

Deal with the Devil

He took a deep breath before making the call he'd been dreading to make for weeks. Nick hoped there would be no answer but of course there was. There always was.

"Hello."

"Barbara?"

"Nick. Surprised to hear from you."

"I know. I wasn't planning on calling."

"Didn't think you would after our last conversation."

"You mean the one where I fired you."

"You mean the one where *I* dissolved our contract?" she said and Nick sighed.

"Look, I haven't had a chance to talk to Arnie about all of the paperwork. I know it's stalled."

"That's not really my problem, Nick. We're no longer business associates."

"Barbara, please. I get it. You need to hurt me. Okay. But that's not why I called."

"Why *did* you call, Nick. I'm busy signing on a new client so I don't have time to chat."

"Cianti?"

"I'm afraid I'm not at liberty to say."

"Fine. I called because I need a. . .favor." He said in a low whisper and then he heard her break out in a laugh that he was familiar with. It was her are-you-effing-kidding-me laugh. He'd heard her use it on more than one occasion. He expected it but he had no choice."

"What's in it for me?" she asked.

"You haven't even heard what I'm asking for. . ."

"Doesn't matter. What's in it for me?"

"I'll come back. Books, films, publicity you name it. I'm yours. I'll do the circuit, whatever you say."

"Well, this is a change of heart," she said in a tone that indicated she was mildly interested.

"I need the favor."

"You'll be all in?"

"Absolutely."

"Fine. What do you want?"

"A jet and a place to stay."

"I can have the jet ready in twenty-four hours but what place?"

"The beach house."

"The beach house?" She sounded genuinely curious.

"I need a secluded place, away from everyone with some level of security."

"It's for her isn't it?" Barbara asked her voice surprisingly softening.

"Yes."

"It's come to that?"

"We're out of options." he admitted. What was the point of lying when it might help convince her?

"Nick. . .I'm sorry, she said and he was taken back by

her kindness.

"Can you help me out?"

"Crazier things have happened in that place. I'll have Ambrose make the arrangements and I'll send the new contract to Arnie Schaefer. There'll be new adendums to it, you know," she said and Nick knew it meant trouble for him.

"I do."

"How soon do you need the plane?"

"Tomorrow."

"How. . .how long before I can expect you back in New York?"

"Barbara. . .I'll contact you."

"The movie premier is a three months away Nick." Nick did the math in his head, given the waiting periods after the medical evaluation Emily would have, and then the applications before finally. . .there was a lump in his throat. . .he couldn't get past the thought.

"I understand," he said.

"Then we have a deal." Barbara said. "Keep in touch." The call ended and Nick stood where he was, certain that he'd made a deal with the devil for a second time. He'd expected that. What he didn't expect was to see Emily standing behind him. Had she heard the call?

"No,"she whispered.

"Did you hear?" he asked and she nodded.

"Why did you go back to her?"

"It doesn't matter. I'm not going to let you do this for me anymore, Emily."

"I can find my way back home."

"I know you can. But we're together now and there's paparazzi almost everywhere we go here. Can you imagine what it'll be like at your house? Not to mention that you haven't gotten you parents to agree to let you stay there while you do this. Emily, let me help."

"But you just signed yourself over to her, your books, your movies. . .I thought you said no one *ever* got out and you did and now you're going back to her. Nick, no. I can't let you do that."

"It's done." He reached out for her.

He held her kissed her on the head. She had covered it with a soft knit cap to cover the hair loss from the chemo. Both she and Caroline got cold easily and often, so they kept a good supply of caps and blankets on hand even though it was already late summer. Soon it would be Labor Day and fall would begin, but Emily's life would end.

"Nick," she murmured, turning her face up so she could kiss him.

"Em. It's going to be ok. I promise," he said as he kissed her back.

He picked her up and carried her back to her bedroom where Mel was waiting. Nick covered her with the blanket Abbie had made for her. Mel sprawled himself across her legs as he always did before she drifted off to sleep. Nick sat by the bed, holding her small, fragile hand. His thoughts sped through the different painful scenarios that would play out over the next days and weeks until he had to let her go for good. He tried to take a deep breath but found it hard. Mel whined, reaching over Emily's legs to lick his hand as if to express what they were both feeling.

"Hey, boy," Nick whispered." I know. You don't want to lose her either."

CHAPTER FIFTY-ONE

Going Home

Dr. Kimberly Lee, Emily's oncologist in Portland was their first stop after traveling on the private jet that Barbara sent to collect them from Nebraska. Before she left Emily made another effort to contact her parents who vehemently disagreed with her choice to leave and who, having dropped the lawsuit, could do little about her final plans—but still had much to say. They begged her not to go. They begged Nick not to let her follow through with it.

"Do something," Meredith Bernstein-Fischer had said grabbing Nick's shirt and pounding her fists against his chest.

"Mom!" Emily had yelled. "Stop it! It's my choice! Not his! Not yours!"

"Please, Emily. Reconsider. Think of us. Think of your faith. Don't turn your back on it. . .on your family." Rabbi Fischer had interjected, but Emily wouldn't change her mind.

"I came here because I want to die peacefully. At *home* not *here* in Nebraska, not in some hospital, but in my own bed surrounded by *my* family. Why won't you do this last thing for me?"

"How can you *ask* such a thing of us?" her mother had cried as her father enfolded her mother in an embrace.

"Mom, please. You'd rather watch me die in pain? Or in a coma or by starvation?"

"There are plenty of peaceful ways you can leave this world. Hospice would give you some of those options. Why won't you just look into it?"

"I'm tired. I'm so tired, Mom. I'm going to die no matter what you do or where you put me. *I* want to say when. I'm tired of this disease taking pieces of *my* life. *I* want to say when, Mom. *I* want to decide, for once, what happens to me."

"What about you? You *still* have nothing to say?" her mother turned her glare on Nick.

He sighed. "It's not about what I want, Mrs. Fischer. I don't want to lose her either but I'm not forcing her to stay, living like this for me. Not anymore."

"So that's it. You're leaving and we'll never see you again." her mother sobbed.

"I'm going but you can come with me. You can be there with me, Mom."

"No. I can't." Meredith Bernstein-Fischer broke away from her husband's embrace and ran to her room leaving the three of them alone in the dining room.

"Papa?" Emily had asked, but her father had crossed his arms and looked down at the table.

"No, Emily. This I cannot do. I cannot break the commandments or witness them being broken," he said looking away.

That's when they had left.

Now they sat in Dr. Lee's office waiting for the first step Emily had to complete as part of her application: she had to make her first oral request. She had to *ask* for permission to use the Death with Dignity Act. Then there would be a fifteen-day waiting period, followed by a second request, a written request, a forty-eight-hour waiting period and then they would be able to pick up the necessary medications. Nick's head had been swimming with information when Emily was doing chemo, with reference to side effects and everything he needed to do to help her while she was undergoing treatment. In comparison, these last few steps in the process seemed so simple. Too simple. But here they were, sitting in Dr. Lee's office, with Emily, ready to utter those four words he dreaded hearing more than any other in his entire life—I *want* to die. When Dr. Lee finally came in, Nick wondered if he'd have the strength to sit through the appointment.

"Emily." Dr. Lee held out a hand which Emily took and held for a long moment. It was clear that she had a strong bond with this physician. Emily smiled as she turned toward him.

"Dr. Lee, this is Nick."

"I recognize him. I hope you don't mind my saying that I'm a fan of your work."

"Thanks."

Dr. Lee opened a file she'd carried in with her. As soon as she did, she was all business. She didn't waste any time getting to the point.

"I wish we were meeting here under better circumstances. But, I've had a chance to review all of the paperwork from Nebraska and Ohio where Gina Manzitti has her clinic and I have to concur with the result. I'm very sorry, Emily." Dr. Lee looked up and made sincere eye contact. "We've talked about this before but I'd like you to reconsider palliative care one more time."

"I can't," Emily said.

Dr. Lee nodded.

"What about hospice?"

"No."

"There are some new drugs that can help with pain management. . ."

"No."

"I had a feeling, based on our previous conversations, that you'd say that. Okay. Then, I'm ready. Go ahead and tell me what you want to do, Emily."

Nick braced himself and Emily took his hand.

"I want to die in my own bed surrounded by my loved ones but not in hospice, or a hospital or drugged up. I want to use the Death with Dignity Act." Her voice was strong and determined.

Dr. Lee sighed.

"Alright, Emily. Let me start the process. I'm guessing you know that this is only the first request and that there's a fifteen day waiting period, not to mention that I have to do some additional consultations on your case. Then, we'll come back and see if anything's changed, if not, you'll send me a written request and after that there's an additional waiting period before the prescription can be picked up."

Emily nodded.

"Fine. If either of you have additional questions you'll contact me?"

"Yeah," Emily said. Dr. Lee took her hand and squeezed it tightly. "It's so good to see you. You've always been one of my favorite patients. You know that—right?" Dr. Lee flashed her a smile and Emily returned it with one of her own.

"It's obvious. What's not to like?" Emily teased and Nick felt a surge of love for her. He'd missed her sense of humor.

After Dr. Lee left, Nick and Emily sat for a moment before getting up and leaving the room. In silence,they walked hand in hand down the hallway leading to the lobby of the medical building, until they got into the car.

"This is really happening," she whispered.

Nick's heart constricted.

"Yeah." "I don't know what to think."

"It's what you wanted, isn't it?"

"Yes."

"Then be. . .okay."

"Be okay," she repeated and he reached out to hold her hand.

"So now we know. . ."

"What?" she asked.

"For the first time since this all started, since I met you, I know the date. I know how much time we have."

"You're right." she said, with tears in her eyes.

"What do you say we go use some of that time?"

"Doing what?"

"I'm sure we can figure something out," he said leaning over and kissing her.

"Nick?"

"Yeah?"

"Thank you."

"For what?"

"For being here and letting me . . ." She started to get

choked up.

"Em…" he said taking her into his arms.

"For staying with me," she cried.

"Always," he said and he meant it, even though inside his heart was shattering.

CHAPTER FIFTY-TWO

Story of My Life

Emily's request was approved. Nick didn't know how to feel about it so he decided to shelve his feelings until it was all over. In the meantime, he dedicated himself to taking care of Emily and making their time together at the beach house as meaningful as possible. Time was ticking away and, before long, Emily felt it was right to let Caroline and Aaron know about the date. They had already said their goodbyes before Nick and Emily left Nebraska. It left Emily devastated and it must have done the same for Caroline, because she and Aaron showed up at the beach house a few days ahead of the date Emily had set.

At first, when Caroline arrived, Nick thought that Emily might change her mind and turn her away, given how passionately they disagreed about how Emily wanted to end her life. Instead, Emily had run straight into Caroline's arms the moment she'd stepped foot in the house. They'd wrapped their arms around one another and headed for the back deck where they had spent the last few hours talking and crying. Nick had checked on them from time to time and they would send him away with requests for little things like hot tea or a small sandwich for them to share. Nick felt he could breathe a little, especially now that he had Caroline's husband Aaron to help him pass the time. But it had taken him a while to let the unease he'd expected to come with Caroline's visit to subside.

Dying had brought them together. Religion had set them apart. It was the friendship that had survived as they sat side by side in wicker rockers staring out into the ocean, hands clasped, fragile bodies wrapped in blankets to keep out the invisible cold that always seemed to be nipping at their extremities. Caroline wore the cap that Emily had crocheted for her during one of her many chemo sessions and Emily lightly clutched the no-sew lap blanket that Abbie had made for her. Nick watched them from the kitchen. Neither one of them seemed to be speaking or, if they were, it was a wordless conversation.

"She hasn't come here to change her mind." Aaron said as he and Nick sat passively watching a ball game.

Nick had been sitting on the edge of the couch, elbows on his knees, nervously tapping his foot.

"Are you sure?" Nick couldn't keep the accusatory tone out of his voice.

"Yes."

"How can you be sure?"

"I have faith."

"Faith?" Nick said, thinking back to the night of Emily's accident. "That's not what happened the last time."

"Caroline never meant to upset her, Nick."

"She ended up in the hospital, Aaron." Nick realized he had raised his voice and instantly lowered it to an angry whisper. "She almost died!"

"I'm sorry. Caroline was devastated, Nick."

"Emily knows what she wants, Aaron. I hope Caroline understands that."

"She does. We both do."

"Then why is she really here?"

"To say good-bye."

The words struck Nick like a sledgehammer. Somehow, even as he accused Caroline of trying to usurp Emily's plans by using their friendship as a way to manipulate her, Nick had to admit that he had been counting on it all along. He had hoped that Caroline would find a way, even now, that she had come with a hidden agenda, wrapped up in her zealous faith and soft manner, to convince Emily that living, even through the suffering, was worth it. Instead, Aaron had confirmed what he had not wanted to hear; Caroline had accepted Emily's choice. She didn't like it, she didn't agree with it, but she had accepted it. The last obstacle to Emily's final decision had dissolved before his eyes. The final conversation, the one he had hoped Caroline was having with Emily as they sat on those wicker chairs looking out over the sea was *not* about staying but about leaving. It was a last *goodbye.* Nick could feel a lump in his throat. He turned back to the TV and pretended to watch more baseball.

After another hour or so, Nick stood up and went to check on Caroline and Emily. As he made his way through the kitchen and was about to open the screen door he heard Emily's voice choked up with emotion.

"Nick loves me," he heard her say.

He quietly stepped back into the kitchen.

"We all love you, Em."

"But this is different. You have Aaron."

Caroline was silent for a moment. "He won't be alone, Em. . ."

"Please, Caroline. You promised."

"I'm not talking about religion, Em. I'm talking about us. He'll have us. Me and Aaron and Abbie. We'll be his family."

"But what if you. . ."

"Die?" Caroline squeezed Emily's hand. "It won't change things."

"Nick is going to have a really hard time."

"Yeah, he is. We all are. That's love, Em."

"Sometimes, I'm sorry that I met him."

Emily was crying now and Nick tried not to let her words affect him, but they hurt. They hurt deeply even though there had been a time he'd had the same thought about her.

"No you're not. You're heart's hurting because you don't want to leave him, Em."

"I don't. But I can't. . ." Her sobs drowned out the rest of the words. Nick's own eyes were moist with tears. Caroline wrapped a frail arm around Emily as Emily rested her head on her friend's bony shoulder. They stared out at the sea a bit longer before Caroline began to sing. Her shaky soprano began to swell into the *Old Rugged Cross* before Emily politely stopped her.

"Do you know any other songs, Caroline?" she asked.

"I'm sorry. I know I promised but. . ."

"I'm still a little bit Jewish."

"Jesus was a Jew," Caroline said softly.

Nick heard Emily sigh.

"How about a compromise?"

"Ok."

"How about Abbie's favorite song?" Emily said.

Caroline laughed. "No. Not that!" she begged in a tone that assured Emily they would most certainly sing it.

"You know it by heart don't you?" Emily teased. Caroline laughed again and began to sing the words to One Direction's *Story of My Life*. Emily joined her in the chorus and the women kept singing until they broke out into peals of laughter and then into tears, interrupted by the intermittent sounds of sobbing Nick heard weaving through the song. He finally walked away and returned to the living room where Aaron was sitting, still staring at the TV. Mel sat at Aaron's feet. Tears were streaming down the big man's face. Nick marveled at the way Aaron could let people see what he was feeling and not care.

"Are they singing?"

Nick nodded and sat down. Aaron didn't make an effort to wipe the tears from his face or pretend that Nick hadn't seen him cry. Nick felt uncomfortable to the point that he finally had to ask Aaron if he was okay. Caroline's husband shook his head yes.

"Are you sure?"

Aaron smiled and at last, wiped his eyes with the back of his hands. "Yeah. Nick, I'm okay. I just really hate that song."

He grinned and both men started laughing. It felt good to laugh. There would be plenty of time for them to cry, to grieve, and he knew it would be here before they knew it. For both of them.

CHAPTER FIFTY-THREE

Sunset

They were listening to Ed Sheeran's *Thinking Out Loud* on the record player. Nick knew that he wouldn't have the lifetime with Emily that was promised by the song. All he had was now. Suddenly he kissed her, not because he wanted, to but because he *needed* to and that need superseded anything else. She kissed him back. So this is how it was going to end. Not with her death but with his. The old Nick was gone. Dead. The new Nick was raw, vulnerable and about to lose the only person, besides Alex, that he had ever truly loved. She was so small and fragile in his arms and he fought back the tears. He promised himself he wouldn't make it harder on her than it needed to be. He promised her a perfect weekend. Then he promised her he would sit quietly by as the preparations were made and the medication was mixed. Finally, he promised her that she would have her favorite blanket—the one that Abbie made—Mel sprawled across her legs, her favorite vinyl playing and his hand to hold while she *fell asleep*. Nick tried to wrap his head around what it all meant but all he could do was think about the fact that time was ticking away. He held her closer and kissed the top of her head.

"What's that for?" She snuggled in closer.

"Just because."

She turned to look at him. "You promised,"

He shrugged. "What?"

"None of this sad business, Nick. It'll ruin the story," she said, cupping her hands around his face and kissing him. "You know, I miss that beard."

Nick laughed. "That's a weird thing to say."

"Is it?"

"A little."

"Really, I miss it. I mean this clean-shaven thing is good too, if you're bestselling novelist Nick Simon, I mean. But. . ."

"But what?" He saw that she was getting a little emotional.

"I liked the way you looked. I miss Simon."

"I'll grow it back out."

She shook her head. "Don't be silly, there's not enough time. . ." She stopped and their eyes met.

Nick was the first to look away but Emily turned his face back toward hers. "Look at me," she said,

He resisted at first. Then he quickly glanced up. "I am," He gave her a sad smile.

"Do you hate me?"

"Hate you?" he asked incredulously.

She nodded.

"No. Of course not."

"I would hate me." Her tears began to fall.

"Emily, no. You know how I feel about you. I could

never hate you."

"If things were reversed, Nick, I *would*. I would hate you for doing this, for leaving me behind and making me watch. I'm a horrible person for doing this to you."

"You're not a horrible person. You could never be a horrible person, Em. And I chose to be here. You're not making me do anything. Come here," He pulled her to him, holding her tightly as she cried.

"*Now* who's ruining the story?" he whispered in her ear.

She laughed. "When you write this scene make sure you cut out the part about me crying, okay? Make me super strong and resilient and determined. None of this wussy stuff." She wiped her eyes, and this time he laughed.

"Emily, this is between you and me. I'm not going to write about this. This is *our* story and the only people who need to know what happens are in this room."

"I *want* you to write about it, Nick. I want you to tell our story. How we met and what you were wearing. How we kept running into each other. And. . .Chester," they both said at the same time and laughed.

"No, Emily. I want to keep this just for us."

"Well, if you change your mind, when you make it into a movie make sure Emma Stone plays me."

"And who would play me?"

"I don't know. . .but he better be just as hot." She turned back around and leaned against him again. She yawned. He kissed the top of her head again. Then he felt the slow and steady rhythm of her breathing.

"Emily?" he whispered in her ear.

When she didn't answer right away, a cold wave of panic swept every inch of Nick's body.

"Emily?" he said again, this time a little louder.

"Hmmm?"

"Nothing, I was just checking to see if you were still awake."

"Ummhumm," she answered.

Nick smiled. He maneuvered her off to one side, slipping out from under her and picking her up. Then, slowly he made his way to her room, carrying her so she wouldn't wake up. He pushed the door open with one foot and saw Mel sprawled across the bed.

"C'mon, boy. Make some room."

The Malamute moved to the foot of the bed and Nick laid Emily down, covering her with Abbie's butterfly blanket. Once he'd tucked her in Mel made his way back up the bed and sprawled across her legs. Whining, the dog looked up at Nick, who gave him a pat on the head before taking one last look at Emily, peacefully sleeping in her bed. After a moment, he forced himself to turn and walk away. Watching her sleep made him nervous and he found it almost impossible to observe her for more than a few minutes without wanting to wake her up, just to make sure she was still okay. He stepped into the living room and looked around. Every inch of the beach house now had Emily's touch all over it—from her record collection, which he'd had shipped to the house, to her colorful bags hanging from the chair, and her art supplies lying on the table. What would he do with them when she was gone? How could he make himself listen to them or worse put them away? It was unimaginable so he stopped thinking about it and decided to go outside and sit on the deck.

When he opened the door, the sweet smell of the ocean hit him and he could almost taste the saltiness traveling on the waves crashing on the nearby beach. He slumped down on one of the deck chairs and exhaled. It was happening. It was really happening. In two days Emily would finally get her wish and he would be forced to live in a world without her. Nick ran a hand through his hair. He couldn't believe how much things had changed. How much *he* had changed. He looked up at the stars. Maybe he could make a wish? Say a prayer? He doubted it. Not after everything he'd done. Things just didn't seem to work that way. He sighed.

He looked up. He thought he heard the doorbell ring. *At this hour?* He took out his phone and looked. It was one in the morning. Who could it possibly be? Nick got up and made his way back inside the house and to the door. He went to the security system and pushed the button for the camera. Nick was shocked. Standing near the gates to the beach house was the last person he expected to see. It was Rabbi Fischer.

CHAPTER FIFTY-FOUR

The Arrival

"You look surprised to see me," Rabbi Fischer said as Nick escorted him from the gate to the beach house. Nick didn't say anything for a moment.

"I am."

"How. . .how is she?" Nick could hear the sadness and worry in his voice.

"She's. . .fine. A little weak and in pain but as well as can be expected."

The rabbi let out a long sigh and Nick opened the door to the house, letting him inside first. He looked around for a moment and smiled.

"It's a beautiful house."

Nick nodded.

"Thank you. It belongs to a friend."

"That was kind," the older man said.

"Yes," Nick said, leading him to the living room and offering him a seat on the couch.

"I suppose you're wondering how I found you."

"The thought had crossed my mind." Nick admitted

and the rabbi reached inside his jacket and pulled out a bright purple envelope.

"My daughter. . .Emily sent this to me. A final goodbye I imagine."

"You haven't read it?"

"No, and I don't intend to."

"That seems cruel, Rabbi."

"I know but I didn't want the last contact I received from my daughter to come from a piece of paper." He waved the envelope. "That's why I'm here."

"I hope you haven't come here to preach at her. I don't want her upset. I promised her that the next two days would be peaceful."

Rabbi Fischer hung his head and Nick noticed that something was missing. He wasn't wearing a yarmulke. He'd *never* seen the rabbi without it and according to Emily he'd never ventured in public without it— until now.

"I'm not here as a rabbi," he said quietly. "I'm here as a father." They sat in silence.

"What about her mother?" Nick asked and Rabbi Fischer sighed.

"She. . .couldn't make the trip and I couldn't ask her to do something her heart won't allow her to do."

"You came."

"Yes," he said sadly. "I don't agree with what my daughter is doing. My faith says it's wrong and *every* instinct I have as a father tells me to protect her even if it's from herself. But. . ." He paused and Nick could see there were tears in his eyes.

"But what?"

"I asked God for an answer to my prayers."

"And?"

"Emily's letter arrived in the mail."

"So it changed your mind?" Nick asked.

Rabbi Fischer smiled.

"Have you ever heard of Abraham and the sacrifice of Isaac?"

"Vaguely," Nick admitted. His family had only really attended church on the holidays so any stories from the bible were scarce in his mind.

"The teaching centers around Abraham and his son Isaac. One day God spoke to Abraham and told him to take Isaac into the mountains and offer him up as a burnt offering on the altar. Abraham was confused and saddened by God's request but he did as he was commanded. He took his child into the mountains. He waited for a sign—for anything that might spare him from carrying out the sacrifice but no sign came. So, Abraham bound his son and placed him on the altar and lifted the knife into the air. Just as the blade was about to come down an angel stayed his hand and told him that God had tested his faith and that he had passed this test."

Nick said nothing. Liev Fischer stared at the envelope in his hands.

"You're Abraham and Emily is Isaac, is that what you're trying to say?" Nick asked.

He nodded.

"But you're not holding the knife in this story. Emily is."

"It doesn't matter, Nick. It is a test of faith. I know that now. It's a sacrifice I'm being asked to make. To let go of my daughter. Until now I was waiting for a sign, for anything that would spare me—spare her—from it. Now I know that I won't be spared from this sacrifice unless it's God's will."

"It's Emily's will." Nick said.

Liev Fischer looked up, his eyes filled with tears."

"Is it?" he whispered.

Nick wondered if Emily's father was questioning his own faith.

"Maybe you shouldn't be here."

"I *must* be here, Nick. Just as Abraham was on that mountain. God has called me here."

"What if Emily doesn't want you here?"

"I'm willing to go, but I don't think she will ask me to do so."

"How can you be so sure?"

"Because of this," he said and lifted the letter up again for him to see. "I know my daughter. If she didn't want me to come she would not have sent this."

"But you don't even know what's inside. It could be a letter telling you to stay away."

"It's a drawing, Nick. It always is. When she was in the hospital over the years she *wrote* us every day and when we went to open the envelopes there were drawings inside."

"Drawings?"

"Yes. Drawings of Emily with us, her mother and I. That's how we knew she missed us," He took the envelope in his hands and began to open it. Then, he pulled out a neatly folded piece of paper that Nick recognized as a piece from her sketch pad. He unfolded it, took a long look and smiled then turned it around for Nick to see. It was a drawing of a child, who looked very much like a young Emily, sitting on her father's lap but she had drawn him as he was now, salt and pepper hair, bushy brows and beard and a yarmulke on his head. He was looking down at her with a loving smile and the child—Emily—was looking up at him adoringly. It did something to Nick to see the drawing. He felt a lump in his throat.

"She needs me to be here." He whispered and Nick couldn't say for certain that he disagreed.

CHAPTER FIFTY-FIVE

Sunrise

"Papa." Emily said weakly as Nick carried her out to the couch the next morning.

Mel followed, jumping on the couch and stretching himself across her feet. She was cold most of the time so his body warmth was a welcome respite.

"Emily," Her father whispered and came to her. He kissed her forehead and gave her a gentle hug. There were tears in her eyes.

"And Mom?" she asked, looking around almost expectantly.

Rabbi Fischer looked away and coughed, clearing his voice before he said anything.

"I'm sorry. She wasn't feeling well enough to travel."

"Oh," Emily said, and flashed her father a brief smile. "I understand."

Nick was certain that she didn't. How could she? How could anyone? Then he thought about his own mother and Alex. *That was different.* Emily's mother wasn't being physically threatened she was *choosing* to let Emily do this alone. He wondered if she would be able to live with herself afterwards. Nick couldn't imagine it. Not anymore.

"Do you want something to eat?" Nick asked,knowing what she would say.

She shook her head. The chemo had made her nauseous and she had never really regained her appetite.

"You must eat something, Emily, to keep up your. . ." Her father said and then stopped himself.

Nick knew he'd been about to say *strength.* Emily looked at her father, smiled, and then she looked back at Nick.

"Maybe I should eat something," she whispered.

He nodded.

"I can make you some toast." "Okay."

Suddenly the door to one of the back bedrooms opened. Aaron and Caroline came into the living room and sat down.

"Hey guys." Aaron looked over at Emily's father.

"I'm Liev Fischer." He shook Aaron's hand.

Caroline smiled and held her hand out, too. "I'm Caroline and this is my husband, Aaron. We're pleased to meet you," They sat looking at each other for a moment until Nick finally got up and headed for the kitchen. The open plan of the space made it easy for him to see everyone as they sat conversing in the living room. Emily had initiated it all, of course, and slowly they all participated, first talking about the weather, then the area itself, the beach house and finally they came to the reason they had all come together.

"A volunteer will be coming to the house later," Emily said, her voice soft and tired.

"A volunteer?" Her father asked.

Emily nodded. "Her name is Sara and she'll also be

here tomorrow."

Everyone became quiet.

"Is she. . .is she the one who will. . ." Caroline couldn't bring herself to finish the sentence so Nick did it for her.

"No. She won't mix the medication."

"But won't she administer it?" Caroline asked and Nick shook his head.

"No. I'll do that," Emily whispered.

Nick thought he saw Emily's father physically shrink. Caroline reached out and took Emily's hand. The two friends sat side by side, making eye contact often but saying nothing. Mel lifted his head and whined. Emily talked to him in hushed tones but it felt as though even Mel knew what was happening. Time was short.

Nick kept working in the kitchen making some green tea and toast for Emily, who thanked him when he brought them out and set them on the coffee table in front of her.

"Caroline, did you want tea and toast? I'm making some eggs for Aaron and myself, and I have some fresh fruit for you, Rabbi."

"Thank you, Nick." Liev Fischer took an apple from a bowl that Nick offered him. Aaron got up and made his way over to the breakfast counter.

"You better let me help you in the kitchen, Nick. I make some mean scrambled eggs and from what I hear all you ever did in LA and New York was tend bar."

"Ok. You got it."

Nick laughed and ceded his spot near the stove. Aaron really was a great cook, as proved by the fact that, after a long day at his construction job, he cooked daily for Abbie and Caroline. Aaron started searching in the cabinets for pots and pans. Then he opened the refrigerator and started scrounging for eggs and extra ingredients. While he did that, Nick went back to sit on the couch with Emily, wrapping an arms around her shoulders. Emily nestled into him and Mel inched closer to the two of them, resting his furry head across both their laps. Caroline glanced at them and smiled. Nick knew she was happy for them but also heartbroken. She didn't agree with what Emily was doing any more than her parents did but out of her love for her friend and her faith in her god she had made the long trip to Oregon with Aaron. She was willing to be a witness to something she herself would never choose. Caroline's journey would take her on a different path and she was willing to suffer the necessary pain as part of that journey. How different both women were, and yet how similar. Both were willing to live as few were, on their own terms, ignoring the opinions of others, including each other's, regarding how they chose to face their own deaths. It was those around them, Aaron, Abbie, her parents and Nick who were having a hard time coming to terms with what was soon to be their reality—a world without Caroline and Emily. Caroline, with her devout faith, and Emily, with her strong will, didn't seem to have the same doubts.

Nick watched as Aaron found his way around the gourmet kitchen deftly as any professional chef he'd ever watched work in any of the fanciest restaurants in New York or LA. He could tell that he really loved what he was doing and he suspected that he would do it full time if it wasn't for the fact that they needed every cent he was making to go toward Caroline's treatments. Nick knew that, even as hard as Aaron was working, there was a stack of bills sitting on their table back home. He had seen that stack and watched as Caroline gingerly touched each one, a look of worry and fear, not for herself but for her family, cross her face. Nick wanted to help, but neither Aaron nor Caroline would accept his offer. They were proud, hard-working people who didn't like the idea of taking charity. At first Nick had thought they refused his offer because of who he was and because he'd left Emily and returned to New York, but as he'd gotten to know them better, he realized that it was on principal that they'd said no to his money. He intended to speak with Aaron again, but knew that it was neither the time nor place to do so. In the meantime, he sat back and reveled in the feeling of Emily safely wrapped in his arms and blocked out any thoughts beyond that moment. The minutes would tick away quickly enough without wasting the remaining precious time with worry and frustration.

They ate in silence, the women nibbling on their toast and barely touching their tea, Rabbi Fischer ate a second apple and Aaron served Nick a giant helping of scrambled eggs. They were delicious and it felt more like a vacation weekend than a weekend of goodbyes. When they were done, they sat quietly looking at each other and Nick wondered when Emily would begin to take each of them into the back bedroom to start her goodbyes. There was a buzz at the gate and Nick got up to go check the cameras.

"Who is it?" Emily called.

Nick was sure that she was hoping it was her mother or even Derrick.

"It's Sara," he said, trying to cover the disappointment in his own voice.

"Oh."

"I thought you said she was coming tomorrow," Caroline said in a panic.

Emily took her hand.

"It's okay. She's just coming to check on me. It's part of the process."

Nick thought back to the bottles of pills that they'd picked up from the pharmacy earlier in the week sitting next to the lamp in the bedroom, their contents full and menacing. Each passing moment was a moment closer to the end of their time together and Sara's presence was a stark reminder that Nick would soon have to let go.

CHAPTER FIFTY-SIX

The Volunteer

Sara was a pleasant, attractive blonde in her sixties who took Nick's hand immediately in her own and held it tight. Since their return to Oregon, Emily had been meeting with a volunteer from an organization dedicated to advocating for those who chose Death With Dignity. It seemed to help her process what was happening and prepare her for what was to come. He could have participated in the sessions with her but he couldn't bring himself to do it. Emily told him she understood and let him wait for her on the beach or in the bedroom while she met with Sara.

"You must be Nick," she said and he nodded.

"Emily's told me so much about you, I feel as though I know you."

"Really?" he said, somewhat embarrassed.

"I mean that in the nicest possible way," she said.

"Thank you."

"Is Emily expecting me?"

Nick nodded.

"Good. I'm just here to check on her and see how she's feeling today. I'm also here to answer any questions you might have. Has anything changed since we last spoke?"

"Well, her best friend and her father arrived unexpectedly within the last two days."

"Oh," she said, looking concerned. "Have they changed their minds? Are they supporting Emily's decision?"

"No. But they want to be here for her. They want to be able to say goodbye."

"That's good. What about Emily's mother?"

"She didn't make the trip."

"I'm sorry to hear that. I know it would have meant a lot to Emily. But sometimes those we love can't agree with every decision we make, particularly one like this."

"No. They can't."

"Is Emily still determined to follow through?"

"Yeah," Nick said and the word seemed to stick in his throat.

"How are you holding up, Nick?"

Nick didn't know what to say. "Does it matter?" he asked and she smiled.

"Honestly, my job is to be here for Emily. But I also know how hard this must be for you. My husband made this choice and even though I was resentful at first, looking back, I understand it. That's why I'm here to be an advocate for Emily, but I'm also here to be a shoulder for you. I was where you are now three years ago and a wonderful volunteer knocked on our door that day and all I wanted to do was lock the door and hide. I hoped that if I didn't answer the door maybe the nice man would go away. But he didn't and I opened the door. Do you know why I opened the door, Nick?"

"No."

"I took one look at my husband and I saw the look in his eyes, the pain, the suffering and the pleading. He *begged* me to open that door. Randy *never* asked me for much, let alone begged for anything. That day he did and I had to ask myself if I loved Randy, truly loved him. It took me a few moments, I'm ashamed to say, but I finally opened that door. There's not a day I don't miss him. But I know I did the right thing."

Nick could see the tears welling up in her eyes. He didn't know what to say but knew that her words hit home somehow.

"Emily will be wondering where we are," Nick said, changing the subject.

Sara let go of his hand and smiled. "Lead the way."

She followed him up to the beach house. The moment Sara stepped into the house, Nick felt a shift in attitudes and emotion. He could sense the tension emanating from Liev Fischer and even Caroline, who sat protectively near Emily.

"Hi, everyone," Sara said, then she greeted everyone individually—saving Emily for last. She gave her a gentle hug before taking a seat across from her on the other side of the coffee table.

"Well, I've come today to check on Emily and to answer any questions she or you might have about what will happen tomorrow."

Sara folded her hands on her lap and waited for someone to speak up. No one did. Nick had taken his seat back on the couch with Emily. Sara looked at each one of them intently until her gaze rested on Emily and she directed her next question to her.

"Emily, what can we do to make this transition as peaceful as possible for you?"

Emily looked at Nick, then at Caroline and finally at her father, who was doing his best to avoid looking at her or at Sara.

"I just want everyone to know how much I love them and how much it means to me that they're here. I know it can't be easy for you."

Nick marveled at how composed she was and how, as always, she was more concerned about how others were doing than about what she was feeling.

"We love you, Em." Caroline said tearing up as she reached out for her hand again.

"I love you too," Emily said, managing a smile that broke Nick's heart.

Emily's father suddenly got up and turned away from the group, finding his way over to the farthest corner, his shoulders heaving, his face covered by both hands.His sobs were audible to everyone, especially Emily who couldn't hold back her own tears. She slowly left Nick's embrace and with his help got up and made her way over to him.

"Papa?" she asked in a childlike voice. He turned and took Emily into his arms and cried, kissing her forehead and face over and over while speaking to her in Hebrew.

"*Ani ohev otach,* I love you, Emily," he cried, causing Emily to sob even harder.

Nick wondered if Sara would step in at any point to let the rabbi know he was only making it harder for Emily to let go. As if reading his mind Sara turned to Nick and smiled sympathetically.

"Everyone needs to work through this process in their own way."

"Sure," he said and had to turn away himself.

Sara placed a hand on his arm. "*Everyone*, Nick," she said, looking directly into his eyes.

He avoided Sara and looked instead in the direction of Emily and her father.

"Don't forget yourself in this process. That's important, Nick. This isn't happening just to Emily. It's happening to everyone she loves."

Sara let Emily and her father take their time and, before long, decided it was best if she left. Nick walked her out.

"I'll be here at 10 o'clock tomorrow evening," she said and he nodded to acknowledge the time.

"Are you okay?"

"No."

"That's the first honest thing you've said so far," she said as they reached the gate.

"What do I do now?" Nick asked as she walked through. She stopped and took his hand in hers.

"You tell her you love her."

"That's all?"

"It's enough, Nick," she said giving his hand a squeeze. "Trust me. It's enough."

CHAPTER FIFTY-SEVEN

The Goodbyes

One by one they spent time with Emily that day. She and her father reminiscing about the good times and the bad as she was growing up. They talked about her mother and Derrick who, despite her father's efforts, would not come. She spent another afternoon out on the deck with Caroline and walked Mel a short distance on the beach with Nick. Before they knew it night had fallen and Nick found himself sitting on the beach alone. The stars were tremendously bright that evening and the constant rhythm of the waves going in and out served as a perfect backdrop to what could have been a last romantic night. Instead Emily was already in bed and Nick was here alone. He breathed in the salty air and exhaled. The countdown was almost done and with each ticking of the clock Nick asked himself *what now?* He tried to stay in the present moment but all he could think about was all of the moments he would spend *without* Emily, back in New York, working for Barbara, making appearances, writing scripts, going to parties. It was the life he'd had before and that seemed unrecognizable now. What would he write about? What would he do? How would he live? So many questions and not one good answer. The worst part was that he wasn't sure he'd be able to hide from this loss like he had Alex's death. He'd thrown himself into his work after the tragedy but this time he felt tired and worn. There was no energy left to give to projects and people that didn't really matter. He looked up at the stars and tried to keep the tears away. It wasn't the time for tears, not just yet. There'd be plenty of time for that later.

"A penny for your thoughts," a voice called out and Nick turned around to see Liev Fischer walking toward him, his pant legs rolled up and his feet bare.

"Hi."

"Hi, Nick. May I?" He pointed to a spot on the beach near Nick. Nick nodded and he sat down. They sat in silence for a few moments before Emily's father spoke up.

"Is it Nick or Nicholas?"

"Nick."

"Hmm. Interesting." Liev Fischer said.

"Why do you say that?"

"I've known many Nick's in my life but almost everyone of them was a Nicholas first."

"My mother named me. She figured she'd beat everybody to it by just naming me Nick instead."

"Sounds like a smart woman." Fischer observed and Nick shrugged.

"Sometimes."

"Sounds like something Emily would say about me." The rabbi laughed.

"Really?"

"Don't all children question their parents' intelligence?"

"I guess," Nick admitted and the older man smiled.

"Does your mother live in New York?"

"No. She passed away."

"Oh. I'm sorry."

"Your father?"

"Him too." Nick said.

"So you're an orphan," The rabbi whispered and Nick nodded.

"Something like that."

"This can't be easy for you."

"I think we've proven that it's not easy for any us."

Emily's father sighed. "I think we can agree on that, Nick."

They sat in silence, listening to the waves.

"What about Emily's mother? Will she be here tomorrow?"

"No. I tried again tonight but she can't bring herself to do it. And I, like you, am unwilling to force the woman I love to do something that she refuses to do."

"So where does this leave you after this is. . .over?"

"I don't know."

"I'm surprised."

"Why?"

"I thought, with your faith that you'd be able to say you'll forgive each other and go on."

"I wish it were that easy. But faith isn't blind ignorance of the facts, Nick. Faith is going forward with the certainty that things will change and that somehow we will cope with that change in the best way we know how."

"What if you can't go on. . .together?"

"I guess I have faith that we'll cross that bridge when we get to it," Rabbi Fischer said. "What about you? What will you do?"

"I have obligations back in New York. I'm back under contract."

"Should I say I'm sorry or congratulations?"

"I don't know. I'm not really thinking about it right now."

"No, I suppose not. Nick. . .there are things I want to say but words. . .words fail me tonight."

"That's okay."

"No, it's not. We've exchanged words over the last few months. They seem meaningless now. They were angry and sometimes very cruel. I'm sorry about that."

"I'm sure Emily knows."

"I've already spoken to Emily. I'm talking about the things I said to you and that Meredith said. Of course, the apology I offer you now can only be mine. I can't speak for her. I can only speak for myself. I am truly sorry and I want to thank you. . .for loving my girl, my Emily." Liev Fischer's eyes welled up with tears as he reached out and put a hand on Nick's shoulder.

"I wish I could have done more," Nick whispered and he knew that the rabbi understood what he meant.

"I know, my son," The rabbi said looking up at the stars. "I know."

CHAPTER FIFTY-EIGHT

The Last Day

Nick had fallen asleep on the deck chair and found that someone had placed a blanket over him. He opened his eyes and watched as the sun rose over the sea. With the cool air enveloping him, he pulled the blanket up higher and closed it tight. He inhaled deeply and slowly exhaled. Today was the day. It was here and it was beautiful. He heard the sliding glass door open behind him and Aaron stepped outside with two steaming cups of coffee.

"I thought you might need this," he said as he handed him a cup and sat down in the chair next to him.

"Thanks," Nick said, taking a sip. It was strong and black. The two men sat in silence, staring out at the sea and drinking from their cups. Aaron finally broke the silence.

"They're up and having their tea and toast," he said.

"Good."

"Emily, knows you're out here, so no need to worry."

"Thanks. I didn't want her to think. . ." Nick started but then he paused.

"It's okay, Nick. She doesn't."

"How's Caroline?"

"A little tired. She had a hard time sleeping."

"Was she up thinking about today?"

"Weren't you?"

"Yeah."

"So was Emily's father." Aaron said, looking back toward the door.

"He was out here with me for a while."

"Looks like you guys pulled an all nighter."

"I don't remember. I think I fell asleep. I woke up with the blanket over me."

"That'd be Liev. I came out to the kitchen for some water last night and he asked me if I knew where he could find a blanket. I asked him if it was for him and he said it was for you."

"That was nice of him."

"Yeah, I could almost say he likes you."

"Really?" Nick asked and Aaron laughed.

"I said *almost*." Aaron patted him on the shoulder.

"Thanks."

"But seriously, Nick, how are you holding up?"

It was the question he'd been trying to avoid answering. He could tell Aaron he was fine but he knew Caroline's husband was an observant guy with a big heart and he knew a lie when he heard one.

"I don't know," Nick answered and, he was being honest.

"That's a good answer," Aaron said. "It's better than what I would've come up with."

"Why? What would you have said?"

"I'd have said I was going crazy. That's the truth. But

in a way, Nick, even with as much faith as I have that God's in charge, I envy you."

"Envy me?"

"You know when it'll happen right down to the hour. I don't," Aaron said with tears in his eyes. "Sometimes I just watch Caroline sleep and I listen to her breathe so I can make sure she's still. . .still here with us."

"I'm sorry, Aaron."

"Don't be. It's hard no matter how it happens. Just know I'm here for you. Today's going to be tough and you don't have to pretend it's not. Emily knows. We all know. It's okay to be real with each other today. To laugh, to cry, to pray and to say whatever needs to be said. We're your family now, Nick. Whether you want it not, we're your family and we're going to be here for you."

Nick didn't know what to say. He wondered if Emily had told Aaron and Caroline the truth about his own family and that he was an orphan but he was sure she hadn't. She wouldn't unless she'd asked him first; it was just how she was. Even so, Aaron's words touched his heart in a way he couldn't explain.

"Thank you, Aaron," Nick said and the two men finished their coffee before returning inside.

Everyone was sitting in the living room when he and Aaron came back. Emily was dressed in her favorite leggings, one of Nick's oversized sweaters, a knit cap and she had her favorite fleece blanket thrown over her lap. Her father had helped her get dressed and the three of them were playing a card game. Their laughter echoed in the room. Emily looked up, her eyes were sparkling and her smile was genuine.

"Nick!" she called out patting the space on the couch

next to her. He sat down and wrapped an arm around her, trying to keep out any other thoughts but what was happening at that very moment.

"Em," he said and kissed her fully on the lips. Liev Fischer cleared his throat and threw him a look of mock disapproval.

"Sorry." Nick said, kissing Emily again but it was clear he wasn't. There was more laughter.

Caroline snuggled into Aaron's arms and the group spent a couple hours playing cards, talking, and generally enjoying each other's company. At one point Emily asked for her sketch pad, which Nick brought her, along with her pencils, so she could draw. Although her hands trembled she was still able to do what she loved while Mel lay comfortably next to her. Lunch came and went with Aaron fixing something for everyone to enjoy. Then Emily asked Nick to go back to the bedroom with her for a bit. Mel followed of course and he took his usual position as they lay together. Nick tried to keep the conversation light and away from the topic of what would transpire later that evening.

"Nick," Emily interrupted him.

"What?" He took her hand in his and caressed each of her fingers.

"Don't you want to talk about it?"

"Talk about what?"

"What's going to happen tonight?"

He didn't say anything.

"Nick?"

"Em. . ."

"We need to talk about it. *I* need to talk about it. I need to know that you're going to be okay."

"Okay?"

"Yeah," she said and he knew he couldn't lie to her anymore than he could lie to himself.

"I don't know that I'll ever be *okay*, Emily," he whispered.

She squeezed his hand. "It won't always be that way."

"It will. . .for me."

"Don't shut love out just when you've opened up to it."

"How can you even talk about me finding someone else?"

"I'm not talking about finding someone else. Actually, it makes me pretty jealous thinking about that," she said, laughing a little.

"I'm talking about plain old love, Nick. Loving your life. Loving yourself. . .once you figure out who you are."

"I don't know anymore."

"It'll take time but you'll figure it out."

He hugged her tight. "I mean I don't know who I'll be without *you*."

"You'll be Nick Simon but just a little bit better version than who you were before."

He closed his eyes to keep in the tears. "I don't know if I can."

They lay quietly together for awhile.

"I'm not afraid, you know."

"You're not?"

"No."

"Are you just saying that to make me feel better?" he asked and she slowly shook her head.

"Don't tell Caroline but I fully expect to see something or someone on the other side. She'll get excited and think all her preaching has finally converted me. Who knows, maybe she's right and I should accept Jesus before I die just in case, but I don't feel like giving my father a heart attack. Either way, I think Jesus will understand. Like Caroline keeps telling me—Jesus was a Jew. Then, he should know what kind of pressure I'm under."

Nick laughed. "Smart-ass to the end."

"Smart-ass to the end."

He kissed her.

Time passed and it passed quickly. Before they knew it the day was winding down and the buzzer at the gate indicated that Sara had arrived. They all gathered together in the living room one final time. Sara sat with them as they took each other's hands and Caroline led them in a tearful but heartfelt prayer. Then Emily looked at her father, who was having a hard time holding back his tears.

"Papa, would you sing?" she asked.

Her father looked at her. "What would you have me sing?"

"Will you sing Shalom Aleichem?" she asked and the rabbi broke down.

"Please, Papa."

After a few moments he composed himself and in a beautiful baritone he began to sing in Hebrew.

"Shalom Aleichem malache ha-sharet malache elyon,
mi-melech malche ha-melachim Ha-Kadosh Baruch Hu.
Bo'achem le-shalom malache ha-shalom malache elyon,
mi-melech malche ha-melachim Ha-Kadosh Baruch Hu.
Barchuni le-shalom malache ha-shalom malache elyon,
mi-melech malche ha-melachim Ha-Kadosh Baruch Hu.
Tzet'chem le-shalom malache ha-shalom malache elyon,
mi-melech malche ha-melachim Ha-Kadosh Baruch Hu."

"That was beautiful." Caroline whispered, tears streaming down her face. "What does it mean?"

Emily smiled. "Papa? Will you tell them?"

Her father translated it for them.

"Peace upon you, ministering angels, messengers of the Most High, of the Supreme King of Kings, the Holy One, blessed be He. Come in peace, messengers of peace, messengers of the Most High, of the Supreme King of Kings, the Holy One, blessed be He. Bless me with peace, messengers of peace, messengers of the Most High, of the Supreme King of Kings, the Holy One, blessed be He. May your departure be in peace, messengers of peace, messengers of the Most High, of the Supreme King of Kings, the Holy One, blessed be He."

After a few more minutes, Emily turned to Sara.

"I'm ready," she said.

Sara took her hand. "Are you sure?"

"Yeah, I'm sure," Emily said.

Nick recognized the determination in her voice.

"Okay." Sara took Emily's hands and gave her a hug. Emily glanced at Nick, who helped her get up and hug her father, who had a hard time letting go of her. Then she came to Caroline and Aaron.

"I love you, Em," Caroline cried and Emily cried with her.

"It's going to be fine, Caroline. You'll see. I love you too."

She went on to hug Aaron.

"I'm going to miss you, Emily."

"I'm going to miss you too, Aaron. You take care of my girls."

"You know it," he said, laughing and wiping the tears

from his eyes.

Nick took Emily by the hand and walked her to the bedroom. They closed the door. Mel was already waiting for them and there on the bedside table sat the medication that Emily herself needed to prepare. With trembling but diligent hands she completed the task. Sara sat near the bed in a chair that Nick had set up for her and he sat on the edge of the bed next to Emily. She looked at the glass from which she would drink and then back at Nick.

"Emily," Sara asked, "do you know what are in the contents of this glass?"

"Yes," Emily answered.

"Do you acknowledge that you are taking them of your own free will?"

"Yes," Emily replied, taking Nick's hand and squeezing it tight.

"God bless you Emily," Sara said as Emily turned to Nick with tears in her eyes.

"You know that I love you, right?" she said and he nodded. Reaching out she hugged him and kissed him as passionately as she ever had. Then just as quickly she drank the contents of the glass before laying down on the bed. Nick covered her legs with a blanket and Mel took up his usual position before Nick went over to the corner where he'd placed her record player and put on her favorite record, Joni Mitchell's *Urge for Going*. As the music started to play, he sat down on the bed again and held her hand. Her eyes began to flutter and her breathing began to slow. She looked like she was sleeping. She looked so beautiful. So beautiful, his girl with the butterfly tattoo.

"Stay with me," he whispered, tears streaming down his face.

"Always," she murmured and he kissed her one final time before she drifted away.

CHAPTER FIFTY-NINE

What Came Next

Nick watched the street signs go by as Daryl drove. He stuck two fingers in his tuxedo collar and pulled. It was choking him. He was about to run a hand through his hair when Daryl cleared his throat.

"You remember what the stylist said, Mr. Simon."

Nick sighed. " I forgot. I won't touch it."

"We're almost there," Daryl said as he pulled up behind a long line of limos. Nick had refused to ride over with Barbara in the ridiculously decked out limo she'd hired for the night. So they'd compromised and he'd agreed to go as long as Daryl could drive him in the SUV.

“You're quiet tonight, Mr. Simon.”

“Is that a bad thing?”

“No. A quiet mind is the seed of all things peaceful,” Daryl said and Nick smiled at his driver’s Zen optimism. “But. . .is your mind at peace? That is the question.”

Nick hesitated before answering. “Sometimes.”

“Is this one of those times?”

“I’ll let you know after it’s all over,” Nick said as the

SUV came to a stop.

"Do you have your speech?"

"You've asked me that five or six times now. Yeah, I have it but I'm not sure I'll need it."

"Faith, Mr. Simon. Have faith," Daryl said.

Nick winced, remembering another conversation he'd had on the topic of faith. He took a deep breath, straightened his tux, checked his pocket for his speech, and waited for Daryl to come around and open the door. As he did, a hundred flashbulbs seemed to go off in his face. There was a whine from the front seat. Mel, laid his head on the console and glanced up at Nick.

"I know. I don't want to go, boy. Don't worry. Daryl will take care of you until I get back," Nick said, petting his soft, furry head. Mel licked his hand one more time before he stepped out of the limo and onto the Red Carpet. The crowd noise was deafening. Nick put on a pair of sunglasses to keep out the glare of the cameras and the setting sun before making his way through the gamut of actors and entertainment news reporters. He was stopped several times and asked to give brief interviews on what he was wearing, what he thought of the actors in the film and of course the Oscar nomination.

"Nick, tell us, what's it like to have your film *The Date* nominated for the Oscar tonight?" a reporter, wearing a stunning Valentino dress, asked. Nick flashed her his usual smile and gave the answer he'd rehearsed.

"It's an honor just to be nominated."

"Both actors have also been nominated and you've been nominated for your screenplay. What an incredible accomplishment." She raised her voice over the din of the crowd.

"Thank you."

"What inspired you to finally write the script?" She asked and Nick thought about Emily and then smiled again before answering.

"My readers of course."

"The book was a wild success." The reporters said. "When did you realize you had a hit on your hands?"

"I didn't."

"It's rumored, of course, that both the book and the movie of the same name were both based on one of your actual relationships. Is that true?"

"I'd rather that people read the book and watch the movie and take whatever they want or need from it without my input or backstory."

"Well, it's a beautiful movie. You should be very proud."

"Thanks again," he said and moved down the carpet toward the next interview. He also posed for several pictures with the actors and even a few with Barbara, who had dressed as if she'd be the one accepting one if not all of the awards.

"Nick," she greeted him with an air kiss as they posed for pictures.

"Barbara."

"You're looking dashing."

"And you look beautiful as always," he said and tried to mean it.

"I should, darling. Yves charges me a fortune. But it's worth it." She smiled as the cameras flashed. They parted, Barbara to have more pictures taken and Nick to find a corner away from all the paparazzi and noise.

When they finally entered the building,

Nick was ushered into a back room where celebrities were mingling before the telecast began. Slowly, they all trickled in and as Nick made it to his seat he met with Cianti, who was stunning and beautiful in a way Barbara could never achieve no matter how much she paid her celebrity stylist.

"Nick?" Cianti asked.

At first he didn't acknowledge her. He couldn't bring himself to do it, not after what she did to Emily.

"Nick, come on, this war between us has to stop," she said and he frowned.

"War?"

"I dropped the lawsuit. I'm Barbara's client and you know I wrote the song for your movie that's been nominated tonight. Aren't we on the same side now?"

"Are we?" He stuck his hands in his pocket and looked down at his dress shoes.

"I read your book. I watched the movie. Nick, I know we've had our differences and God knows you've had your problems. We both have. I didn't know. I know now."

"What do you know now?"

"I know you loved her. *Really* loved her."

"I don't know what you're talking about," he said, trying to brush off her words. He wasn't ready to talk about it. Not even now.

"It's the most honest you've ever been and it's all over that book and the movie. . ."

"It's fiction."

"It's life," she whispered and Nick shrugged.

"What do you want Cianti? Didn't you get everything you wanted from Barbara?"

"Sure, Nick. Almost everything," she said, giving him a look he recognized from their time together on that New Year's Day almost two years ago.

"Well, the show's about to start," he said trying to divert her attention.

"I understand now. I didn't at first. But I do now. I just wanted you to know." She headed toward her own seat near the front row.

Nick went to his seat near the middle of the theatre and sat down next to the director of the movie and one of the producers. The show began with a musical number and a few barbs thrown at each of the movies and various actors by the host. Then, one by one, awards were presented and the recipients tried to give emotional, long-winded speeches, while the show's music director cut them off to keep within the broadcast time limits. In between the awards, each movie was introduced and Nick was nervous because he, as always, hadn't watched the film. He couldn't bring himself to do it. When the popular actress who introduced the film came to the podium, Nick was about to get up and leave when he heard the clip come on and the words he'd found almost impossible to write came to life. As he watched the exchange he found himself riveted to the actress who had gotten every aspect of Emily's appearance and even some of her mannerisms down pat. His heart was breaking all over again.

"How is wanting you to live so we can be together wrong? What's so wrong about that?!"

"Because you want me to keep living for you!"

"What's so bad about that?"

"It's a two way street. It's not just about what you want or what you need, it's about accepting what's actually real and right in front

of you or moving on."

"Then you're right. I don't understand it! I don't get why you think this is the only option. Don't you want to be with me?"

"Yes! Of course!"

"Then why? Why?"

"If you don't know by now, then it doesn't matter what I say. But, I don't have to convince you or anyone else. It's my life and. . . my death."

The audience applauded and whistled for the actors and Nick wondered if he'd be able to make it through the rest of the show. But before he knew it his category was up. A previously-nominated screenwriter and winner read the names of the nominees.

"Now on to adapted screenplay," he said and Nick's whole body tensed. This was the last place he wanted to be. If Barbara hadn't insisted he'd have stayed home with Mel and tried to ignore all of the fanfare. He'd wondered more than once if he'd done the right thing by releasing the book and making the movie but each time he sat down to write all he could think of was Emily and everything that had happened. Initially, he had stopped writing altogether for about three months, which only made Barbara angry and irate. He didn't care. It was only when Daryl was driving him to another meaningless party to meet up with Barbara that Nick had truly considered writing something, *anything* again.

"Mr. Simon, are you alright?" his driver and bodyguard had asked and Nick knew he was not.

Each time they passed another nightclub or bar Nick wanted to scream at him to stop so he could dull the pain with a merciful shot of vodka. If the thoughts didn't stop he'd have to call his sponsor.

"I'm fine."

"You are a much better writer than liar, Mr. Simon."

Nick looked out the window again. "Am I, Daryl?"

"You have not written in a long while," Daryl said matter-of-factly.

"No." Nick admitted.

"Ms. Barbara is not pleased." Another fact.

"No."

"What about you?"

"Me?"

"Do you miss it?"

"There are a lot of things I miss, Daryl. Writing is not at the top of that list."

"Maybe writing will help."

"Help with what? Barbara's bottom line? I'm not interested."

"Help with healing, Mr. Simon."

Nick knew he was trying to help. "Thanks, Daryl, but I can't."

Daryl said nothing more until they reached a stoplight. Then the big man turned around in his seat and took something from his pocket.

"It's time, Mr. Simon," he said and handed him the item. In the dim interior light of the SUV Nick could see it was an envelope. . .a purple envelope. His heart stopped.

"Where did you get this, Daryl?"

"Miss Emily."

"When. . ." There was a lump in his throat. "When?"

"All that matters is that she found a way."

"But. . ."

"She said I was to give it to you when it was time. It is time."

"Time for what?"

"Time to let go."

"But how am I supposed to do that?" Nick's eyes were full of tears.

"I suggest you open the envelope and find out," Daryl had said and returned to driving when the light turned green and there were several honks. With trembling hands Nick pulled at the envelope's flaps and reached in for the familiar folded piece of sketch pad paper. He unfolded it and broke down. It was that same envelope that was sitting in his tuxedo pocket now next to his speech at the awards show. He reached in to touch it.

"And the award goes to. . .Nick Simon for 'The Date,'" the presenter announced and the auditorium cheered. Nick felt numb as people around him, including the director and producer, along with a group of well-wishers congratulated him. He made his way down the aisle and up onto the stage. The presenter handed him the award, which he took and placed on the podium, while he reached inside for his speech. His finger brushed up against the purple envelope and he stopped. He didn't need the canned speech he'd prepared and that Barbara had approved. All he needed was to speak from his heart for the very first time, without caring what everyone sitting in that auditorium thought. Looking up, he scanned the crowd and felt suddenly emotional when his eyes fell on Aaron, Caroline and Abbie. He was glad they could be there. This journey had been theirs as much as it had been his and Emily's. He was so glad to see that Caroline was looking better. Soon after Emily passed, Nick had had a heart-to-heart talk with Aaron and convinced him to let Nick pay for a new experimental treatment that Dr. Gina Manzitti and Dr. Kimberly Lee were working on to combat stage IV metastatic breast cancer. While it hadn't eradicated Caroline's cancer it had at least slowed it down and given her more time with Aaron and Abbie. He paused for a moment to wave at them from the stage and saw that right next to them sat Emily's parents. He wondered if their presence meant that they had finally crossed that bridge Nick and the rabbi had talked about on the beach and made it over together, the way the older man had hoped. He knew it would have meant a lot to Emily. After thanking the actors, producers, his agent and the appropriate members of the awards committee, Nick thanked Caroline, her family and Rabbi and Mrs. Fischer for being there. Then, he stopped for a moment before reaching in his jacket pocket and pulling out the purple envelope. He took out its contents, took a deep breath and looked down at the drawing that Emily had made. It was a drawing of a beautiful emerald butterfly that looked as if it was about to take flight and the words *tell our story* written at the bottom of the page in her handwriting. He swallowed the lump in his throat and spoke up.

"A friend once told me that sometimes love means letting go. At the time I thought he meant that love meant accepting loss. But over the last two years I've come to realize that maybe it means giving the gift of freedom. The freedom for someone you love to do what's best for them even if it's not what you would choose for yourself. I know, it's radical. It's not what we're taught. It's not what we're supposed to do. We're supposed to hang on for dear life and never let go. But that's fear not love. This letting go, it's what I learned from the best human being I'll ever know." He paused and realized he was starting to choke up. "A lot of people have asked me if the book and the movie are based on a true story. . .they are. But that's not the point. The point is if you love someone, tell them, show them, be there, and when it comes time to let go. . .don't be afraid. Thank you." There was a round of thunderous applause as Nick exited the stage and made his way back to his seat. As he sat down he felt something inside of him shift and lighten. He'd finally let go—but he hadn't lost anything, not this time. This time his heart had cracked open, but instead of darkness there was light and instead of spiraling down, it had taken flight. It was freedom. It was . . .*love.*

THE END

Made in the USA
Monee, IL
23 July 2023

39673278R00184